THE RUSSIAN MADHOUSE

RICK BADMAN

THE RUSSIAN MADHOUSE

ARPress
45 Dan Road Suite 5
Canton MA 02021

Hotline: 1(888) 821-0229
Fax: 1(508) 545-7580

Ordering Information:
Quantity sales. Special discounts are available on quantity purchases by corporations, associations, and others. For details, contact the publisher at the address above.

Printed in the United States of America.

ISBN-13:   Paperback   979-8-89389-482-0
                  eBook   979-8-89389-484-4
                  Hardcover   979-8-89389-483-7

Library of Congress Control Number: 2024918680

Table of Contents

After the going away party at the Madhouse when praise was heaped upon Dick and Kate, the empty home in the Madhouse was proof that the place the Thurmans had called home for over three years had to be left for their new home in Russia. They loaded the refrigerator in the levitated flying car with a dozen Thurman sub sandwiches and a couple gallons of Dr. Pepper that they would try to only sample when they longed for their former life in Ariona. They hoped that wouldn't be too often.

It was 40 degrees when they flew from Arizona on a wintery February morning north toward Canada and to Siberia over the top of the world. It was 40 below when they arrived before dawn at the landing pad above the Russian Madhouse. Lights outlined the pad to help them find where to land. The pad descended to the receiving area and after the roof was closed, the temperature climbed to a more comfortable 50 degrees.

Three representatives of the Russian Madhouse approached the vehicle as Dick and Kate climbed out of the cramped cockpit. They greeted the couple with hearty handshakes and kisses on the cheek. "Welcome to the Facility," said one of the representatives. "Your things have been placed in storage since your apartment is fully furnished and the refrigerator and freezer are stocked with what is assumed to be what you like to eat and drink."

"We also have a dozen sandwiches and a couple gallons of Dr. Pepper in the refrigerator in the car," Dick mentioned. "When we make room in the refrigerator, someone can come down for them. They should be good for quite awhile."

"Your android assistant Sam can be sent down for them," said another representative.

"Where is he?" asked Kate.

"He is in your apartment. He'll show you around when you arrive," said the first representative. "By the way. Will you need a day to adjust to the time change? It's a twelve hour difference between here and Arizona."

"We took a nap on the flight here so we will have breakfast first and then go to work," said Dick.

The third representative said, "I hope you have your car locked because there are some people here that will steal anything that isn't locked down."

"If they try to enter the car they will receive a 100,000 volt warning. I'll give the entrance pass to Sam before he comes down here to retrieve our food and drink," said Dick.

As the Thurmans and the representatives walked toward the exit, a robotic towing vehicle approached the car. Since it didn't have wheels, the towing vehicle had to scoop the car up and set it in the bed before carrying it to the next room which was used to store other vehicles workers at the Russian Madhouse owned.

The Thurmans took the elevator down to their apartment that was on the middle level of the Facility. It was a few paces from the elevator which made it convenient to take to the levels where they worked. The door of their apartment slid open to reveal a living quarters that was slightly larger than their first apartment back in Michigan. Sam was sitting on the couch awaiting their arrival. The living room had a couch, two recliners, a wall that contained the extended 3-D TV system, a coffee table near the couch, and two computer systems and office chairs against the last wall. There were EPU headsets on the computer desks that would allow them to work from home if they chose. Some pleasant classical music was softly wafting from the speakers in the ceiling which was an illumination panel otherwise.

The android stood and said,"I am Sam. That stands for Standard Android Manager. I manage your apartment and anything else that is required. I can manage your schedules and be your avatar if you want to go somewhere and aren't physically able to be there. Use an EPU headset to interface with me and experience what I am experiencing. You can also talk through me too."

"Great. I want to take a tour of the Russian Madhouse before I assume my managerial duties," said Dick.

"I would advise that you refer to the Facility as the Facility. Most people call it that because calling it the Russian Madhouse gives the impression that it is an insane asylum."

"I'll try to remember. I guess you're going to give us the grand tour."

"I will start with the kitchen. Follow me."

The Thurmans followed Sam to the crowded kitchen that had a refrigerator/freezer, a rapid-heating oven and microwave combination, an induction stove, some drawers and cabinets, a food processor, a toaster oven, a beverage machine, a sink, a dishwasher, a small table with two chairs, and a flat-screen 30-inch 3-D TV on the wall next to the table.

Sam opened the refrigerator to show it was stocked with the expected items you can find in most American refrigerators with peach ice tea and cherry cola in the double drink dispensors on the outside of the refrigerator door. When the freezer door beside the refrigerator door was opened, there were three flavors of ice cream, frozen meats, vegetables, frozen dinners, and two pizzas under the ice maker.

"I found out what you two liked and ordered it in from the grocery store yesterday since I knew you would arrive today. I'm sorry that we don't have Dr. Pepper. Cherry cola is the closes substitute to it."

Sam opened a cabinet and showed them five types of cereal in plain boxes marked frosted flakes, wheat and barley nuggets, graham cereal, oatmeal flakes, and honey nut oats.

"I trust the variety of cereals suit your tastes." "Very much," said Dick.

"Do you also cook?" Kate asked.

"I've been programmed to prepare over 1,000 menu items and prepare certain foods in various ways. Would you like for me to prepare breakfast for you?"

"That would be nice," said Dick. "I bet you were programmed to fix my eggs the way I like them."

"Scrambled or over hard?" "Over hard."

"And I'll take mine scrambled," said Kate. "That won't be any problem, will it?"

"No problem at all. And would you two like bacon or ham to go with your eggs and toast or English muffins with butter or preserves?"

"I'd like some ham with an English muffin with butter on it," said Dick.

"Same here."

As Sam was preparing them breakfast, Dick turned on the TV which was tuned to the Facility's internal TV station Channel 1.

"The launch of the latest space plane will happen at 2:00 PM this afternoon from hangar 3. It is expected to reach the moon within an hour and then return to be prepared for a test flight to the Mars colony which will take place tomorrow at the same time. It is expected to take three days to reach Mars Base Gagarin.

"In the Department of Medical Advancement and Care, Dr. Sorchen Vlandner has regrown a leg in three days for a former Russian soldier that lost his natural leg in Syria 22 years ago. After a day of rehabilitation and stimulation, the patient is expected to return to his wife and children in Saint Petersburg and resume a normal life. Dr. Vlandner is hoping to reduce the time for regrowth and rehabilitation to two days before introducing the proceedure to the medical community.

"In cultural news, various musicians will perform in the Glinka Recital Hall starting at 7:00 tonight. A reception for Richard and Katharine Thurman will be held in the banquet room between the recital hall and the Rimsky Korsakov Concert Hall after the recital. All are welcomed to attend both.

"If you want to hear President Kursolov's speech he gave last night, tune to Channel 2 for the full speech. It runs for approximately an hour and a half and begins in three minutes. You can hear it again at noon, 3:30 PM, and 10:00 PM on Channel 2.

"I'm Yuri Denovia reporting for the Channel 1 News at 7:00 AM. Have a successful and safe rest of the day. Next will be News From Saint Petersburg and a performance of Kachaturian's ballet 'Spartacus' recorded at the Kirov Ballet Theater."

"Sam," said Dick. "What will they be performing at the recital?

I hope it's not some non-musical noise."

"A pianist named Ivan Bogdanovich will be playing selections from the music of Chopin and Lizst during the first hour and various musicians will be playing pieces by Mozart during the second hour. Since we know you appreciate music of the old masters, we programmed accordingly."

"Good. I was expecting nothing but Russian music since I know how proud you are of your country's composers," said Kate, relieved. "We usually reserve that music for the larger stages. There will be performances of the ballet 'Romeo and Juliet' by Prokofiev Friday, Saturday, and Sunday in the Tchaikovsky Ballet Theater. The starting times will be 7:00 PM all three nights with an afternoon matinee on Saturday at 2:00 PM. Are you planning on attending any of the performances?" Sam asked.

"I could be at all the concert performances every time the doors were open if I had my way," Dick admitted. "But I would eventually get tired of that. I have an idea." he said to Kate. "Why don't we make Friday night date night like we used to back in California. It will be like a reward after a week of work."

"That sounds wonderful," said Kate. "Sam, do you know when all concert performances are scheduled?"

"I receive that information constantly. Ask me what is supposed to happen at any time of the day and if I've received that information, I can tell you. By the way. Dick, you have a morning meeting with the other three administrators at 10:00. They are Sasha Bogorman, Misha Sochi, and Ludmila Crisaloff. You will see them in the conference room next to your office. So if you want to take a tour of the Facility, it would be best if you used me as your avatar. There is an EPU headset in the bottom right hand drawer of your desk in your office. It is programmed to translate all languages used in the Facility to English and vice versa."

"I hope I don't have to wear a translating headset to talk with most of the people here since your President insists on having mainly Russians work here," Dick complained.

"Many know English to some extent. But if you want, there are devices that can be implanted in your brain that will allow you to understand all the languages used in the Facility. They're available in the medical clinic. Many people have them."

"Maybe I should get them before I start working in the electronic entertainment department," said Kate.

"That would be advisable," said Sam.

As Sam was finishing breakfast, Dick and Kate sat at the table and bowed their heads in prayer.

Dick said, "Dear Heavenly Father, bless the food that we are about to receive and bless the rest of this day. May we work well with our co-workers and fit in well on our jobs. Let everything run smoothly without any incidents. May we honor you in all that we do. I ask this in Christ Jesus' name. Amen."

After breakfast, Dick and Kate took a quick shower together in the cramped shower that was just large enough to accomodate two people which was sufficient for them. It felt like being back in their first apartment in Michigan when often they had to shower together to have enough hot water to bathe with.

There was a small flat-screen 3-D TV above the mirror which was shared by two sinks. The music of Kachaturian was appropriately playing the romance music from "Spartacus" as the couple showered which made them feel a bit arroused. They were reluctant to leave the shower while it was being played.

After the couple were done in the bathroom, they went to the bedroom where new clothes were hung up in the closet and placed in dresser drawers waiting to be worn as strains of Kachaturian were coming from the speakers of the 30-inch flat-screen 3-D TV on the wall of the bedroom facing the bed. The clothes they had worn coming to Siberia were placed in the clothes hamper in the wall. Behind the wall was a washer/dryer combination that took the clothes from the hamper and cleaned the items. Robotic hands and systems would remove the dried clothes and either hang them up or fold them and place them in the closet or drawers from behind the closet and dresser. Kate appreciated the conveniences.

After getting dressed, Dick and Kate left their apartment and walked to the elevator. Kate's job was on the top level while Dick's office was a floor below that. Dick kissed his wife goodbye before leaving the elevator and walked a few paces to his office past a kiosk that had a projection of a pleasant looking young woman inside.

"Good morning, Mr. Thurman," said the projection. "Have a pleasant day in the Facility."

Dick's office door slid open to reveal an office that reminded him of the way they used to look like a century ago. The huge desk might have been there when Hitler was threatening to conquer the Motherland. What was out of place was the holographic projection- box computer facing the worn office chair. There was no keyboard. Instead, there was an EPU headset jacked into the book-sized PC on the right side of the projection box.

Before he could don the headset, a projection of the kiosk projection's head was seen in the box.

"Good morning again, Mr. Thurman. You know about the meeting with the other administrators at 10:00 in the conference room. There is also a luncheon meeting with President Kursolov scheduled for noon today in the executive dining room which is down the hall from the offices. Since you and the cooks are the only ones that know about the meeting, it will be a one-on-one meeting in the private dining section of the room."

"Should I tell the administrators if our meeting goes long?"

"I doubt your meeting will last more than ten or fifteen minutes; half an hour tops."

"I guess it's a get-to-know-you meeting."

"Most likely. They were chosen to come here after your last planning session with the President last year."

"Why does the President want to talk with me this afternoon?" "I don't know. He didn't transmit that information this morning.

He might be coming to see the launch of the new space plane this afternoon."

"Did Dr. Davidoff work on it?"

"Yes she did. I was informed that you wanted to take a tour of the Facility. Your avatar might see her this morning."

"It would be nice to see a familiar face today. Which reminds me. Since the meeting is in a little over an hour, I better start the tour as soon as possible. I'd like to start at the Department of Medical Advancement and Care. Could you tell my android—"

"He already knows. He should be at the kiosk for the department by the time you put the EPU headset on."

Dick opened the bottom drawer of his desk and found the EPU headset that would connect his mind to that of Sam's. The moment it touched his head, it was activated. The projected head vanished and Dick sat back to enjoy the tour.

CHAPTER 2

Sam was standing at the kiosk of the Department of Medical Advancement and Care when Dick's headset contacted his cybernetic brain to transform the android into his avatar. What Sam saw and said would be what Dick saw and said in his office.

"Good morning, sir," said the projection that looked and sounded exactly like the one Dick had a conversation with. "May I help you?"

"Yes. I'm Dick Thurman. I'd like to take a tour of the department. Where would you suggest I start?"

"First, I'll summon the android guide to be your tour guide. He will meet you in the dental clinic at the end of the hall."

"Thank-you."

Sam walked down the hall which seemed to stretch beyond the horizon. He passed door after door that led to different divisions of the department. It looked like the tour of just that department might take over an hour. Minutes later, Sam entered the dental clinic where his guide was standing beside the receptionist's window.

"I've come to tour the clinic," said Dick through Sam. "Are they busy in there?"

"There are five patients being cared for right now," said the android. "Two of the most interesting procedures are being done that you should watch. So that we don't disturb the dentists or their patients, we will get in close with insect drones that will transmit what is seen and heard to a receiver. I'll tell you what is being done." The insect drones left their compartment in the wall and flew silently toward the first dental patient who had a mask over his mouth connected by a hose to a device the size of a toaster.

"This patient has five teeth with cavities in them that normally would either be pulled or filled. Today, the dentist is using natural and synthetic material to reconstruct the teeth. A pain bypass on the back of his neck is preventing pain signals from being felt. The nerves at the base of the teeth have been removed and the teeth have been anchored more securely into the jaw. A biosynthetic cement that will keep the tooth material together is blended with it and after it hardens, a thin crystalline glaze will be baked onto each tooth in his mouth to prevent cavities from forming. The glaze has a whitening agent that will keep his teeth pearly white. This procedure has the potential of ending the need for dentures or tooth implants in most cases."

The drones flew over to the next patient who had a larger mask over his mouth that was connected by a hose to a device that was the size of a toaster oven.

"This patient was born with an incomplete lower jaw. Thanks to the pain bypass on the back of his neck, no anesthesia is needed. The reason why he is wearing an EPU headset is to keep his brain occupied while the operation proceeds. It could last over 12 hours. His jaw is being reconstructed with both natural and synthetic materials along with his teeth and additional skin which is being merged with what exists. When he leaves the clinic and goes back to his home in Saint Petersburg, he will be able to eat food like a normal person as if he was never born with a defect. Micromachines are being used to reconstruct his jaw. Most will be removed once the work is done. The remaining micromachines will circulate throughout his body to keep him healthy."

"Imagine how much this dental surgery would cost in the real world. He couldn't work enough years to earn the money for it."

"The dental surgeons and dentists that go out into Russia with the technology perfected in the clinic will charge nothing. All expenses will be paid by BOSS and once dental clinics are set up for the procedures, they'll pay for whatever is needed."

The drones flew back to their compartment and the androids left the dental clinic. They walked down the hall to a door that had the sign DR. FRANKENSTEIN'S LABORATORY on it. It slid open and the androids entered a small reception area where a doctor was talking to a receptionist who was sitting behind a glass partition along with two other receptionists who were talking on the phone with people. The doctor put his coffee mug down on a coffee table that was between four comfortable chairs and greeted the androids.

"Hello, gentlemen. How may I help you?"

Dick through Sam said, "I'm Dick Thurman. I'm here to tour the place."

"Welcome to Dr. Frankenstein's Laboratory. I'm Dr. Vlandner. I spent the first 15 years of my medical career at the Newgate Municipal Hospital in Newgate, New York. But the last three months here have been more rewarding. Let me show you what we're doing in the animal lab."

The androids followed the doctor into a room that was down the hall from the reception area. When the door slid open, the trio entered a bright room where small animals were kept in cages. Two assistants were standing beside two cages that were next to each other. In one cage was an average-sized rat and in the other cage was a mean-looking feral cat that tried to reach the rat through the cage walls. He vigorously swatted at the rat that was in the corner of its cage.

The doctor opened a drawer under the cages and pulled out two syringes. He filled one with micromachines from a bottle and the other with raw material for the replication of micromachines from another bottle.

He pointed the syringe with micromachines at the androids and said, "These micromachines have been programmed to replicate six times before they rebuild the rat's brain into a cybernetic brain. That is why the syringe with the raw materials is so full. Watch what happens."

The doctor injected the neck of the rat with micromachines after one of the assistants held the struggling test creature down with a gloved hand. Afterwards, the doctor injected all of the raw material from the second syringe into the rat's neck. The assistant pulled his hand out of the cage and quickly closed the cage door.

The rat was on its stomach on the bottom of its cage for about a minute. It shook its head and climbed to the top of the cage which was about three feet above the floor of the cage. A cage door between the cages was slowly lifted by the second assistant until the cat squeezed into the rat's cage.

The cat jumped at the rat, but it crawled upside down out of reach of the feline's claws. The cat started climbing up the side of the cage. But it was too heavy to hang onto the top of the cage and fell to the floor of the enclosure. In a flash, the rat jumped onto the back of the cat's neck and bit down hard; snapping the spinal cord of the furry monster. It dropped to the floor of the cage unable to move its legs. It screamed in anger at its attacker, but was powerless to oppose it.

The rat scurried down the side of the cat and slashed the creature's throat. Blood gushed out of the jugular for about a minute until it became a trickle and finally ceased to flow. The cat closed its eyes and died while the rat was in the cat's cage eating its food and drinking its water. The first assistant opened the rat cage door and pulled the dead cat out to dispose of it.

The doctor smiled and said, "The rat is probably the smartest lab rat in the world. It has a totally cybernetic brain and from the way it moved, I think the micromachines are rebuilding its nervous system and muscles. We'll have to transfer it to a stronger cage before that happens."

The trio entered the next room where clear plexiglass enclosures and a huge saltwater tank were located. There was a wolf in one enclosure, an ostrich in a second enclosure, a polar bear in a third enclosure, a frog in a long enclosure, and a shark in the tank. There was a control panel with seven monitors, switches, and dials in the middle of the floor on a desk with a wheeled swivel chair under it. The doctor sat at the desk and flipped the switch to the left of the bottom left screen. The scene was shown on the larger center screen showing the wolf. The doctor twisted a dial to the left of the top left screen until it showed a sheep. With the flip of a switch, the sheep was shown on the screens with the wolf as the prey animal jumped out from behind a rock and jumped in front of its enemy. The sheep was only a robotic sheep with real mutton on it to produce the smell of a sheep, but the wolf thought it was real. The wolf took off after the fake sheep on a treadmill. The scenery in the enclosure changed to match the speed of the animals. The monitor on the plexiglass partition toward the ceiling indicated that the animals were doing 90 kph.

"Do you want the wolf to be like Wiley Coyote and not able to catch up with the sheep or do you want me to reward it for its effort?" the doctor asked.

"Give it a break," said Dick through Sam.

The doctor turned a dial on the desk and the speed of the animals increased to 125 kph. He smiled as he dialed up the speed of the treadmill. 130…135…140…145. The wolf kept straining to reach the fake sheep until the doctor flipped a switch and the prey animal stopped. The wolf pounced upon the sheep and ripped its throat out.

"The wolf has bionic legs, an adrenal gland stimulator, and a bionic heart," said the doctor. "If it didn't have the stimulator and synthetic heart, it would probably die from a heart attack because wolves aren't supposed to be able to run faster than some cars."

The doctor flipped the switch to the left of the screen that was in the center of the collumn of screens on the left side of the control panel. On the main screen appeared the polar bear. The doctor flipped a switch to the right of the smaller screen which showed the bear. The plexiglass partition of the enclosure ascended into the ceiling. The doctor walked into the enclosure and approached the bear as the androids were yelling at him to get out of the dangerous area. But the doctor flung his arms around the bear's neck and gave it a hug. The creature grunted and shook its head.

"Old Snuggles is a real sweetheart. He was in the Moscow zoo for ten years before he was sent here to experiment on," the doctor said as he stroked the bear's chin. "He has behavior modification brain implants that have transformed him from a killer into a giant teddy bear. I can't have him go back to the zoo for fear he'll be attacked and killed by natural polar bears unless he has his own enclosure and tank to swim around in. It would be murder if I had him set loose in the wild. He has lost his instincts of hunting and fighting. He is now a great big lovable pet. He has fathered some cubs for breeding purposes. But a female would either rip him to shreds or reject him if he returned to the zoo like this."

The bear stood and his head nearly brushed the ceiling. The doctor gave him a hug around his middle before leaving the enclosure. He lowered the partition and flipped a switch to the right of the bottom right screen and showed the image of the ostrich onto the main screen. He twisted the dial to the left of the top left screen until it showed a lion. He transferred the image to the screens with the ostrich and a projection sphere descended from the ceiling and projected the image of the lion behind the ostrich which began to run on a treadmill.

The speed indicated on the monitor on the plexiglass partition was 150 kph seconds after the projection of the lion appeared chasing the bird. The doctor turned a speed dial and turned up the speed of the treadmill to 160…170…180…190…200 kph.

"I've been able to top out at 270 kph. I'm glad it's a big stupid bird," the doctor admitted. "If I used micromachines to make its brain like the rat's, I'm afraid it would realize the lion is a fake and would stop running."

The doctor turned off the image of the lion and had the projection sphere ascend into the ceiling. He also slowed the treadmill until he brought it to a stop.

"Look at that frog over there," the doctor commanded. The androids stared at the little green amphibian.

"How far do you think it can jump?"

The enclosure was twenty meters long with a soft wall at the end. "After watching the wolf and the ostrich, I'd say the enclosure isn't long enough," said Dick through Sam. "Watch," said the doctor.

A loud bang was heard and the frog jumped toward the wall. He bounced off of the wall after colliding with it a couple meters above the floor. The distance monitor on the plexiglass partition registered 35 meters.

"Impressive," said Dick through Sam.

"I guess I shouldn't have fed it so many flies this morning," said the doctor. "Yesterday, Hoppity Hooper was still ascending when he hit the wall three meters up. Imagine how far he could jump if he thought it was life or death. That little fellow had to have synthetic skin to cover his hind legs because the skin he was born with couldn't have withstood the explosive action of the bionic muscles. I wouldn't be surprised if one day his legs take off and leave his body behind. I doubt that will happen. But around here, nothing is impossible."

The doctor took a wireless microphone out of his shirt pocket and said, "Okay, Ludmilla. Ready for a morning swim?"

Moments later, a beautiful young woman wearing a tight light blue swimsuit walked through a door near the pool. She climbed over the lip of the pool and swam toward an approaching shark fin. The doctor showed the shark as viewed from below the surface on the main screen. It was a great white that had to measure over five meters in length. Instead of attacking the swimmer, it dodged her and swam away.

An assistant walked through the doorway and flung a clear plastic bag with fish into the pool. The swimmer swam toward the bag and grabbed it. She took a deep breath and plunged to about two meters below the surface. She opened the bag and seconds later, the shark was within arm's reach of the woman. She pulled a fish out of the bag and hand-fed the creature. She kept pulling fish out of the bag and after she emptied it, the giant fish swam away. The woman swam toward the lip of the pool and climbed out.

Dick asked through Sam, "Were you scared out there?" "Not a bit. I enjoy my daily swims with Peter the Great." "As in great white shark?" Dick asked through Sam.

"I wish I could have swam with him like I usually do. But since you two are here today, I had to wear some clothes. Maybe that's why he darted away when we got close the first time. I know the doctor enjoys my daily swims."

The doctor smiled broadly and said, "One of the perks of my job here. At least my wife understands since she's a synthetic."

"Really?" asked an amazed Dick through Sam.

"Yeah. If you attend one of the performances of 'Romeo and Juliet' this week you'll see her perform as Juliet. Next month she'll do the title role of a new ballet composed especially for her by three of the Facility composers. It's titled 'Andria.' I've been at some of the rehearsals and the music is as good as anything Tchaikovsky or Prokofiev composed."

"I'm looking forward to watching her perform," said Dick through Sam. "I hope she doesn't outperform all the other dancers. I was wondering. Since she is basically a mechanical woman, does she weigh more than a human woman?"

"Her synthetic material is lighter than muscles or bone. She probably weighs no more than 75 pounds."

"Is she…you know…uh…" Dick through Sam fumblingly asked. "Just like a real woman? She is more female than many females. Our son and daughter, Trav and Helia, are cyborgs. Yes, I was able to get her pregnant in the same way real women become pregnant. She synthesized the DNA in my sperm and blended it with her synthetic DNA in her egg and three months later, each child was born. Their different-pitched screams took a bit of getting used to because I expected to hear crying. But she knew how to interpret them and after awhie so did I. It was kind of weird seeing them grow up so fast. But they look like humans in every respect. I sort of pity poor Trav. If he marries a human woman, he's the one who will have to be pregnant."

Dick shuddered to think about it.

"If he gets pregnant, I'll try to get back to New York to ask him how it feels."

"Is he back in Newgate?" Dick asked through Sam.

"Someone had to replace me at the hospital after I left. I guess it's because he's mainly synthetic that makes him a better doctor than I am."

"What about his sister?" Dick asked through Sam.

"She takes after her mother. She's in the New York City Ballet. Appropriately, she is the lead character in 'Coppelia' which I believe is performing later this Spring at Lincoln Center. Her mother and I will try to see her back there."

The doctor got up from the chair and headed for the exit. The androids followed him into a hallway past a small cafateria into the hospital ward. There was a nurse and two mediunits behind the counter watching monitors that showed what was happening in the rooms. Dick caught a glimpse of one monitor which showed a couple naked in one of the beds having sex.

"Physical therapy?" Dick asked through Sam.

"That's Mr. Bellindikov in room 5. It took years for Mrs. Bellindikov to convince him he needed to boost his sexual performance. But he didn't want to do it chemically. When his wife found out about the Facility needing test subjects for a new micromachine system to boost sexual performance, she volunteered him for the project. I don't think he minds being a guinea pig."

"Is she…"

"She's synthetic," the doctor said. "She acts just like a human woman only better. She can be aroused and evidently can arouse men too. At least she won't get pregnant unless she wants to be."

"Are most of the prostitutes in the bordello synthetic too?" Dick asked through Sam.

"All of them are. I haven't asked too many people who have gone there if it was like in a regular bordello. But the ones I've talked with like the pleasure units, as they're called. Even a couple women I've talked with enjoyed the experience. Personally, I like my sweet Dollia. She is more than satisfying," the doctor said with a huge smile on his face.

The trio entered room 10 where a patient was lifting his right leg with a weighted shoe on it. There was an electronic stimulation legging on it.

"Corporal Kirov, how are you doing?" the doctor asked.

"Better than I dared believe was possible. Thank-you so much. I feel like I could run a marathon," the man bragged.

"Really?" Dick asked through Sam.

"Well, maybe at least a 5K. It feels like my other leg only better. I'll throw away my crutch when I get home."

"What's the first thing you want to do when you arrive home?" asked Dick through Sam.

"Besides hugging and kissing my wife when I see her, I told my sons Sergei and Peter that if all went well, I would race them to the park and back. They laughed, of course. But the way I feel, I think I can beat them."

The trio left the room and headed for the elevator to the gallery above operation room 2. There were seven other doctors and surgeons in the gallery watching an operation being performed by two humans and three mediunits. The trio found seats near the front where the others were seated. What looked like a small iron lung was over the patient and the surgeons were wearing EPU headets and moving their hands as if they were handling surgical instruments.

The head surgeon spoke to the gallery and said, "This man has not lived a normal life. If his parents weren't as rich as they are, he would have died as a baby. His organs are incapable of functioning normally without external assistance. He has spent his entire life in hospitals and a special medical assistance chamber in his home. But he is his parent's only child and they love him too much to let him die.

"What we are doing is giving him a synthetic heart, a chemical catalyst to replace his liver and some other vital organs, a synthetic digestive system, a small nuclear reactor to provide a sufficient amount of energy, and a new type of micromachine that uses less synthetic materials and more biological materials that one gets from food and supplements. They will circulate through his body and replicate when they need to. Every now and then he will need either a pill or an injection of standard micromachine material.

It's up to him. I would advise that he use the chemical input port of his catalyst.

"For the first time in 21 years he will be able to live a normal life, or at least as normal as possible. He won't be such a burden for his family and might be able to find a nice woman and marry her and have children. He might live to be over 150 for all I know. It depends on how good the micromachines are along with the other synthetic organs."

Dick through Sam whispered to the doctor, "It's too bad the kid's parent's didn't pay for the operation. They could probably afford it."

The doctor said quietly, "They gave the facility a 10 million ruble down-payment and will give another 100 million rubles if the operation is a success. It will allow the Facility to take the medical technology to many hospitals throughout Russia and the rest of Europe."

While the surgery was being carried out, the trio left the gallery and took the elevator to the hospital ward. Dick and the guide were about to go down a hall when the doctor stopped them.

"I'm sorry, but we can't go down there. It's an ultra-clean ward where work is done on bionic limbs and devices. You two would have to wear clean suits and be sprayed down first. So I guess this is the end of the tour. Dick, I hope I will see you at the recital tonight."

"I wouldn't miss it," Dick said through Sam.

The doctor shook Sam's hand and left the ward to go back to his laboratory. At least Dick assumed he was doing that.

CHAPTER 3

Sam left the android that had accompanied him in the medical division and took the elevator to the Department of Science and Technology a level below where the administrative offices were located. The department occupied three levels including the level where the offices were located which were near the Transportation Division of the department. Dick figured he would be spending enough time working in that division that he didn't need a tour.

He had heard that scientists and engineers were working on adjusting the environment to modify what the world was experiencing; global cooling. For years they were formulating plans to try and reverse global warming. But when sunspot activity nearly ceased, they had to change their goal: make the world warmer safely without compounding the problems that they believed had caused a warmer climate. They didn't want to believe the sun played a major factor in shaping the climate. But with the temperatures plunging to levels not experienced in some places for the last few centuries, something had to be done to prevent another ice age.

Sam left the elvator and faced the familiar projection at the kiosk inside a reception area.

"Welcome to level B of the Department of Science and Technology. On this level there is the Division of Industrial Technology, the Divison of Materials and Products Fabrication, and the Division of Environmental Research. Hallway 1 leads to the Division of Industrial Technology. Hallway 2 leads to the Division of Materials and Products Fabrication. Hallway 3 leads to the Division of Environmental Research."

Sam headed down the third hallway to a door that was at the end of the hall about half a kilometer away. When he reached it, a red light above the door came on and a man's voice asked, "Who are you?"

"You are looking at my android assistant Sam. I am Dick Thurman. Am I allowed to enter for a tour of the division?"

The light turned green and the door opened. Sitting at a reception desk was a young woman who asked him, "Do you know who you want to see?"

"I would like to see someone in environmental research."

The receptionist pressed a button and asked, "Is Dr. Bronkowski available?"

Moments later, a young man entered the room. He looked like he was half the age of Dick. He extended his hand and Sam shook it.

"Who am I talking to through this avatar?"

"Dick Thurman. I'd like to see what you're doing in here." "Sure. Follow me."

The man and android walked through the doorway into what looked like a TV station monitor room. Half a dozen men and women were observing work being done inside and outside the Facility. They were also manning controls.

On monitor 1 there was a saucer that measured about ten meters in diameter. It was on the ice somewhere north of the Facility. It lifted from the ice and when it was around 100 meters up, it began beaming plasma beams down upon the ice that rotated under the saucer to melt a hole which was expanded to a kilometer in diameter. The beams rotated at 100 RPMs and produced a warm air cavity under the saucer because ice didn't reform. Steam began to rise slowly from the sea inside the cavity.

The saucer rose as the camera pulled back until it reached a kilometer above the ice. The hole was 10 kilometers in diameter and steam formed a cone to fill the cavity.

A camera on a drone that was further away than the camera on the ground showed the saucer climbing to 10 kilometers and the hole expanded to 100 kilometers and the cone of steam filled the cavity like a conical cloud. When the beams stopped boiling the water and the saucer flew away, the cone of steam expanded into snow which was blown by the wind or sank to the hole which was free of ice so far. The snow that fell onto the hole dissolved into the sea as rain due to the warmth of the water.

"Dr. Bronkowski, what did I just see? I know it was more than a glorified science fair experiment."

"I wanted to see if water could be drawn up as steam from the sea. It's around minus 50 degrees centigrade out there. I thought that when the beams were shut off, the steam would become ice and not snow. But the latent heat of the beams warmed the air enough to turn the steam into snow and the water in the sea is still warm enough to not turn back into ice. At least not completely.

"Imagine if there were 100 saucers over open water using rotating plasma beams to generate huge clouds of water vapor. Since water vapor is a powerful greenhouse gas, it can be used to warm the atmosphere. If I wanted to make the atmosphere colder, I would use ice whales to form small icebergs. I wish we had had 100 of them half a century ago. They might have moderated the climate enough to stop some of earth's deadliest and costliest hurricanes we experienced before I was born."

On monitor 2 was another saucer on the bottom of the sea. The woman at the controls flipped a switch and seconds later, bubbles started forming around the saucer. Within a minute, the bubbles totally obscured the view.

"How hot is the saucer?" the doctor asked the controller. "I've got it up to boiling. Do you want it hotter?"

"Turn it up to 500 degrees centigrade."

The woman twisted the temperature dial to 500 degrees centigrade and through the mass of bubbles was seen a blurry red object which was the saucer.

"This is another way to create water vapor, in a round about way," said the doctor.

On monitor 3 was the camera that showed the first saucer on the ice. The water that had not turned back into ice in the hole that had been melted began to bubble as the saucer-produced bubbles surfaced. Bubbles of ice floated in the wind away from the hole, shattering when they slammed into other bubbles or ice they landed on.

On monitor 4 there were seven saucers flying in a V formation that were glowing white hot.

"If there could be 100 squadrons of these saucers circling the earth generating fields of heat in excess of 1000 degrees centigrade, eventually the atmosphere would warm enough to reverse the period of global cooling we are experiencing," claimed the doctor.

"But since the sun is involved in how our climate is, wouldn't they have to be in the air constantly?" Dick asked through Sam.

"That's the problem. Each saucer costs around $50 million even at the Facility's discounted price for construction. That's $35 billion. It costs approximately $100 a day to keep each saucer flying a year counting fuel, maintenance, and personnel expenses. At least the nuclear fuel is processed nuclear waste which at one time they wanted to deposit in salt mines forever. Eventually the saucers will wear out and have to be replaced. The second alternative is much more expensive initially, according to computerized projections. Watch monitor 5."

A sphere that was 10% of the diameter of the moon was shown near it. It suddenly glowed like the sun and emitted waves of electromagnetic energy. The waves slammed into the Van Alan Belts and the upper atmosphere of the earth.

"I call this a mini-sun. It would be basically hollow. But there would be one of the most powerful nuclear reactors inside that would power the system to generate the equivalent of miniature sunspots that would do the same thing as real sunspots do only focused on this planet. It is estimated to cost over $5 trillion. The annual maintenance costs might exceed $100 million. But if it were built, it might supply enough radiated energy to reverse the effects of a spotless sun."

"That is genius," said Dick through Sam. "What would it do to the moon if it were so close?"

"It would be positioned far enough away from the moon to not be drawn too much to it. People would have to get used to seeing the sun in the day and the mini-sun at night. But if it can warm up the earth, people will appreciate it."

"And what if what you are doing here does too good a job and we start experiencing another period of global warming?"

"Watch monitor 6."

Something that looked like a giant centipede was on a body of water as seen from a camera floating somewhere a lot warmer than the Kara Sea. Suddenly, ice began to surge from what looked like feet at the end of each leg. Within a minute, ice collided with the camera and rocked it.

"That is an ice centipede. Then again, you probably expected me to name it that. It is located off the coast of New Guinea and measures over

150 meters in length. It takes nitrogen out of the air, condenses it into liquid nitrogen, and turns the water it comes in contact with into ice. This is faster and possibly more efficient than an ice whale. If ever the earth warms up too much, fleets of these things will form ice islands probably large enough to be seen from space."

"That was truly incredible. Is there anything else you're working on?"

"Follow me."

Sam and the doctor entered a huge room where robots, technicians, and engineers were working on saucers, centipedes, and other devices. The doctor walked over to one of the devices that was being built that was the size of a school bus. It was an oval shaped flying craft that was testing scoops that opened and closed on top and below the craft. It was open in the back, ready to have the power system and engine inserted. Cables were used to power the device for testing.

The doctor said, "This is a scrubber. It doesn't look big enough to do the job it is called to do. But if 100 were built, they could do an amazing job in removing certain chemicals out of the atmosphere. We know that when a volcano spews material into the atmosphere, it can make the climate colder for awhile. That has happened often. What this would do along with maybe 99 other scrubbers is fly over a volcano and suck in the ash and chemicals produced, condense it, compact it, and form solid blocks in many cases which would be discharged either in desolate areas or at places where the material could be recovered and possibly used for various purposes. Entire buildings might be built from the material discharged by a volcano. In fact, the Facility will see if it can interest the Russian Antarctica base in using material spewed by Mount Erebus and other volcanoes to be used as building material."

The doctor and Sam walked over to four other devices that were simple looking. They had two flat plates that measured ten meters long by a meter wide by 10 centimeters thick that were joined at a right angle. Behind the plates were hundreds of angled metal cross pieces that connected to squared metal arms that were a meter square that ran the length of the plates. Behind where the plates met, there was a larger metal box that measured three meters wide by two meters high by four meters long that connected to the arms behind the plates with a dozen metal tubes that were 5 centimeters in diameter.

"These are field generators and emitters," said the doctor. "Once the reactors are installed they will be placed in orbit between the earth and the moon. A fifth device I call the discharger will be located in the middle of the field that is generated to discharge it toward the earth in the same way a sunspot discharges energy toward the earth in a flare. This system should cost no more than $250 million and might be nearly as good as the mini-sun. It depends on the amount of energy I can discharge. I should have the system up within the next couple weeks for testing. We will do ground testing first outside when the emitters are at least a kilometer apart. The discharger will have to be held in place suspended from a drone. I just hope the field that is discharged doesn't create a square crater that is too deep."

The doctor and Sam walked over to a familiar looking device. But it was a bit larger than Dick had seen before and slightly different. It was the size of a jet fighter, would be piloted, and had dozens of 2-centimeter pipes over the rear portion of the fuselage raked back at a 45 degree angle close to the surface of the craft. It looked like a bee which is used to boil storm clouds away by means of hot pipes. But there were also vents under the pipes as if it were a wasp which is used to flash freeze storm clouds with condensed nitrogen. There was a cockpit in the front with a technician in the seat.

"Stand back," the technician shouted.

The doctor and Sam stepped back several paces until they were several meters away from the craft. The pipes began to glow red and then white. They felt the heat as if they were standing near a forge.

"This is a piloted version of both a bee and a wasp. When I read about the experiment that was conducted in Indiana a few years ago when a team of storm chasers used bees and wasps to attack tornado clouds, I knew I had to build a larger version of them to attack not only tornadoes, but also hurricanes. Sometimes pumper vessels aren't able to stop hurricanes from forming. So a squadron of these will try to destroy those monster storms. I knew that the head of NOAA was wrong when he claimed it would require a nuclear device to destroy tornadoes and hurricanes.

Ironically, a nuclear reactor powers this device."

Moments later, the pipes cooled and were retracted into the device. That was when the vents began blowing extremely chilled air that was colder than the windiest winter blast.

"That cold air comes from compressed nitrogen being pushed out at over 300 kph. We're lucky the vents are pointing away from us or else we might get frostbite. How low a temperature are you programmed to withstand?"

"I can function normally down to minus 110 degrees celsius. Anything lower and my joints will begin to stiffen. If I were out in space I would need a space suit to insulate me. I would also need it to protect me from the extreme heat of space, to some extent. I can go out there like I am now and not experience much degradation. I just don't know how cosmic rays would affect me during extended periods of exposure."

Dick asked through Sam, "How do you take devices out of here to the surface?"

"There is an elevator at the end of the room that can take things the size of this up to the surface where they can be taken to one of the hangars where they can be prepared for launch. The centipede needs to be disassembled and brought up in sections where it will be brought to one of the hangars where it will be assembled. At least it's not too large for the largest hangar. And then it will be taken by VLVs to where it is needed. If it needs to arrive faster, it can be placed in sections into cargo planes. But when you consider the assembly time, it might be easier and a bit faster to fly it by VLVs to where you need it since they can fly at upwards to 700 kph when they are carrying something the size of a centipede. An aerodynamic shell would be placed over the device in the hangar before it's brought out where four to eight VLVs would attach cables to the shell."

"How will you place large objects like the emitters and dischargers into space? They look too large for a space plane to put into orbit."

"They'll be shot into orbit by GSLP in sections. Robots will assemble the sections and help handle them. We'll be able to give the devices directions. But the robots will fine tune the arrangement of the devices. I'll put them into space inside a GSLP projectile. When they're not needed, they will go back in the projectile to protect them from cosmic rays and space debris. They'll also be recharged in the projectile."

"First or second generation GSLP?" Dick asked through Sam. "Second. It rquires a bit more energy due to the rotating beams.

But the beams also shield the projectile from harmful things out there. In the Space Research Division they've sent stuff up to the Russian moon colony and to Mars Base Gagarin using the second generation GSLP system. It took three months to land cosmonauts on Mars aboard conventional rockets. With second generation GSLP we can send tons of materials to Mars in as little as six hours." "Then why are they going to send the new space plane there tomorrow?" Dick asked through Sam.

"Many space travelers want to see what's out there so they can avoid collisions. Inside a GSLP projectile you're like what American Mercury astronauts felt like; spam in a can. Once we can perfect repulsion-drive engines, a trip to Mars might take as little as 15 minutes even when you consider taking off from here and landing on Mars."

"How close are we to having repulsion-drive engines?" Dick asked through Sam.

"You'll have to ask them in the space division. I just use what they give me."

"I'll make sure to visit them there before the end of the day. I want to see Dr. Davidoff. I haven't seen her since I met her in Moscow."

"Like so many people here in the Facility she's brilliant."

"She's also a bit easy on the eyes. She's around my age, but she still looks great," Dick said admiringly through Sam. "I also think it's wonderful that she's a Christian. How many people at the Facility are Christians?"

"I don't know the number. But it's safe to say the churches will be crowded this Sunday. So go early to the one you want to go to. I'll be sleeping in on Sunday because I'll be attending Sabbath services at the synagogue. My father Solomon would love the synagogue here and Rabbi Jacob Bernstein from Queens, New York."

"How many Americans are at the Facility?"

"I'd say at least 15% of the people who work here are from America. Then again, at least half of the people here are Russian. President Kursolov insisted on that."

"Naturally. I'm hoping they're the best that can be found in Russia."

"I heard that for every job opening, even for bussing tables, there were between five and 30 applicants. Extensive background checks were made to make sure the right people came in. Free food, housing, health care, and nearly everything else were very tempting. The higher than expected pay and perks are very attractive and should allow many to retire early. That will let other qualified people come here and work."

"I know BOSS invests much of my salary into companies associated with the Madhouse in Arizona and stock options in BOSS Investments. Whenever I do retire I should be set for life." "I remember when I was a kid I used to hear people say that people talk about the weather but they do nothing about it. Here at the Facility we are going to finally do something about it. I wish this stuff had been around half a century ago. We wouldn't have had all the turmoil and fear over climate change. I rarely heard people blame the sun for causing it even though the sun has been involved in climate change from day one. I'm glad America, China, India, and Russia didn't buy into the panic despite so many millions wanting those countries to waste trillions of dollars combatting it. I remember people saying when I was a kid that by the middle of the century, if we did nothing, we would have global disasters. They were right about the disasters. But it won't be from a sun that is too hot or too much pollution. Our scrubbers will handle the air pollution. Then again, greenhouse gasses that are there could increase our average temperatures around the world now that we need the heat. But with volcanoes and a lack of sunspot activity, it will take more than greenhouse gasses to raise the temperature.

The world needs us to succeed."

At Dick's office door were the three other administrators.

"I'm sorry, but I'm about to have a meeting," Dick apologized through Sam. "I need to leave because I'd rather experience a tour of the Facility through Sam or in person. I have some questions I'd like to ask and I don't think Sam may come up with them. See you at the recital tonight?"

"I'm not a big fan of classical music. Now if there was a science fiction convention, you couldn't keep me away. But since we're doing what a few years ago was considered science fiction, talking about hard science is more interesting."

Sam left the weather division and entered the reception area where the information kiosk was located. He sat in one of the chairs located there and went into dormant mode. With no one coming in, no one was going to say it looked weird to see someone sitting in the reception area with his eyes open and not breathing as if he were dead.

CHAPTER 4

The door electronically became transparent to reveal who was outside. Dick put his EPU headset in the bottom drawer and opened the door from his desk.

Dick stood and shook the hands of the trio and motioned toward the chairs they could sit in. But they weren't interested in sitting.

"Mr. Thurman, we need to talk in the conference room," said Sasha. "We have some charts and graphs and other information we want to share with you and the conference room is set up for the presentation. Also, it is electronically more secure in that room and so sound proof that you could fire a gun in there and no one would hear it outside the room."

"Then let's go," Dick said before the quartet left the office and entered the conference room where they sat at the conference table after the door slid close.

Misha turned on the holographic projection system which showed the internal layout of the Facility. It was enormous; even larger than the original Madhouse. The factory complex had five levels; each able to accomodate an entire factory assembly floor. Since WW II it had expanded to 12 levels with three of them off limits for some reason.

Ludmila said,"One of the main reasons why we three were chosen to be administrators was because members of our families worked here at one time or another. My great-grandfather worked here when it opened in 1941 building tanks and planes. He eventually became a designer and stayed with the Facility designing tanks and planes; most never used. But he was a fine designer and many of his machines were tested here on the bottom level which at that time during the '50s and '60s was the fifth level down from the top." She pointed at that level of the projection.

"My father used to conduct experiments for the GRU in the forbidden zone," said Misha as he pointed at the bottom levels of the Facility.

"My mother was a doctor in the hospital which is still being used today. You have visited that part of the Facility during your tour through your avatar," said Sasha.

"How did you know I was touring the Facility?" Dick asked expectantly.

"I interfaced with your EPU headset without you knowing it," said Sasha.

"You know, I thought someone was watching me. I guess it's old cold war historical paranoia. Everyone in America assumed when they went to the Soviet Union that they were being watched. I bet your relatives might have thought the same thing if they got the chance to visit America."

"My parents were in the Leningrad Symphony," said Ludmila. "They visited America a few times with the orchestra and in other groups of performers. Their handlers made sure they weren't turned by your CIA or others who wanted to 'rescue'them from communism. They were more interested in making music than being citizens of a country that would always be suspicious of them or put them on a pedestal as if they were deity. They were fine performers. But they weren't great performers. The Soviet Union allowed you to be above average as they were and made your life comfortable. Then we lost much of the security we depended on when the Soviet Union became just Russia. They still made a living. But it was harder. That is why I joined the government after I finished college."

"I feel honored to be a part of the Faciity. But I'm sure you have more than a history lesson to share with me."

For the next 20 minutes, Dick had to sit through some boring statistics, charts, graphs, performance records, materials orders, and requests. He pretended he was interested. But when the trio of administrators realized he was bored, they wrapped up the meeting and left a little disgusted with Dick. Dick sensed their disapproval even though they smiled as they left the room. At least he had the chance to tour more of the Department of Science and Technology. Dick had Sam travel down hallway 1 to the Division of Industrial Technology. The meeting with the other administrators informed him that they were doing work on factory equipment that he might find interesting.

At the end of the hall was another red light and a man's voice said, "We are conducting testing inside this room. Please wait a few seconds and then I will be able to allow you to enter."

Sam waited about a minute before the door slid open and he was allowed to enter what looked like a factory. A man inside a lifting suit trudged toward the door. The powered suit was at least three meters tall and looked like it had been used for awhile. There were scuff marks on the device and yellowish orange paint was duller than it originally was. The suit opened in the rear and the operator exited. He shook the hand of Sam.

"Good morning," he said. "I'm Gregor Novachec. I run this little operation here. I bet you want to be taken on the grand tour."

"That's right. I'm Dick Thurman. What exactly were you testing that I wasn't allowed to observe?"

"See that steel girder on the top of the rack over there?"

There was a girder that measured 10 meters long by half a meter high by 5 centimeters thick on top of a rack five meters above the floor.

"I carried it from a pile of girders at the end of the room and placed it up there."

The man reached inside a box beside the door of the suit and handed Sam a hardhat.

"I know you're an android. But if I drop that girder on your head… You know, if I were to drop it on your head, this hardhat wouldn't keep you from becoming mashed metal and synthetic material. But I need to obey the safety regs. You understand."

"Yeah, yeah," Dick said through Sam. "Could I watch you lift the girder off of the rack and take it back to where you got it from?" "Knock yourself out. Just stand here and I'll try not to stomp you like a bug with my big feet in a fit of anger."

The feet were at least two meters long and half a meter wide. The legs of the suit were jointed in the middle of the feet. Magnetic pistons in front and behind the legs were connected to the feet to allow the legs to bend forward and backwards for stability when lifting something. The operator trudged to the rack, extended the arms of the suit, grabbed the girder, and easily brought it down to the floor where it was gently placed on two levitation carts.

"This girder weighs at least six tons. I hope you're wearing insulated shoes," the operator advised.

"Why?"

"You're going to feel a little tingling in your feet and legs when I turn on the carts."

The operator turned on the carts remotely from inside the suit. The fields they produced caused the rebarb in the floor to become magnetized. If Dick had physically been there, he would have felt the current surging through the floor. It wasn't enough to do serious damage. But it would have felt as if one's feet and legs were touching something that was shorting out.

"I hope the fields don't bother you. I've been trying to adjust the fields, but they're not cooperating."

"Back in Arizona we had the same problems with our lev carts there. Ionize the air on the floor more and repel off of that. You'll still get a surge in the rebarb. But it won't feel like your feet and legs are in a light socket."

"I'll make the adjustments later. For now you'll have to withstand the pins and needles as I move them over to the pile."

The operator directed the carts to the pile which was more than 100 meters away. They glided to the pile in less than a minute. The operator picked up the girder after he lowered the carts to the floor and placed it on the pile with a loud clang. Sam followed the lumbering suit which acted as if it were sticking to the floor a bit several meters behind it.

"Will my feet not feel like I'm slogging through mud after I adjust the carts?"

"It should be a little easier. Just don't extend the fields too much or follow too close. You might be drawn to the carts too much," Dick through Sam advised. "You might try using multiple fields and boundary fields to keep the displacement fields from spreading out too much."

The operator exited the suit and approached Sam.

"Follow me to the platform conveyor system I've been working on lately."

Sam and the man walked over to something that looked like a trough on the floor that stretched 100 meters in length. It was several centimeters high and a meter wide with a dozen platforms that measured two meters long. The trough had a 10-centimeter lip on both sides and each platform followed a track in the lips.

"I used to work in a warehouse in Moscow that used rollers to move things from the trucks to inside the receiving area. There were hundreds of rollers; each with bands and motors and lots of problems when they weren't maintained well. Sometimes small objects would drop between the rollers if the conveyor was stretched too much. This platform conveyor uses levitated platforms that can carry upwards to three tons of material and glide smoothly down the trough. The platforms can glide without power or be moved by linear induction from turtle speed to a nice jogging pace.

"When a platform gets to the end of the trough, it drops down and moves below the upper platforms back to the start of the trough. When each platform reaches the beginning of the trough, it is lifted to the top to be used. The platforms can be spaced out or against one another to prevent things dropping off the platforms. Even if that happened, the lower platforms that are going in the other direction will be lifted when they get to the beginning."

"Could you demonstrate?"

"Sure. In fact, I've had fun platform surfing. What I do is drop the platforms and leave one platform in the top lips. There are thirty platforms in the trough that easily fit in the bottom of the trough. I leave one platform in the top lips, run as fast as I can toward the platform, and either jump onto it or do a belly flop on it. Since it's rather hard, I usually place cushions on the platform before I dive onto it. I sometimes place cushions at the end of the trough to land on. But if I do it right, I can jump off of the platform before it comes to the end of the trough. "

The man picked up a controller that was connected to the trough by an electrical cable. He sent all of the platforms to the end and dropped them to the bottom lips. He popped one platform to the top and walked to the back of the room. He ran as fast as he could toward the trough and when he was a few meters from the platform leaped like he was long jumping. The platform glided down the trough on his knees and hands. In less than a minute he was at the end of the trough sprawled on his stomach after the platform came to a sudden stop.

"Are you all right?" Dick asked through Sam.

"Yeah. I usually end up like that," he said as he was getting off the floor. "I'm sorry that there's nothing more to see. I've only been here a few months and there are a lot of things I'd like to work on after this. I'll work on making the carts a little less shocking after you leave. Maybe the next time when you're here for real we can have a platform race."

"You'll probably beat me because I haven't long jumped since college and back then I wasn't all that good."

Sam left the room and headed for the elevator because he wanted to see Dr. Davidoff more than he wanted to see how materials were formed. He took the elevator to the level where the Space Division was located and entered the reception area where the familiar kiosk with the familiar projection were located.

"Good morning, sir. Welcome to the Space Research Division of the Department of Military and Space Research. Who would you like to see?"

"I'd like to see Dr. Davidoff. This is Sam the avatar for Dick Thurman."

"She is in hangar 3 preparing for her flight to the moon. Take the elevator to the top level, exit it and walk to the horizontal elevator car, and push the button corresponding to hangar 3."

Sam got in the elevator and took it to the top level. On the destination panel were hanger 1, hangar 2, hangar 3, the GSLP launch site, the distillery, the greenhouse complex, Smirnoffgrad, and Konstanigrad. He pushed the button corresponding to hangar 3 and in two minutes was leaving the elevator car and taking another up to the hangar floor where technicians were preparing the space plane for a flight to the moon. A technician approached Sam.

"May I help you?"

"I'm Dick Thurman using my avatar Sam. I want to see Dr. Davidoff?"

"She's doing her preflight ritual. She's in the break room having a late breakfast and probably praying. If she's praying, please don't disturb her. She wants God's protection even if it probably won't be any more dangerous than flying a regular plane. After over 20 flights for the Facility she hasn't been close to losing it all. But there is always a first time for everything. It's tomorrow's flight that could be dangerous since she is flying to Mars."

Sam headed for the break room that was in the corner of the hangar at the back. When he saw her head bowed and her eyes closed he waited for her to finish before entering the room.

Dr. Davidoff smiled and said, "Good morning. Who are you an avatar for?"

"Dick Thurman."

Her smile widened. She said, "Sit down. Let's catch each other up since we last met."

The doctor walked over to what looked like an old-fashioned automat vending machine and opened the doors where two breakfast sandwiches, some waffles, and a tangerine were located. She placed the plates on a tray and slid it to the microwave to heat up the sandwiches and waffles. She also picked up a couple packets of syrup, a fork and knife and napkin, and placed an insulated mug under a tea dispenser to receive a mug of hot Earl Grey tea. She talked as she approached the table where Sam was sitting.

"I had heard you and your wife were here. How do you like the Facility so far?"

"I think I could get used to the place. It's so good to see you again."

After she sat down she reached out her hand and clasped his for a moment before withdrawing.

"I wish I wasn't too forward. I've thought of you a lot since the day we met in Moscow."

"Same here. But I'm married."

"So am I; to my work. Many of my friends in the old life ended up burnt out or married to men who wanted them for their bodies. But the body falls apart. A few found some decent men. But those were the lucky ones. Unfortunately, a few commited suicide."

"Are you happy?"

She clenched her lips, took a sip of tea, and said, "I guess I am.

Let me pray grace before I forget." Both bowed their heads in prayer.

"Heavenly Father, thank-you for this meal and thank-you for bringing the avatar of Dick Thurman here to see me. May my flight be uneventful and may tomorrow's flight be the same. I need you to protect me and guide me in everything I do. I ask this in Christ Jesus' name. Amen."

Dick through Sam talked about how things had gone since the time in Moscow to let her eat her breakfast. She filled him in on how her life had been since they met before entering an exercise room to work off some nervous energy. There were some weights and a treadmill in the room that looked like they had been there since the hangar was used by the Soviet Air Force. Sam followed her in.

The doctor took off her top and hung it on a hook on the wall next to the small locker room door. At least she was wearing a sports bra which relieved Dick. She walked over to the treadmill and set it at jogging speed. After it started, she stepped onto it and began jogging.

"I hope you're not too tired for your flight after this," Dick commented through Sam.

"I'll be fine. I try to jog a couple kilometers everyday. It would be nice to do it outside in the fresh air on the runway. But the air is a bit… brisk today. I was thinking. Why don't you accompany me to Mars tomorrow."

"I don't know if I can allow Sam to do that," said Dick through Sam.

"I want you, not your avatar, to accompany me. The trip to Mars will take at least three days since it is on the other side of the sun at this time. I'll have to fly wide of the sun to get there. It's going to be more dangerous than I've been letting on."

"So you want to have company if you plunge into the sun?" Dick asked sarcastically through Sam.

"I said I'll fly wide of the sun; not into the sun."

"I guess I'll have to slather on some sunscreen before I go. I hope they have some SPF 1 million. I'll probably need to trowel it on."

"I've designed the plane with an electronic windshield. As long as the cameras and sensors aren't knocked out of commission we'll be fine."

"I thought you were using an electronic windshield because I didn't think I saw a real one. You won't feel like you're flying blind will you?"

"Once I turn on the screen, it will be as if I had a real one. There are a lot of advantages to having an electronic windshield. When we fly in the direction of the sun, the screen will cut down the level of light so it won't blind us. If sensors detect something in our way, the screen will magnify the view of the object."

"I don't know if you're a big fan of 'Star Trek.'"

"I grew up watching it. I thank the inclusion of Chekov for that. But sure. I liked the next generation better."

"When I was a kid, I asked one of the people involved with 'Star Trek' why the Enterprise had so many windows. Electronic ones would be better. He told me that Gene Roddenberry liked windows, so they put in windows. I still think electronic ones are better. One tiny rock flying through the windshield at 100,000 kph can end your life."

"Speaking of 'Star Trek,'there are several electronic entertainment producers that produce that type of programs for the Facility's channel 5. Your wife might be working with some of them. Ask her about it when you get home."

"I will. I just hope I'm not too tired when I come along with you tomorrow."

A big smile came to the woman's face.

"When I get back from the moon I'll probably eat something, pray for awhile for God's protection, and then go to bed so I'll be ready for tomorrow's flight. Most of the trip will be on autopilot. But just the same, I need to be alert."

"What type of engine does your plane use?" "Repulsion-drive."

"Then it's not going to take you three days to reach the Red Planet. It might take you three hours."

"I'm not going to ask too much from my engine during the trip." "Do you have enough fuel for the reactor?"

"I'll have enough fuel for a trip to Andromeda and back." "So you're going to travel at hyperlight speed?"

"I don't know. I can't promise you that. But if I do, I do. We'll just have to see if the engine I built is capable of hyperlight speed. If not tomorrow, at least some day in the future. How fast can your flying car travel?"

"It uses a field engine; not a repulsion-drive engine. But if I work on it and make some adjustments, I might have an engine that is similar to a repulsion-drive engine. I might have to totally rebuild my field engine or build a totally new vehicle. I just don't know."

"If you need some help, I'll be more than happy to help you. You have to remember, I am a rocket scientist."

"What you will be flying is as much a rocket as a housecat is a tiger. Did you ever think you'd be flying to the moon let alone Mars?"

"To tell you the truth, yes. I also thought someday I would travel to Mars. I just didn't think I'd do it in a space plane of my own design."

"Are you thinking about landing on the moon?"

"Yes. I have both wheeled and levitated landing gear. It depends on the surface I'm landing on. The wheeled landing gear I'll be using to takeoff from the tarmac out there will rotate inside the fuselage to the levitated landing gear. I'll use field ionization of the surface of the moon to repel off of. I might be able to descend like the LEM did 70 years ago. I might even have a smoother landing than the American astronauts did back then. Then again, I have repulsion-drive engines in the belly of the plane that will be deployed to land with and ascend off of the surface of the moon."

"So you have a space suit inside the plane?"

"Yes. I even have a Russian flag I want to plant on the surface. I know there are a couple already there planted by cosmonauts at the moon bases they occupy. But I'll be the first Russian woman to land on the moon."

"If we go to Mars and you meet with the people at Mars Base Gagarin, will I also have a space suit or will I have to sit in the plane until you're done?"

"I've got four suits on the plane of various sizes. You might find one that will fit. They're there for future flights."

"I wish I could go with you today. But as you said, you don't know if any of the extra suits will fit me and you probably don't have time to check since you'll be in the air by 2:00. And that's… Oh no. I've got a meeting in less than half an hour. I'll see you tomorrow then."

"See you then."

Sam walked out of the training room and headed for the horizontal elevator car. Dick was tempted to check out the distillery. But that would have to be during another tour of the Facility. He was about to have lunch with President Kursolov and didn't know if he would be early or on time.

CHAPTER 5

When Dick removed his EPU headset he was startled by the sight of President Kursolov sitting in a chair facing him.

"See anything interesting?" he asked.

"I was using Sam as my avatar to tour the Facility. I thought I would have a little more time before you showed up."

"There's a lot I want to see before I return to Moscow. I of course want to see the new space plane takeoff at 2:00. But I want to see some other things. I heard about the distillery where Russian Madhouse Vodka is made. They say it packs a punch without making you drunk. I've got to sample some of it and maybe take a bottle or a case home with me."

"I was shocked to see it on the destination panel in the horizontal elevator. I know we have a bar here. I didn't know we brewed our own private brand of vodka."

"I heard that it is the only liquor that has micromachines in it that can change alcohol back into sugar in the stomach so you can't get drunk. It sort of defeats the purpose of drinking. But at 110 proof, I've got to down some of it to see if it tastes like real vodka."

"Well then, let's have lunch."

The men stood and walked down the hall to the executive dining room. They entered the private room at the back of the dining room and sat at an intimate table next to a larger table that could accomodate upwards to eight people.

As soon as the pair sat in their seats, a projection sphere descended from the ceiing and hovered over the middle of the table. The projections of menu items were shown to both men as if they were on plates in front of them. About the only things missing were the aroma, taste, and texture of the food. If you wanted a certain food item, all you had to do was pretend you were eating it by using your utensiles. The item would disappear and another item would appear in front of the men.

Before the food and beverages arrived, the President asked, "How do you like it here at the Facility?"

"So far I like it a lot. I was taking a tour of the Facility through my avatar Sam. There are many good people here. I hope we please you and the people of Russia and the rest of the world."

"Do you miss Arizona?"

"It was hot and dry out there. I was glad I worked underground." "As opposed to cold and snowy."

"At least I work underground here too. I'm definitely going to enjoy going to so many concerts and ballet performances. I hope being so eager to arrive by curtain time doesn't cause me to work too fast and sloppy."

"You have an extended 3-D TV. You could always record what you want to see and hear later."

"I know. But being there with an audience is more exciting. I know you didn't come to talk about vodka and concerts."

"I want to check out the military research being done here. I don't want another Israel to happen to us. We have enough enemies out there that want to humiliate us. I trust you weren't partly responsible for our defeat," he said as an accusation.

"I was working on cars in Arizona. I had nothing to do with weapons. And you don't need to worry about me having divided loyalties. I will do all I can for the Facility."

"I heard that you and your wife came here this morning in a flying car. Is that true?"

"Yes it is. Would you like one?"

"If you could build a flying limousine I would like to have one.

I'm sure that won't be much of a problem, will it?"

"I've been thinking about designing the next generation of levitated flying cars for my car company Thurmeyo Motors. I believe I can design you a limousine that will be able to glide a few centimeters above the ground or a roadway, fly into space, and even fly to Mars like the space plane you'll see this afternoon."

"Will it be huge like the space plane?"

"Not if I can help it. It should be large enough to carry at least five or six passengers. But it will be small enough to be parked in a standard-sized garage. That's my goal at least. Once it's ready, I'll contact you. Do you want me to accompany you this afternoon?"

"No. There are some things I want to see that you might not be interested in. I definitely want to go to the distillery which can happen after I watch the test flight. I won't stay around to see the good doctor past the time she reaches the moon which I assume she will land on. I know you're not a drinker. So going to a distillery may not interest you. Am I right?"

"Exactly. I'd like to be at hangar 3 when she returns. The entire trip should take no more than three hours if all goes well."

A wheeled robot entered the room and slid the plates, glasses, napkins, and utensiles toward the men on two trays. The surfaces of the trays were magnetized to hold everything to the trays. Metal plates on the bottoms of the plates and glasses latched onto the trays so they wouldn't slide. When the robot removed what looked like probes from the sides of the trays, they ceased to be magnetic. The robot left the men to eat in peace.

Dick bowed his head to pray over his meal while the President buttered a slice of rye bread and took a few bites.

"Do you always pray before your meals?" the President asked. "Yes I do. I've been a Christian most of my life and it's a habit of mine. Are you a Christian?" The man smiled and laughed.

"I was wondering if you would have the nerve to ask me. Even though the Facility is your baby, I can have you sent back to Arizona immediately, if I choose."

"You won't insult me if you say no."

"My father and my grandfather grew up under the Soviet system and were good communists. My great-grandfather was proud to say he was good friends with both Lenin and Stalin. If he had had the chance, he would have shot the Czar and his family. He died while the Soviet Union was intact. He would have never believed his great-grandson would become the leader of Russia. If you look at me you will know what the man looked like. He reluctantly shaved off his mustachio when deStalinization went into effect during the early '50s. But he grew it back after Khrushchev died in 1971. He considered that man a clown. He wasn't allowed to say that when the bald fat man was in power. Personally, I feel Khrushchev was removed just in time because when he gave his 'we'll bury you' speech at the UN, your people thought it was a threat. It was actually a foolish boast. He thought that the Soviet Union could outproduce America's defense factories and the factories that produced consumer goods. But our economy at the time was incapable of matching the industrial strength of America. America would have buried us."

"My grandfather was so worried about the 'Red Menace' as it was called. At least he didn't foolishly construct a bomb shelter to protect his family from atom bombs. But I think if he could have afforded it, he would have brought in a front-end loader and would have dug as deep and big a hole as he could have and would have poured the cement. But after the Cuban missile crisis and the threat of a missile attack seemed more distant, he gave up on the idea of putting in a bomb shelter. As time went on, he became more glad he gave up on it and lived a normal life in Michigan. He was still worried that someday the missiles would fly. But it wasn't worth losing sleep over."

"I've only met a handful of Christians in my life. I had been taught that you people were weak-minded. But if Christians were willing to go to prison for their faith when it would have been so easy to deny their Lord, I thought they were insane. But since the Soviet Union dissolved and Russia was going to pieces, Christians remained faithful to their Jesus. Instead of opposing the government, they tried to live peacefully and honored Russia. They weren't terrorists which one would have expected from oppressed people. They've gained my respect. But I'm not ready to become a Christian. Not just yet."

After the meal, the two men went their separate ways for awhile. Dick decided to go to his design and fabrication studio which was larger than the one he had back in Arizona to work on the levitated flying limousine for the President. The President didn't go to the Department of Military and Space Research as one might expect. Instead, he headed for Dr. Frankenstein's Laboratory. He had heard about something he had to see to believe.

He was met by Doctors Trachel Hovernan and Sorchen Vlandner at the reception area in the Department of Medical Advancement and Care by the kiosk. They shook hands and headed for the area that Dr. Vlandner had told Sam and his guide was a restricted area. As the doors opened, the President thought he was entering a gym. Men and women were pumping weights, running on treadmills, and to the President's amazement, flying near the ceiling.

"Who is responsible for these magnificent humans? They are humans, aren't they?"

Dr. Vlandner said, "They are enhanced humans. I usually show visitors my pets to impress them. But these people are why I came from Newgate, New York to Siberia. Back there, enhanced humans are almost common. But that's because Newgate was founded by people from another dimension. I met one of those enhanced humans from another dimension named Drozin Kanfibulac. He works in New York City for a graphic novel company called WOW. But he is also Mr. Amazing. He describes himself as the Swiss army knife of superheroes. He became what he is through training. My people here have the help of technology. Let me introduce you to some of them."

The three men walked over to a woman who was using a weight machine that relied on magnetic resistance and attraction instead of big weights which had to be pushed or pulled. According to the monitor, she was benchpressing 1275 kilograms. After ten reps, she sat up on the bench and hadn't broken a sweat.

"Very impressive, young lady," said the President. "You have arms of steel."

"Actually they're ultra-stressed crystalline molecular solid materials and synthetics. My legs are of the same materials. I have so many bionic parts that I sometimes feel like an android. Only my brain is biological and even that organ has implants."

"You were very brave to volunteer to be remade into what you are."

"I didn't have any choice. My organs were failing and I was as weak as a kitten. I decided to go all the way and become bionic."

"Now that you're bionic, or enhanced as the doctor calls you, what are you going to do with those abilities?"

"I've always wanted to be an Olympic athlete. But since I'm so enhanced, I'll probably go on tour showing people what is possible and recruit people to be enhanced. I also want to run and swim around the world."

The trio walked over to where two men were running on treadmills. They were viewing 3-D scenes of outdoor locations in front of them on screens that went from the floor to over two meters up. According to the speedometers on the screens, each man was running at 100 kph. They recognized the Russian President and picked up the pace. Within a minute, the men were racing at over 150 kph. Since each screen was set to end the scenes after a certain distance, eventually they passed the finish line. The man on the right finished first. Both men had covered 100 kilometers in less than an hour. When they stopped running, the scenes froze and seconds later the screens went blank.

"Very impressive," said the President. "You two remind me of that American TV program 'The Six Million Dollar Man.' Have either of you seen that program?"

They both shook their heads no.

"How fast can either of you run and for how long?"

"I can run for two hours with no problem at upwards to 160 kph for short stretches," said the man on the left.

"Same here," said the other man.

"These two are bionic like that Amercan Steve Austin. They are just like the young lady we left," said Dr. Vlandner.

The trio walked over to the area beneath where a man and a woman were flying like Superman. They descended like feathers onto the floor.

"This is Ivan Korsakov and his wife Irena," said Dr. Vlandner. "They are big superhero fans and volunteered to be turned into superheroes. They also have agreed to join the Russian military and fight terrorists and whomever the government views as a threat."

A man walked up behind the President and aimed a gun at his head. Ivan jumped between the gunman and the President a split second before he fired his weapon. The slug vaporized as it struck Ivan's head. More shots were fired with the same results. The wife appeared beside the gunman, grabbed his weapon, and wadded it up as if it were made of paper. The President was more than impressed. "If you liked that demonstration, follow us to the elevator that goes down to the forbidden zone," Dr. Hovernan said.

The trio walked to the locker room and into the shower room. Dr. Hovernan reached in his pants pocket and pushed a button on a controller.

A door opened and the trio entered a hallway that led to a secret elevator. They went down to the second from the lowest level and entered a room where a woman was nursing a baby. Two men entered from another room and stood in front of the mother and child.

"This woman is a single mother from Smirnoffgrad," said Dr. Hovernan. "She is a teacher at an elemetary school with a lot to life for. She thinks that one or two of the men who teach there might be fond of her."

One of the men handed the other man an 11 mm pistol and told him, "Shoot the woman and her child."

The man with the gun aimed without hesitation at the head of the baby while the woman was pleading for her life and the life of her child and shot him in the head. As the woman screamed, the gunman shot her in the head. He handed the gun back to the first man who immediately shot him in the head.

Instead of dropping dead, the man who had been shot stood and looked at the one who shot him. The bullet popped out of the wound which closed up in five seconds. The President's mouth dropped open in astonishment as two robots picked up the corpses and carried them out of the room.

"The one you thought was going to drop dead on the floor is Corporal Sergei Kalishnkov," said Dr. Hovernan. "He was dead for five days before we brought him back into the land of the living. He is part bionic, part cybernetic, mostly human, and absent a soul. After one dies, his soul goes to wherever souls go. It could be Heaven, or Hell, or maybe another dimension. I really don't know. Being without a soul makes him the perfect soldier. He won't question an order and will not feel any guilt."

"Were the woman and child androids or humans?" the President asked.

"They were exactly how I described them. We'll lie about them and dispose of them. Then again, we could replace her and her child with synthetics that will seem totally human. If we're successful, no one will know the difference," said Dr. Hovernan.

"I'd like to talk with the soldier," the Preident said. "Go ahead," the doctor said.

"Corporal, do you know that you were dead for five days?" the President asked.

"That's what they told me, sir."

"What's the last thing you remember before you died?"

"I was on guard duty more than a month ago when I felt a sharp pain and moments later everything went black. They told me here at the Facility that a bullet went through my heart from possibly a Muslim sniper. The next thing I remember is waking up in a hospital bed."

"I've never talked with a formerly dead man. Do you feel any different?"

"I feel better than I have felt in years. I don't have nightmares much about my death. I just hope I can go back to the base and hunt down the man who shot me. At least I won't leave him in any shape that will allow him to be resurrected."

"And you felt no guilt about killing a woman and her baby?"

"I was given an order and obeyed it. I no longer feel guilt. If I was told to kill you with my bare hands I would most likely snap your neck."

"I'm glad no one around here hates me enough to kill me." "My comrades were glad they weren't sent to Israel," said the soldier.

"If you were told to go to Israel knowing it might mean certain death, would you go?"

"Yes. But with the micromachines circulating through my body, I'm a lot harder to kill. They will repair any damage to me in seconds. For all I know, I could have my head cut off and I would grow a new one."

"Come along," said the first man to the soldier before they left the room.

"I could have an army of souless formerly dead soldiers for the military within a year or two," bragged Dr. Hovernan.

"How long can someone be dead and still be brought back?" "So far I've been able to revive someone who has been dead for eight days if they are well-preserved. After that, you might as well build a robot or synthetic."

The trio left the room, got back on the elevator and took it back to the shower room where Ivan and his wife were preparing to shower together.

"Excuse us, please," Dr. Vlandner told them before he and the other doctor and President left the locker room.

"I hope the weapons demonstration isn't a big letdown after what I've seen this afternoon," said the President.

The men left the gym and headed back to the reception area where they parted company. The President went to the floor where the latest weapons were going to be demonstrated.

When the elevator door opened, over a dozen people applauded him as he entered the reception area. He smiled and shook their hands as they told him their names and how wonderful it was for him to pay them a visit.

"I didn't expect this kind of reception since this was supposed to be a secret. I guess my dynamic personality is too powerful to hide. Who is going to show me some weapons for my approval?"

They all raised their hands. He chuckled a little. A man and woman stepped forward.

"I'm Irena Markowitz. I have designed some very powerful weapons that soldiers can use. I've incorporated them into an advanced fighting suit that soldiers will wear. My partner, Yuri Danoloff, has developed some armored weapons systems that should please you. We won't have another Israel debacle with our weapons."

"That's what I want to hear. Take me to them."

The President and the two weapons developers were followed by the others into an observation room where the weapons tests were going to be safely viewed on a wall-sized 3-D screen. The developers entered another room where Irena suited up and her partner entered a tank. Within a minute, Irena glided half a meter above the floor in a fighting suit and softly touched down on the floor.

In a deep voice, Irena said, "We have found that people pay attention to a deep authoritarian voice more than to a woman's voice unless she's angry. I'm at a conversational level. I can amplify my voice so that I can be heard clearly a kilometer away."

She lifted her right arm that had a multi-barreled weapon in its hand.

"This is a charged particle beam shotgun. It can be used to hit multiple targets simultaneously."

The room was flooded with over 100 flying and surface drones and robots. A field was projected in front of the suit that scanned the attackers in a split second. The barrels of the weapon began to move independently and fired charged particle beam energy projectiles at each target. Within three seconds, each target was destroyed. The people viewing the test applauded.

Into the room a robot that was three meters tall, just as tall as the fighting suit, started firing lasers beams at Irena. An electromagnetic energy shield around the fighting suit scattered the laser beams into harmless light beams. The shotgun blasted the beam weapons with energy projectiles and began carving up the robot with energy beams, making it a pile of metal and plastic pieces in six seconds. A robotic vacuum entered the room, vacuumed up the debris, and left the room.

"If my suit hadn't had the force field, the lasers might have damaged it. But lasers are only concentrated beams of photons. The force field spread out the laser beams and made them as weak as a flashlight beam. If missiles had been fired at the suit, the force field would have vaporized them and protected me from the explosion. But I have an even more powerful weapon on my left arm."

A metal wall that was a meter thick was brought into the room on a levitation cart. The cart landed with a clang onto the floor.

"This wall is made from carbon steel similar to what is used by warships. It is twice as thick as what battleships have used. Watch me turn it into Swiss cheese."

Irena aimed a power ray cannon at the wall and proceeded to punch holes in it. Multiple beams wrapped around energy projectiles punctured the wall with holes that measured 4 centimeters in diameter. It took half a second to punch a hole. When Irena accidentally fired a blast that lasted more than half a second, the wall behind the steel wall was punctured. In two minutes, the wall became too weak in some places and fell to the floor with a clunk. The vaporized steel reformed either as dust on the floor behind the wall or collected on the wall in the room as well as the door. The hole that was punched accidentally in the wall at the back of the room was filled with searing steel dust that eventually solidified. Irena had to use a power ray beam to cut the doors apart where the steel had welded them shut.

"If we had a battalion in which all of its soldiers were wearing fighting suits like mine and were armed with my weapons, it could march or..." She silently lifted off of the floor and hovered a meter off of the floor. "Fly to any enemy position or capital and instantly defeat it. We should have had my suit and weapons in Israel. We still have Islamic enemies we need to crush. And Beijing better watch out. If China ever went to war with us, we could destroy it on the ground if 1,000 suited soldiers were fielded."

The doors opened and in glided something that looked like a giant computer mouse. There was a 150 mm hole in the top portion of the tank and 20 mm power rays on the top portion and the bottom portion. The top portion lifted like a head on a neck that was 20 centimeters in diameter. As it was extended to a meter above the bottom portion of the tank, another steel wall that was more than a meter thick glided by the tank on a levitation cart. Irena left the room to give the tank more room to demonstrate its abilities.

Once the doors closed, the tank began blasting away at the wall.

But instead of punching 100 holes in the wall, three holes were punched through it which exploded the wall due to electromagnetic repulsive expansion of the energy projectiles. After the wall was torn apart, a hole large enough to allow a man to leave the tank formed at the rear of the weapon.

After Yuri left the tank, he turned toward the spectators and said, "This tank is the most advanced tank in the world. It is also the most powerful and capable tank in the world as well as most expensive. It is built from 120 layers of crystalline molecular solid materials sandwiched over multiple-layer force fields. It uses three injection reactors; one for the fields, one for the weapons, and one for the motive and levitation fields as well as the remaining systems. It has no visible hatch for the driver, gunners, and engineer/communications officer to allow them to enter the tank.

It uses something called solid energy. The fields are so dense at the hatch area that they feel solid as long as you're wearing an insulated glove. If you didn't wear a glove like what I have on, you could burn your hand. If you weren't wearing an access ring, you couldn't enter the tank.

"This tank looks like a giant computer mouse. Since it had no windows or ports to see through, it could be called a blind mouse. It uses sensors to allow occupants to see out. It doesn't need lights at night or during bad weather. It uses a triple-field motive system; one motive field and two repulsive levitation fields that can lift the tank a couple meters above the ground. If I were to extend a displacement field and couple it with my motive field, the tank could fly. It may weigh over 20 metric tons. But if it could fly, I might call it Dumbo or a bumble bee since they aren't supposed to be able to fly since their bodies are so bulky.

"It has virtually unlimited range since it's nuclear-powered. But it has a practical mission range of two weeks even if it were at the bottom of the ocean. It is sealed, has a urine-to-water system, an air recycling system like a submarine, frozen food storage, and a microwave to heat up the food for four people for two weeks. If we had had a dozen of these in Israel, there's no way the earthquakes could have swallowed them."

The President stood and said, "I should have waited another couple years before trying to invade Israel. The next time we have a major war, I want 100 tanks and at least 1000 fighting suits. Could this be possible by 2042?"

"If we had all our defense factories doing the job, yes we could," Yuri said confidently.

"That's what I wanted to hear. Do it."

The President left the room and headed for the elevator to the top level to take the horizontal elevator car to hangar 3. But since it was a half hour before the takeoff, the President went past hangar 3 and arrived at the distillery to sample some Russian Madhouse vodka.

When the President got off the elevator, he smelled the strong aroma of alcohol. He smiled broadly. A man wearing a lab coat approached him and shook his hand.

"It is an honor to have you here, Mr. President. Do you want a tour of the distillery?"

"I don't have time for that. I want to see the space plane taking off and landing on the moon. After that I can come back for a case of Russian Madhouse vodka. Maybe two or three if I like it."

"Come with me then. We can share a bottle in the tasting room." The two men passed by stainless steel stills and entered a room where a man and a woman were sampling adult beverages and spitting them into sinks after swishing them around in their mouths. They would swish some water in their mouths to cleanse the palate. The man in the lab coat reached behind the counter and pulled out two bottles of vodka. One was cherry flavored and the other was caramel flavored. The President looked surprised. "I have never tasted caramel flavored vodka."

"It makes the vodka go down a little smoother. Want to try it?" "Sure."

The man poured from both bottles into four glasses about half full.

"You sure I can't get drunk on this?" asked the President with a tinge of doubt.

"I could give this to a baby and the only crying would be when it goes down. But the only aftertaste would be either cherry or caramel."

"Salute."

The men downed the glasses with cherry vodka first. They grimaced as the 110 proof liquor passed their tongues and throats. But within a minute, the micromachines changed the alcohol back into sugar and the taste of cherry was in both men's mouths. They downed the caramel vodka and didn't make such ugly faces when the vodka went down. The caramel aftertaste made the President smile broadly.

"That was fantastic. What other flavors do you have?" "Traditional, lemonaide, honey, tea, raspberry, peach, apple, pear, apricot, and orange. At least those are the flavors we've been selling. I'm trying to develop more flavors."

"Where are you selling it at?"

"With Smirnoffgrad and Konstanigrad so close we've used those cities as test markets. I've sold over 100 cases so far and I've only been distilling Russian Madhouse for five months. Think how many cases I could sell in Moscow and Saint Petersburg."

"Send a case of all the flavors to Moscow. How much does a case cost?"

"For you it's free."

"That's all well and good for me. But I'm going to serve it at state dinners and to foreign visitors. I'll be a salesman for Russian Madhouse. I need to know how much should be charged."

"For domestic consumption, 10,000 rubles since there are 20 bottles in each case. At least 12,000 for foreign markets."

"If the other flavors are as fine as what I've sampled, the prices are low. I think Russian Madhouse vodka will make the Facility famous."

"I hope we don't have to call the Facility the Russian Madhouse even though that is its official name."

"Keep distilling the best vodka in Russia and you eventually might not mind. I'll definitely be back for a tour after the landing. Can you have the cases sent to Moscow after I leave?"

"Do you want it sent by tube or in a cargo plane?"

"Send it by tube. It's almost as fast and maybe a bit safer. I'd hate to have a plane crash and cases of vodka are the major casualties." The President shook the man's hand and left to go to hangar 3.

The man went to work collecting cases of vodka to send to Moscow. After finding what he needed, the man placed the cases in a tube transport capsule and sent it to the tube station he had used to send cases of vodka to the two cities he sold Russian Madhouse to. Instead of having the capsule head east, he sent it west toward Moscow. The vodka would be waiting for the President. The man included a recorded holographic message which included the President drinking some of the vodka and his comments.

While the President was being shown some wonders in the areas that were off limits, Dick was in his design and fabrication studio trying to come up with a levitated flying limousine that had a repulsion-drive engine for trips to Mars Base Gagarin and the Russian moon base. He also encountered some things he wasn't expecting.

CHAPTER 6

The big advantage of being one of the administrators at the Facility was the design and fabrication studio that was a bit larger than the one in Arizona. Since Dick enjoyed drawing vehicles and not relying totally on a CAD system, there was an electronic drawing board that allowed him to move the images three dimensionally to aid the designing process. Whatever he drew in one perspective would be shown in other perspectives. Instead of erasing mistakes, he would turn his stylus upside down and electronically erase the mistake. If something he had drawn became hidden, the board would take this in consideration.

There were some features of the board that he hadn't had back in Arizona. If he wanted to do some interior designing, he could record what he had drawn and save it in memory. When he went back to designing exterior views, what had been recorded could be reapplied to the interior views and if the changes changed what had been recorded, that would also be taken in consideration and shown. After drawing a preliminary design of the limousine, Dick plugged in an EPU headset to get a good look at the vehicle in its full-size form. He could walk around the vehicle and even enter the unfinished cockpit.

The scissor driver door opened and Dick slid into the seat before the door closed and the left hand controls slid out of a panel to the left of Dick's leg.

"Hi, Dick," said a man sitting in the passenger side of the vehicle. "Who are you? How did you get in here?"

"My name isn't important. What I have to tell you is. President Kursolov wants to remake his military with formerly dead soldiers and give them weapons that are superior to anything the United States and China have."

"I wouldn't put it past him. If the Russian Madhouse is anything like the Madhouse in Arizona, almost anything is possible. Tell me something I might not know."

"There is a Chinese spy here. I've been watching him because that's my job."

"Who is he?"

"He uses the name Joseph Simmeroff. He is working in the Department of Military and Space Research. He looks like a Mongolian and claims to be from a small town in Eastern Siberia. He went to Moscow and earned a degree in engineering at the university. But he was bioengineered in a secret military lab in China. He has biosynthetic skin, a partially cybernetic brain, and micromachines circulate through his body. I'm sorry to say that he wouldn't have been possible without the medical technology developed by the Madhouse in Arizona."

"How do you know all this?"

"I'm a watcher. My job is to keep track from an adjacent dimension what goes on in this dimension. I'm not supposed to interact with people in your dimension directly. But since I'm using a transdimensional interface communications device, technically I'm not interacting with you directly."

"What would you advise for me to do?"

"If you meet the man who calls himself Joseph Simmeroff, don't let on you know he is a spy. Don't even hint you know what he is. We need to make him believe he is getting away with technology theft for the Chinese government."

"Tell me he isn't succeeding."

"We are intercepting his communications with the Chinese. So he thinks he's accomplishing his mission."

"Are you sending him false information?"

"Constantly. We're also sending false information to Beijing so his people will think he is successful. It's advanced technical information. But it isn't what they're developing here. It is almost as good, but not quite. The Chinese might have developed it eventually. But it won't be as good as what is being developed here or in Arizona."

"Why are you talking with me in the first place? How long have you been watching me?"

"Longer than I'm allowed to tell you. Just don't tell anyone we've had this conversation because I could get in trouble for telling you anything."

"Are there some other things I should know?"

"Be careful tomorrow. Dr. Davidoff may be a Christian. But she is still a woman who sometimes fantasizes about her former life. Being alone with her on a trip to Mars could lead to serious trouble, if you know what I mean."

"I'll be careful. I will have to tell my wife so she'll know where I'm… I'll take her with me."

"Good idea. The good doctor will appreciate having someone there to keep her in line. Also, you would hate to have people whisper behind your backs about an affair. She is still a beautiful woman. You and her might be forced to leave if everyone thinks you two had sex aboard the spaceplane. Having your wife come along will prevent giving into temptation. I think both women would agree."

"I really don't know her all that well. I must admit that I have seen her naked pictures before I met my wife and, I'm almost ashamed to admit it, but after we were married. But I eventually stopped looking at pornography."

The watcher stared at Dick in disbelief.

"I'm also a telepath. Most people in Newgate are. So you tell me you've stopped looking at pornography."

"Okay, I sometimes am weak and I… Okay, okay. Sometimes I've experienced it in EPU programs. With my wife here, there is no way in the world that I'm going to go to the brothel in the Facility. I love my wife a lot. I'm also very honest with her."

The watcher gave him that disbelieving stare again.

"You're like my dad and mom rolled into one. It was as if they were telepaths. They always knew when I was up to no good or tried to hide something. Yes, there are things we don't tell each other. I'm sure there are things she has done that she'll never tell me about. And I'm not going to ask her about them. If she's not guilty, why should I make her feel guilty?"

"There won't be any watchers aboard the spaceplane. At least not that I know about."

"I'll be on my best behavior tomorrow and for as long as the journey lasts."

"Just make sure you tell no one about what we were talking about. I could get in trouble and we don't want the spy to know he has been made. I'll let you get back to work."

The man vanished and Dick went back to designing the limousine. He also thought about Kate and wondered if she wanted to take a trip to Mars with him and a former nude model.

CHAPTER 7

Kate was having an interesting first day on the job. She didn't know what to expect because she knew Russian culture was a bit different from American culture. She didn't realize how different.

The first person she met in the reception area was Maria Shapulla. She looked young enough to be her daughter. She wasn't beautiful. One could say she was cute. But after the first few moments, Kate knew she was more tough than cute. It started with the hearty handshake the young woman presented.

"Good morning, Mrs. Thurman. I'm Maria Shapulla. They call me the Protector around here. My dad was a boxer and dabbled in the martial arts. He taught me what he knew and thanks to him, no one around here tries anything untoward against me. And no one can mess with any of my friends," she proclaimed.

"Are there any people around here I ought to watch out for?" "Follow me to your office where you will be working. When people see me with you they'll know they can't mess with you."

The women walked down the hall past the open doors of offices where employees were standing and greeting both of them. Kate glanced at them and smiled and said hello. One of the men leered at the women as they passed his door.

Kate's office was spacious as she expected since her husband was an administrator. There was a computer with five screens; a larger main screen and two smaller ones on each side of it. There was also an EPU headset jacked into the mainframe. There was also a small kitchen with a refrigerator, a coffee maker, a microwave, a sink, a table, two chairs, and a 3-D TV on the wall above the table. There was even a small bathroom and a recliner for her to relax in and catch some Zs.

"I could live in here," Kate commented.

"That's what the Facility intended. I have a few of the same amenities in my office because there are times I get so busy that I lose track of time. A quick nap or a bite to eat and I'm good to go. You'll appreciate this arrangement quickly."

The women sat at the kitchen table where Kate asked, "Who was that creepy guy back there?"

"That was one of the people you need to watch out for. He's Boris Shenova. He produces… uh… how can I say it without making him sound like a pervert?"

"Does he produce pornography?"

"Hard core. He would have fit in well working for Larry Flynt or other pornographers in California half a century ago. I don't know why they let him come here in the first place unless it's his connections in the electronic entertainment business. Either he knows the right people or the industry thought it was safer to send him here. I really don't know. And it doesn't help that he has sold hours of pornography to the public."

"Maybe President Kursolov views him as a money-maker for the Facility and likes the income flow."

"I wouldn't doubt that. We sometimes call him Mr. Channel 10. That's the adult channel here at the Facility."

"I remember when I was a girl accidentally seeing the Spice Channel at a motel my parents and I stopped at. It was kind of a sleazy place. But it was cheap to stay at and late at night. When I saw a bunch of naked women in a doctor's office at a nudist camp I asked my mom why they were letting someone who claimed to be the doctor touch them in their…you know."

"That sounds tame compared to some of the garbage he has produced. But there is a market out there for it. Maybe a bigger market for his EPU programs. He's probably working on one of those disgusting EPU programs right now."

"I'll make sure I don't take him up on his offer to sample his work."

"Good idea. I hate to say there is a woman around here that is almost as bad as he is. She must have been busy because her office door was closed. Sometimes he's used her in programs he has produced and he has appeared in some of her's. We sometimes call her Miss Channel 10 and she doesn't mind."

"I'll try to avoid her too. Who can I make friends with here?"

There are five men and three women here that you can be close friends with besides me. The others, I don't know. I just hope they don't brown nose you because you're the wife of an administrator." "Can I schedule a meeting with everyone tomorrow at 10:00

AM so I can set down some rules?"

"I don't know. Some of the people here like to take their stuff to Moscow and Saint Petersburg to sell to the stations and networks directly. A couple have contracts with electronic entertainment companies headquartered in those two cities. Besides, most people like the freedom of working here and don't like to be told what to do. You'll make some enemies if you lay down the law."

"Is there any way to have some order around here? I don't want the Electronic Entertainment Department to bring shame to the Facility."

"As long as we make money for the Facility, we can make whatever we want even if it's raunchy."

"I was working with micromachines interfacing with brain implants back in Arizona."

"You mean your Mind Trips system?" "Yes. How is it doing in Russia?"

"My grandmother used to tell me about old women selling opiates on the streets of Moscow. Today they sell Mind Trips kits they are given for free by the Madhouse in Arizona to help them make a living so they can keep a roof over their heads and not starve."

"No problems, I hope."

"None so far. I heard about the problems you experienced in the United States a few years ago. It looks like you solved them."

"That's good to hear. What I was working on before I left Arizona was a companion brain unit for children that was safer than what adults use and maybe not as frightening to use. I could make it seem like a toy that is totally harmless."

"Wonderful. I have a neice and a couple nephews that might go for something like that. You will need to go to the tech lab to work on such a device. It's down the other hall from the reception area." "I hope I don't sound paranoid, but how do the others feel about me starting here?"

"As long as you do a good job and don't meddle in people's business, you'll be accepted here. If you need children to try out your companion brain for children, there are two nearby cities that send people here. They're Smirnoffgrad and Konstanigrad. They each have around 50,000 people. That may not sound like too many. But you have to consider that they were little more than rustic villages 20 years ago. But the President wants to open up Siberia like previous leaders did and with the stress on mining, manufacturing, and oil and gas drilling, those two cities have grown from a couple thousand to what they are today. With the help of the Facility, they could grow to over 100,000 each within a decade thanks to increased manufacturing demands. We also have a source of workers for the Facility. They're already being used for testing purposes."

"What if I need you for some reason? What's the best way to get ahold of you?"

"Call me on the phone. Each person working here has their own work number. My number is 9 since I was the ninth person to be hired. Your number is 37. If you're in a hurry, either shout out my name or number. Just say phone 9 or phone Maria Shapulla. If I'm in the department, I'll pick up immediately unless I'm busy with something. It will be a speaker phone so don't shout out something you don't want people outside this office to hear. If I'm not available like when I'm at home, you'll have to physically use the phone. Speak my name into the receiver and my home phone or my I-phone will alert me. You'll either get me or my AI program. Have you set up an AI program yet?"

"I had the one in Arizona set here." "Does it simulate you well?"

"If I didn't know I was talking to a computer I'd swear I was talking to myself."

"I'd better get back to work. We can have lunch in the cafateria or in our offices. Want some company?"

"Sure. Where is the cafeteria?"

"Down the third hall. The projection at the kiosk in the reception room can tell you how to get there. One o'clock?"

"Sounds good. I hope I can tear myself away from what I'm doing then."

Maria left Kate's office and entered her's. Kate left soon afterwards and headed for the tech lab to continue her work on the companion brain for children.

The office doors were closed as Kate passed down the hall and walked down the second hall to the tech lab. She entered the lab and moments later realized she should have had the brain implants that would allow her to communicate in the languages used in the Facility implanted when someone spoke to her in Russian. She stared at him and hoped he would speak something in English. He knew what was wrong and opened a drawer in a desk and pulled out a metal Altoids container and handed it to her.

"Swallow three blue and three green," he said with a Russian accent.

Kate opened the container and saw some light blue and light green capsules that were the size of similar medicine capsules. She swallowed them after the man gave her a bottle of water to make the capsules go down easier. They stood staring at each other for a couple minutes before he spoke again.

"We keep those capsules in the drawer to give to those that should have gone to the clinic for brain implants."

"Can you understand me now?"

"Yes. If you had gone to the clinic, they would have injected the implants into your jugular. Micromachines would have constructed the implants and attached them to the audio and visual portions of your brain."

"So I can also read Russian?"

"Like a native. You can also read other languages. The words will look out of focus until the implants have adjusted to the new language you're reading. I guess you don't have them in Arizona."

"Not to my knowledge."

"It takes longer for the implants and micromchines to enter the bloodstream if they have to go through the digestive system. But it's less dangerous. What can I do for you today?"

"Back in Arizona I was working on a companion brain for children. I brought a flash drive with the information and drawings of what I was working oh back there."

She handed the man a flash drive and he inserted it into a computer. The first drawing appeared on the 3-D screen as a compilation of a few drawings.

"Your contacts are too small," the man pointed out. "They need to penetrate the skin."

"But it will hurt kids."

"Not if you use a pain bypass first before you apply the companion brain to the side of the child's head. I heard they're developing localized pain bypass pads that reroute pain signals away from the nervous system and to the pads. I don't know exactly how they work. But they are supposed to provide pain-free conditions for as long as they are worn over an area where you don't want to feel pain. Puncturing the skin won't be felt."

"That's good to know. But I still need for it to be small enough for a child's hand yet capable of inserting days of information into the brain."

"How many layers of encoding are you up to?"

"Five."

"According to the scale, this thing is the size of an Oreo cookie. You want to make it smaller?" "If I can."

"You've made a lot of work for yourself. But I'll help you if I can. By the way. My name is Andre Pushkin."

"Kate Thurman," she said as she shook his hand.

"I'm not going to give you special tretment just because your husband is one of the administrators at the Facility."

"I hope not."

"Good. Let's get to work. And since your husband is probably too busy to go to the clinic for brain implants, remind me to give you the container and you can give the capsules to him when you get home. Remember. Three capsules are for the audio center of the brain and the other three are for the visual center of the brain." "Remind me to leave for lunch at 1:00. I'll be eating with Maria Shapulla."

"I'm glad you two met. She'll help you out real well around here. Let's get to work."

For the next few hours, Kate and Andre worked on the companion brain which involved testing on themselves and androids since there were no children available. Pain bypass pads were sent to the tech lab and proved to be effective. A call went out to Smirnoffgrad and Konstanigrad for children to volunteer to test the companion brain and by noon there were a dozen children ranging in age from 3 to 14 to test out the device. There were only four devices made so they had to be shared which proved difficult since the younger children were fussy and the older children were reluctant to remove the device and give it to another child. Some of the androids had to assist Kate and Andre to maintain a degree of order and gather test results.

Lunch time couldn't come fast enough for Kate. She left the tech lab shortly before 1:00 and entered the cafeteria where Maria was standing at the counter with her tray sliding plates of food onto it. Kate grabbed a tray and joined Maria.

"I'm glad you could join me," said Maria.

"Not more glad than I am. I thought I'd have a relatively easy time working on my companion brain. But we had too few devices for too many kids testing it out."

"Does it work?"

"Yeah, it works. But I think I'm going to have to restrict it for children 10 and older. The younger children couldn't handle the increased knowledge and sometimes cried because their biological brains couldn't process it like I thought any brain could. I was wrong and I hope I haven't psychologically hurt them permanently. How has your day been so far?"

"Less hectic than yours. I've been working on a historical EPU program about the invasion of Russia by Napoleon. I want it to be as accurate as possible and have enough variables programmed into it so that freestyle programming won't allow too much nonsense. Sure it would be nice to use jets and tanks at the Battle of Borodino. But come on. Even the use of percussion caps for the weapons is a stretch."

"I sort of wish I had been working on an EPU program today. But I've started work on the companion brain for chidren and I like to finish one project at a time. I remember when I was a young child that I loved learning new things all the time. I hope brains haven't changed too much since then. Do you distribute your programs to schools or electronic entertainment venues?"

"Both. My biggest seller so far has been Atilla the Hun. It is both educational and fun to participate in. It appeals to boys more, as one would expect. Most want to join him instead of oppose him. But there are some that want to be a Roman general fighting against him and his horde. What do you like to work on most of the time?"

"There are some books I have turned into multi-books. The works of Jules Verne and H.G. Wells have gained a new generation of enthusiasts thanks to the multi-books I produced. I should have tackled something easy like the Foundation books of Asimov," she said sarcastically.

The women walked to one of the small tables and put their trays down. Kate said grace before eating as Maria sat patiently waiting for her to finish.

"Not many people pray before they eat," said Maria. "Are you offended?"

"Oh no. I sort of respect you for doing that. I'm not a Christian. But I'm not like some people who think the world would be better off without Christians. I've heard some people blame Christians for praying for God to punish the Russian military and that's why it lost in Israel. Do you think it was the wrath of God down there?" "Yes. I know the Bible predicted it would happen. But just like Satan likes to oppose God when he knows he will eventually be defeated, President Kursolov defied God. Why do the people in Russia still like him?"

"The people of Russia have always supported strong leaders. He reminds them of the legendary man of steel; Joseph Stalin. As long as the nation doesn't go under financially or looks weak, he can stay as President for as long as the Russian Constitution allows him to remain in power."

For the next half hour, the women talked about themselves and people in the department. Kate appreciated all the advice Maria gave her and subconsciously thought of her as one of her daughters; especially when she talked about the loss of her natural mother and the alienation she felt from her step-mother.

The rest of the day went a little smoother for Kate. There were two more companion brains made to test and the youngest children went home which left Kate and Andre with six children that didn't need to share devices. She found that a portion of the information that was fed into the biological brain by the companion brain was retained after the device was removed. She also made an innovation that could be used by regular companion brains. Information could be transmitted from a computer to the device with the simple flip of a switch.

Kate told Andre, "I wish I could have used my companion brain for younger children. If only their brains were more developed."

"Actually, they can be more developed. Down in the medical department they're working on micromachines that can rebuild portions of the brain into a cybernetic brain," Andre mentioned. "I gave you implant components and micromachines to let you speak, read, and understand other languages."

"I'd like to know if my Russian is understood by you. You sound like you're speaking English to me."

"Your Russian is fine. But I hear sort of an echo that sounds like English."

"I'm glad you said that. I thought I was going crazy when I heard Russian at the same time you were talking English. It was like when interpreters seemed to be talking over those they were interpreting. It's as if a microscopic interpreter is in my head."

"I've never heard anyone describe it like that. But yeah, that's basically what it is like. Do I sound like a Russian?"

"You sure do. I guess I sound like an American to you."

"You do. You sound like what an actor on an American TV show sounded like before I got my implants. I understood a little bit what they were saying. But after I got the implants, they were speaking perfect Russian though with an American accent."

"I'll order in some containers of micromachines and building material. I hope they tell us the ratio between micromachines and building material."

Andre picked up the phone, punched in the number for the medical department, and in seconds got ahold of an AI system to order in the material that was needed.

"The AI said the containers will be sent up within a minute or two."

"Will they send them by tube?"

"Yes. That's how the material the fabricator used to make the companion brains and information inserts got here. I know they used to use pneumatic tubes to send things from one place to another. Now they use linear induction in a vacuum tube. About the only difference is that the containers are quiet when they travel.

There isn't that sucking sound anymore. At least not as much. About the only time you hear anything is when the container is opened." "The tube is clear like the old pneumatic ones. That's nice because sometimes people want to open the containers before they're locked into place. After the brakes are extended, the green light comes on. Sometimes if you're quick enough you can open the container before the light comes on. I had a friend back in Arizona that pretended that it was a game. Could you beat the light? She did a few times."

"At least the containers can't open unless they're locked in place." Moments later, the container appeared in the small container tube. When the tube door was opened, the capsule that was the size of a loaf of bread was pushed out of the tube by the braking sections. There were a dozen 100 milliliter containers of micromachines and a dozen 500 milliliter containers of material that could be used to make more micromachines and brain implants. There were also 30 syringe needles and two syringes plus two encapsulation devices that could draw either micromachines or the material needed for the formation of micromachines or implants into them to make either red or yellow capsules. After emptying the tube container, it was returned to the tube and after the door was closed, the brakes were retracted and the capsule sped back to the medical department. "Now that we have what you need, how much of each do you think is needed per child?" Andre asked Kate.

"I don't know. The capsules I used for Mind Trips had 10 mg of micromachines suspended in either saline solution or filler materials. Let me look at an encapsulation device."

Andre handed Kate one of the devices. There was a digital control on the device she could easily hold in her hand. A person would flip open the cover of the control and punch in how many milligrams of active ingredients would be required per capsule. Since both the micromachines and the material required for construction purposes were suspended in saline solution, the encapsulation device would measure the amount of active ingredients was removed from a container and place it in a gel capsule along with the saline solution. The capsule would be sealed before coming out of the enapsulation device.

"Back in Arizona the encapsulation device we used couldn't be held in your hand. I guess you just insert the one end into the container you're removing material or micromachines from, close it, make sure there is enough capsule material in the device, and then push the red button below the digital readout. The light will come on when the capsule is ready. I hope there is enough capsule material in the device."

"It depends on how many capsule you want to make. Each device is set up to make 60 capsules. Just pop open the back of the device and place a slab of capsule material in it. In less than a minute a capsule can be formed, filled, and sealed. Push the button at the bottom and the capsule compartment will open.

"We have a larger encapsulation device that can make a bunch of capsules at one time. But for testing purposes, making one capsule at a time is sufficient."

"How many capsules will be needed to increase the brain capacity of a child?" Kate asked.

"One 10 mg capsule of micromachines and one capsule with 100 mg of construction material should be sufficient to increase the IQ of a child 50 points."

"That much?" Kate asked.

"I don't know. I thought it sounded good, so I said it. I have no idea what will happen. But one capsule of each sounds right. We can start with that and go from there. We could also use syringes. But I think most people would rather down a couple capsules and wait a couple minutes for them to kick in than get jabbed by needles in the neck."

Kate and Andre made twenty capsules of micromachines and construction material and placed them in Altoids containers and set the tins on the table where the containers of micromachines and construction material were.

Before calling one of the children over to the table, Kate suggested to Andre, "If we expect these kids to take the capsules, maybe we should take a couple capsules first and see how they affect us."

"Are you serious?"

"Like a heart attack. Back in Colorado I used myself as a guinea pig when I tried out the modifications I made on my Mind Trips system. They thought I was insane back then. But things worked out. After that, Mind Trips became a world sensation."

"Really?"

"That's what I keep telling myself. So maybe it's true. Have you ever tried Mind Trips?"

"Yes I have. Sometimes when I have a rough day I take a couple drags on a vaping unit before I go to bed. Your system really makes the nights pass better. Nothing but good dreams."

"I guess I was successful then. I still have some water in the bottle I drank from earlier. I'll down a couple capsules first and then you can do the same thing if I don't turn into a cyborg."

Kate took a red and a yellow capsule and downed them with a swallow of water. She stood motionless for a couple minutes and then her face began to contort for several seconds. She then began to laugh.

"Got you," she said.

"Do you feel any different?"

"Not really. I think I…uh…oh really?" "Oh really what?"

"You think I'm crazy for taking dangerous chances."

"That was what I was thinking. Maybe the micromachines made you telepathic."

"I'm sorry for reading your mind."

"Actually I was thinking how brave you are. I admire your guts." "You got me back. I guess we can give them to the kids to make their brains better suited to use companion brains. But before we do that, maybe we should give the capsules flavored coatings to make them go down easier. Since the yellow capsules are micromachines and the red ones are construction material, we could give the yellow ones banana flavoring and the red ones could taste like cherries. Give them a candy shell and they won't stick together in the tins." "That could be done. I'll order up what we need from the food people."

Minutes later, two tube capsules came to the tech lab. One had the flavoring equipment and plenty of banana and cherry flavoring while the other had the equipment needed to form the candy coating along with the coating material. All 40 capsules were given flavoring and coating to keep them from sticking to other capsules. After the capsules were flavored and coated, the children that were testing the companion brains were offered capsules to help their brains.

Each child swallowed a red and a yellow capsule and after they did their job, they all thanked Kate and Andre except for one 11-year old boy who bit into the capsules because he thought they were candy. He didn't like the saline solution and thought the metalic aftertaste was nasty. But each child found they could learn more thanks to the cybernetic parts of their brains. This gave Kate hope that maybe younger children could benefit from the capsules tied to the use of companion brains. But the ones that had been in the tech lab earlier were either back home or on their way.

When it was a few minutes before 2:00, the children wanted to see the flight of the new spaceplane that was going to be piloted by Dr. Davidoff. They all headed for the cafeteria where a 40 inch flat screen 3-D TV was located. There were a few workers in the department seated in front of the TV waiting for the takeoff. President Kursolov was standing to the right of the rocket scientist with his arm around her shoulder. She looked nervous while the President felt excited; not just because she was going to make the Facility and Russia proud. But also because he had wanted to put his hands on the woman since she was a nude model. He had to show a degree of self-control not to squeeze a breast.

CHAPTER 8

With the cameras of the Facility, Russian TV, and the world broadcasting the event, President Kursolov smiled and said, "Today is a wonderful day for the Facility and Russia. This woman beside me, Dr. Maria Davidoff, is about to do something no woman has ever done. She is about to fly to the moon and plant the Russian flag next to the American flag at Tranquility Base where American astronauts, Neil Armstrong and Buzz Aldrin, became the first humans to walk on the moon."

Dr. Davidoff looked at the President a bit troubled. He looked at her and smiled broader.

"I know it wasn't her original plan. But the symbolism is what matters for the first female flight to the moon in a craft that could become the prototype for a space fleet that will bring tourists to the moon, Mars, and beyond. If her trips to the moon and Mars are as successful as I believe they will be, I will give the Facility the money needed to design and build at least 20 spaceplanes. I will have this hangar expanded into an aircraft assembly plant similar to what it was nearly a century ago when the motherland was threatened by the Nazi war machine.

"A few years ago, an American named Dick Thurman approached my government about the need for a facility like this which would be similar to the one he worked for in Arizona. At the time I was intrigued. But we have many research and development companies throughout Russia. But in time I saw the logic in having one facility do what a dozen or more companies do. It also helped to have BOSS kick in over 5 trillion rubles to make the Facility a dream come true.

"This brilliant scientist and engineer could usher in a new era in transportation. The people who are at the three moon bases, one

American, one Russian, and one Chinese, arrived there atop rockets that were a generation or two beyond what were used to land the first men on the moon. I want the moon to become a tourist destination for normal, everyday people. I want passengers to board planes similar to what she will be flying in Moscow, Saint Petersburg, even Volgograd, to fly to lunar cities that will grow from the bases that they are today.

"I remember when I was a child the articles on the Internet about how the Americans never landed on the moon. It was a hoax to fool the world into thinking American technology had done the impossible. The supposed live broadcasts were recorded in a studio. This time, there will be no doubts. Cameras aboard the plane will broadcast to the world every second of the flight. And after she lands, however that is done, she will plant the Russian flag and project from the surface of the moon a holographic message for the world to read. People will be able to step outside and if the skies are clear, they will read in the three languages of the people who are there now, PEACE."

The people assembled in the hangar applauded him for nearly a minute. He kissed the doctor on both cheeks and sent her off amidst more applause to her spaceplane. The intakes were open so the repulsion-drive engines could be compression-field engines sucking in air, compressing the air between electromagnetic fields, and using linear induction and bursts of electromagnetic discharges to shove the compressed air through the engines. In the upper reaches of the atmosphere where the air was too thin to compress the intakes would be closed and the engines would use field repulsion to push the plane to the moon.

Since the engines had no moving parts unlike a conventional jet engine, only the rush of air and the sticky sound of tires pressed against asphalt were heard. Once the tower and the orbital sensors that monitored the position of objects in space between earth and the moon said the way was clear for at least another 10 minutes, the plane took off. It barreled down the runway at over 300 kph, opened the nose vent to blow the nose into the air, and quickly climbed into the stratosphere nearly straight up. The force field around the plane protected it from the air friction the craft encountered when it was soaring toward space at hypersonic speed. By the time the plane was 10 kilometers above the earth it was doing over Mach 15 and increasing its velocity rapidly.

Inside the plane, the doctor was concentrating on what was ahead of her. The sensors of the plane helped her maneuver past orbiting debris that wasn't detected by the orbiting sensors. She didn't fear having her craft punctured by any of it since the force field protected the craft from objects ranging in size from dust to boulders traveling at over 40,000 kph.

Once the plane was above 35,000 kilometers, the doctor relaxed a bit and began a commentary on the flight that was braodcast back to earth. To show the plane was actually on course to land on the moon, the doctor swiveled her seat around to face the camera behind her which showed the moon becoming increasingly larger. "Hello. My name is Doctor Maria Davidoff. I am hurtling toward the moon at speeds greater than any rocket ever achieved. You may see at the bottom of your TV the monitors that show the increasing speed of this plane and the decreasing distance between the earth and the moon. As you see, I'm not coasting toward the moon to save energy. I have plenty of fuel in my reactors. Once this plane reaches a speed of 2 million kph, it will begin coasting toward the moon. That will happen… three, two, one, now. I'll coast for a few minutes before opening all four of my nose vents and turn on my forward repulsion-drive engines to slow the craft to a manageable speed. If that isn't enough, I'll have to turn this plane around and use the primary engines to slow it dramatically. I hope I won't have to do that. Oh, I'll just go ahead and slow the craft in a couple minutes so I can allow you to continue to see the moon all the way there."

The doctor swiveled her seat around and when the moon was within 50,000 kilometers, she shut off the primary engines, opened the nose vents, and switched on the forward engines. The velocity of the plane decreased dramatically until it reached 1,000 kph. By then the moon was so close that the people watching the broadcast could easily see the lights of the three moon bases and the buildings below.

The American base was near where the first travelers to the moon landed; Tranquility Base. The doctor opened the landing gear doors and swiveled the landing gear so that the field repulsion gear could slow the descent of the plane to 10 kph. When the plane was 100 meters above the American flag, it slowed to a meter a second. The bubble of the displacement field pushed at the flag and nearly knocked it down.

The doctor landed softly on the surface of the moon 10 meters away from the flag that was tilted at a 50% angle. She slipped into her space suit, opened a cabinet where the Russian flag was leaning against the back wall, and picked up a carbon fiber bag that contained a flag holder that would drill into the moon before the flag staff was inserted, a small folding shovel, and a holographic projector. She hoped she could right the American flag without it falling over because she didn't have a second flag holder to secure the flag in place.

Panels descended from the ceiling of the craft near the hatch to produce an airlock chamber just large enough for one person to stand in it. Seconds later, air was sucked out of the makeshift chamber and the hatch opened to allow the doctor to leave the craft. A drone with a 3-D camera flew out of the front landing gear bay to let people see the doctor descend to the surface of the moon down the ladder. Since it was difficult climbing down the ladder with a flag in one hand and a bag in the other, she dropped the bag onto the ground and bent over to drop the end of the flag staff to the ground while propping it against the side of the plane.

She stopped for a few seconds before stepping onto the surface of the moon, gathered her thoughts, and finally hopped off of the bottom rung of the ladder. She faced the camera and tried to channel the spirit of Neil Armstrong.

"I thank God, the Creator of the moon and the earth, for allowing me to step foot on a world I have since I was a child longed to walk upon. I consider myself more than just the first woman to reach the moon. I am more like you who are seeing this broadcast than one of the astronauts that is less than 200 meters from where I'm standing."

Her heart was beating rapidly due to nervousness. She nearly dropped the flag as she grabbed it and the flag holder out of the bag. She walked over to where the American flag was located, drilled the flag holder into the moon a couple meters from the first flag, and inserted the Russian flag into the holder. She saluted the flag and seconds later righted the American flag out of respect.

As she was walking over to the bag, a couple astronauts approached her. They had been watching her approach to the moon as she descended and also seeing the broadcast on the TV in the cafeteria. When she turned around they were a few meters away. She was a little startled, but soon calmed down. She dropped the bag and approached the astronauts.

The astronauts tried to communicate with her. But since they used different radio frequencies, they had to communicate by hand jestures. Both astronauts beckoned for her to come with them to Tranquility Base. She followed them by duplicating their bouncy gate to the base. A few minutes later, the airlock opened inside the main building and the trio entered the assembly room which doubled as the cafeteria. Security cameras inside the room trained on the doctor and the eight astronauts that worked on the base as the doctor removed her helmet and placed it on a table. The two that had gone outside to meet her removed their suits and placed them in their lockers.

The base commander, Captain "Wild Bill" Peters extended his hand and shook the suited hand of the doctor.

"Welcome to Tranquility Base. Let's drop expected protocols.

Call me Wild Bill. It is a pleasure to have you come here today." "I'm Maria Davidoff."

"I know who you are. We've been watching you on TV. Pretty exciting isn't it?"

"More than I thought it would be."

Bill turned to one of the other astronauts and said, "Jim, go get the bear."

The astronaut walked over to a table in the back where a small teddy bear holding an American flag in one paw and a Russian flag in the other was sitting. He handed the bear to the captain.

"This is something we threw together at the last minute. Your comrades at the Russian base a few miles from here brought over the Russian flag and we taped it onto the left paw with good old fashioned duct tape. We have a box of bears with flags in their paws in one of the storage rooms. I knew one day I'd get the chance to hand one out to a visitor."

"You better get a lot more bears because I intend on being the first of thousands of tourists to the moon."

"I heard the speech your President made. I hope he's right. Why don't you take off your suit and stay awhile?"

"I'm sorry. I need to return home so I can attend a recital tonight."
"God, I wish I could travel between the earth and the moon so fast. It

took us a few hours to get here which I thought was fast. But it only took you minutes. What do you have in your ship?" "Repulsion-drive engines and a reactor to power them. That's all I can say. You know. State secrets."

"Bull shit. You're a scientist and I got a degree in astrophysics at the accademy in Florida; God bless Donald Trump for the Space Force. State secrets was the excuse for us not knowing more about flying saucers and alien life. You can tell me what you used to get here so fast."

"Would former President Trump have told former Russian President Putin how to build tanks and fighter planes?"

"So it's more a competition thing. Once our Madhouse helps NASA and the Space Force more, traveling between the earth and the moon will be more like a weekend jaunt."

"If that's the case, you're going to need boxes of bears once the tourists start flooding the area. Will your government or the Madhouse build the city you will need up here to make this a tourist destination?"

"I sure hope so. If a lot of those tourists look as good as you, I might stay up here a few more years. I hope I wasn't offensive when I said that."

"Not at all. A lot of men are thinking dirtier thoughts than that due to my past which I won't bring up."

"I won't ask."

"If I come up again, I'll try to remember to bring a present with me."

"How about a case or two of that Russian Madhouse vodka?" "We can have as many cases sent up by GSLP projectile as you want. Just tell us the flavors you want and we'll send them up. It won't be free except maybe for the first couple cases; professional courtesy."

"Sounds good to me. If it is as good as I've heard, I'd personally pay for them. You can have a case of cherry and a case of apple sent up for us to sample."

"I'll tell them at the distillery to send them to the GSLP launch facility. I hope the Facility doesn't think it's too frivolous a reason for sending vodka to the moon."

"Call it a sign of friendship between Russia and America. The good will jesture could send the sales of Russian Madhouse vodka through the roof."

"You Americans always seem to be trying to make deals to enrich yourselves."

"Hey, I'm in the Space Force. I already make good money. But if I can make a little more on the side, as long as it's legal, I'll do it.

My dad made a lot playing poker at the Air Force bases in Iraq and Afghanistan and he got to keep the cash. So who knows?"

The doctor shook the hands of each man there before putting her helmet back on and entering the airlock with the teddy bear in her left hand. She bounced back to the plane and placed the teddy bear on the top step of the ladder before removing the holographic projector out of the bag, setting it on the ground about 20 meters away from the plane, and turning it on to project the word PEACE in letters and symbols that were 300 kilometers high in English, Cyrilic, and Mandarin. She picked up the bag to collect moon rocks and dust to put into it. Minutes later after collecting enough rocks and dust to fill the bag up to a mark inside the bag, the doctor sealed it shut with a simple zipper at the top. She set the timer on the projector to allow the word peace to be shown for an entire month to prove she had actually landed on the moon.

When she opened the hatch control next to the ladder she pushed the button to open the hatch and a moment later had to chase the teddy bear as it flew after the hatch opened and knocked the toy off of the top step. She also dropped the bag which landed on the ground. It's tough carbon fiber construction kept it from tearing open. After placing the bag and bear into the temporary airlock, the doctor climbed the ladder and entered the spaceplane. The drone that had followed the doctor to the American moon base and back entered the front landing gear bay before the engines were switched back on. The surface of the moon was ionized below the landing gear which levitated the plane a few centimeters above the ground. To prevent bending the American flag over again, the doctor glided the plane over the surface to an area 100 meters away before expanding the displacement field to lift the craft to a height of 100 meters above the moon.

The trip back to Earth was faster and when the plane rolled back into the hangar, all of the people who had seen the doctor off were still there. The President gave the doctor kisses and a hug. The doctor handed the bear to him before walking over to Dick to kiss and embrace him. She was looking forward to the next day when he would accompany her to Mars. She was taken back a bit when he told her that his wife Kate would come along. But she finally conceded that there would be talks of hanky panky going on aboard the plane if they went together without Kate accompanying them. Only Mr. Channel 10 would fantasize about a three-way happening on the trip.

CHAPTER 9

The rest of the day seemed to drag for Dick even though he was busy working on the flying limousine for the President. He was looking forward to the recital that night and the trip to Mars the next day. Sometimes he was grateful the fabricator caught his mistakes before going ahead and forming some of the components.

Dick decided to go home around 5:00 to shower and eat a light dinner with his wife. He was surprised she wasn't home when he got there. He told the sound system to play some Mozart while he showered and ate. By the time he had Sam prepare a taco salad, Kate walked into the apartment. Dick was sitting at the kitchen table sipping a tall glass of peach tea.

"Sorry I'm a little late. I was working on my companion brain for children in the tech lab and lost track of time. Then I was intercepted by Mr. Channel 10 before I reached the elevator," Kate complained.

"Mr. Channel 10?"

"Boris Shenova. He produces pornography that is regularly shown on Channel 10."

"I'm amazed they allow such things here."

Kate bent over and kissed Dick on the lips before sitting at the table.

"It's good to be home. How was your first day on the job at the Facility?"

"It was interesting. I had lunch with President Kursolov before he ended the afternoon watching Dr. Davidoff fly to the moon and back. Did you get a chance to watch the flight?"

"Oh yeah. Andre and the kids accompanied me to the cafeteria to watch it. Which reminds me."

Kate pulled the Altoids tin out of her pants pocket and handed it to Dick.

"You didn't go to the clinic for the translator implants did you?" she asked.

"I didn't get around to it. What's in the tin?"

"Micromachines and construction material. Three are for the audio portion of the brain and the other three are for the visual portion."

Dick opened the tin and removed the capsules. He downed them two at a time with a swallow of tea.

"Back at the tech lab we coated capsules in banana and cherry flavoring. One kid thought they were candy and ate his."

"What did you expect? At least you can take a break tomorrow." "Oh?"

"Dr. Davidoff is flying to Mars and wants me to go with her. I told her I want you to come along so people won't talk about us having an affair behind our back. She agrees."

"I have a cousin who is at Mars Base Gagarin. My Aunt Olga in Volgograd told me that before we left Arizona. We could see him when we arrive. Won't he be surprised."

"I think we're going to spend a little more time on Mars than she did on the moon. Sam is fixing a taco salad for me. Want one?"

"Sounds good."

After Sam finished Dick's salad he began to make one for Kate. He brought both bowls to the table and stood waiting for another command.

Dick looked up at Sam and said, "Thank-you, Sam. You can go to where you normally go when you're not needed."

Sam walked down the hallway toward the bedroom and entered a cabinet where he recharged.

"I never thought I would have a great tasting taco salad in Russia," said Dick. "When we get back from Mars I need to test the President's new limousine I'm constructing."

"I bet it's a flying one. Am I right?" "You got it."

"What do you think of Kursolov?"

Dick thought for a moment and said, "I hope he's not using the Facility to become another Stalin. I know he knows it was the Madhouse in Arizona that destroyed his best planes before they could attack Israel. If he got the chance to punish America for destroying his military he would."

"I have that feeling too. I pray I'm wrong." "Same here."

After dinner, Kate took a shower and put on an evening dress while Dick changed his clothes and put on a suit. They entered the Glinka Recital Hall 15 minutes early which they were glad they did since the recital hall was filling up. By the time the pianist walked on stage the hall was packed. He walked over to the computerized keyboard, touched a couple buttons, and turned toward the audience. Since he was dressed in the style of an early 18th century musician, Dick wasn't surprised what came next.

"Good evening," he said. "In honor of Richard and Katharine Thurman, I have changed my musical selections to the music of Bach. I will be performing the Two and Three Part Inventions For Harpsichord by J.S. Bach. Enjoy."

The keyboard artist played perfectly and with his powdered wig and Baroque era clothes on made the Thurmans imagine he was the great composer at the keyboard. The first half of the recital was over too fast for them.

During intermission, more chairs and music stands that had computerized score display units on them were brought on stage. A display unit was also placed on the keyboard for the keyboard artist to play from. Before the intermission was over, more performers dressed like musicians from 300 years before took their seats.

The keyboard artist stood, faced the audience again and said, "To continue the theme of this recital, we will be performing the orchestra suites for flute and orchestra by J.S. Bach."

The flutist stood and raised her music stand. The keyboard artist raised his head for a moment and when he dropped it, the musicians began to play. The second half of the recital was played as flawlessly as the first half and received a standing ovation which prompted the performers to play a flute concerto by Bach. After the second standing ovation, the musicians left the stage and the audience left the recital hall and entered the banquet hall next door. Inside the banquet hall were long tables loaded with finger foods, beverages, small Thurman submarine sandwiches, and a cake that had a Russian flag made from vanilla, blueberry, and cherry frosting on the left third of the cake, an American flag made from vanilla frosting for the stars and white stripes, blueberry frosting for the blue portion of the flag, and cherry frosting for the red stripes on the right third of the cake, and a middle section that had caramel frosting with block letters made from dark chocolate frosting that read: WELCOME TO THE FACILITY RICHARD AND KATHARINE THURMAN. The table with the cake was beside the table where two young women took Dick and Kate. The young women loaded plates with what the couple wanted to eat and cut generous slices from the bottom of the middle section of the cake that had no writing on it. The couple were also given cups filled with Dr. Pepper that had come from one of the gallons they had brought with them from Arizona.

People would come up to their table, set their plates and cups down, and shake their hands before making some small talk. But when Dr. Sorchen Vlandner and his wife Dollia came to the table, Dick stood and shook the couple's hands.

"Honey, this is Dr. Sorchen Vlandner and his wife Dollia. Dollia is not only a ballet dancer, she is an android," Dick said excitedly.

"I like to be called a synthetic," Dollia corrected Dick.

"We have two children," said Sorchen. "Our son Trav has taken over my practice at the Newgate Municipal Hospital in Newgate, New York. Our daughter Helia is a ballet dancer in New York City."

"Hold it. You have children?" Kate asked, shocked.

"We are like any other couple," said Sorchen. "We love each other very much and after we married decided we wanted children."

"How did you two meet?" Kate asked.

"When I started working at the Newgate Municipal Hospital 15 years ago I saw her working with children and nursing babies in the maternity ward and fell in love with her."

"Wait a minute. You can nurse babies? How's that possible?" Kate asked, perplexed.

"Let me start at the beginning. When I met Sorchen, I knew from the start he was different. I was used to people treating me like a thing and accepted it as normal. But he treated me like a person with feelings and value."

"In the dimension I come from, synthetics have had human equivalence rights for centuries. When I found out she had a soul, I knew she was someone I wanted to be with for the rest of my life." "We waited until we were married before we had intimate sex.

In order for me to become pregnant, I synthesized his DNA in his sperm and blended it with my synthetic DNA to produce conception. Our son Trav was born first and our daughter Helia was born a year later. They both developed at a rate three times faster than humans do."

"Did you nurse them?" Kate asked.

"Yes. Since they are cyborgs, my mother's milk has micromachines and construction material in it. When I nursed human babies my milk was formulated to be more nutricious than standard mother's milk."

"I gave miromachines to kids today and they didn't hurt them," said Kate.

"I guess I could have given the babies micromachines then. Oh well. If some woman gives me her baby to nurse it, I might blend in some micromachines. I hope the woman isn't shocked when her six month old baby looks like he's 18 months old and runs her ragged." "We have a synthetic called Sam in our apartment. What would happen if he had sex with a human woman?" Kate asked.

"He's the one who would become pregnant and give birth since human women can't form a synthetic DNA," said Sorchen.

"Too bad Dick couldn't carry at least one of our kids. He'd know what real pain feels like," Kate proclaimed.

The Vlandners moved to the cake table and cut slices from the American flag before moving on.

A few people later, a Mongolian-appearing man came up to Dick and Kate's table, put his plate and cup down on the table, and shook their hands.

"Welcome to the Facility. My name is Joseph Simmeroff. I work in the Department of Military and Space Research on weapons."

Dick swallowed hard and said, "Nice to meet you. Do you like what you're doing in the Facility?"

"Very much. Few people in my region get the chance to work in a place like this."

"Maybe I'll get the chance to see your weapons being tested in the future." said Dick.

"I'd like that."

Dick kept staring at the man as he cut a slice of cake and walked away. Kate shoved Dick's shoulder.

"Excuse yourself," Kate insisted.

"I'm sorry. President Kursolov was in his department watching a weapons test. I should have asked him if the President got the chance to see anything he built."

"I think there's something you're not telling me." "When we get home. I can't tell you in this crowd."

After most of the people and most of the cake were gone, the two young women placed food on a platter for the Thurmans to bring home with them. One of the women pulled a bag out of a fanny pack and placed it over the food and platter. She pulled an inflation device out of the pack and inserted it into the bag to pump up the bag. The other woman took a small spray can out of her fanny pack and sprayed the bag which hardened. The inflation device was removed and the bag was sprayed again so air couldn't come out of a hole since the spray sealed it close.

"How do I remove the bag?" Kate asked.

The woman who sprayed the bag said, "Crack it like an egg. The bag is vegetable-based. So if any of the pieces fall into the food, you can still eat it if you don't mind the nasty taste of the spray."

"Thank-you," said Kate.

Dick carried the platter home while Kate carried the remaining Dr. Pepper. After he placed it on the kitchen table h realized something. There wasn't enough room in the refrigerator for it to keep the food fresh and the Dr. Pepper was going to become flat. Kate dumped the remainder into an insulated jug and crammed it into the refrigerator. Dick cracked open the bag and wrapped fruit, cheese, and sandwiches in plastic wrap and stuffed them as best he could in the refrigerator and freezer.

Sam entered the kitchen and said, "There are vacuum containers on the bottom shelf of the cabinet to the left of the sink. I'll show you how to use them."

Sam opened the cabinet and pulled out two hard clear plastic domes and two plastic plates to set the domes on. There was a valve on the top of each dome. Sam opened a drawer and laid a small vacuum pump between the domes.

"If you want to prevent air from drying out your food, put it on one of the plates, put a dome over it, swivel the dome until it clicks in place, insert the vacuum pump into the valve, and pump out the air. What do you want vacuum sealed?"

"The cake and the nuts."

Sam took the pieces of cake and placed them on one plate and the nuts on the other. He placed the domes over the plates, twisted the domes until they clicked in place, and inserted the vacuum pump into the valves. It only took a minute to create a vacuum under each dome. Sam put the vacuum pump back in the drawer and was about to leave to go back into his recharging chamber when Dick asked him a question.

"Do you have a soul?"

"Yes I do. It is different from a human soul. I have a memory and operation core. It allows me to function normally and collect memories. It is the essense of me. Without it I would be no better than a robot."

"Is there such a place as android Heaven?" Kate asked.

"Not in the sense of living forever in a place that is perfect like Heaven. My soul should last me for at least 150 years. When my memory capacity is at maximum, my core will be removed and the information will be stored in the cloud. Without a core I would still have basic functions. But with a new core installed that is engineered specifically for me, I will be able to go on for another 150 years unless the soul has been improved. Then I might function for two or three centuries. I would have access to my original memories due to the cloud. But as long as no one erases my core, I could theoretically exist forever."

"How about cyborgs?" Kate asked.

"If they are offspring from a synthetic that has a soul, they too will have souls. It's all in the programming. They might have hybrid souls since they are the product of a human and a synthetic."

"Let's say you met a human woman who wanted to marry you and raise a family. Would you actually get pregnant and give birth to a cyborg?" Kate asked.

"That is correct. Human women can't form synthetic DNAs." "Have ever been pregnant?" Kate asked, a little embarrassed. "No. I'm only a year old. I was constructed in the National Robot and Android Institute in Moscow and programmed there. I have no authentic emotions like love, hate, fear, or anything else that makes humans human. They are programmed responses to stimuli and conditions. But if you respect me,

I'll respect you. If you ask me to kill someone, I would ask you why. If the person were endangering either one of you and you could be killed unless I killed them, I would kill the person who seeks to do you harm. But if you wanted someone dead who was just a pest, there would be no valid reason to kill them. I would naturally refuse."

"Do you believe in God?" Dick Asked.

"I believe the one you call God, the one who you believe created the universe, does exist. The universe didn't just happen. It is too complicated and at times natural laws have been violated. There has to be something or someone who is responsible for the way things are. I had a creator and so did you two. To me it is only logical that God exists."

Dick and Kate looked at each other and smiled.

"We had better get to bed. We're on a trip to Mars in the morning and we don't want to be too tired to enjoy it," said Dick.

"What about that thing you said you would tell me about when we got home?" asked Kate.

"That can wait. We've had an enormous day. I know. We can go to hangar 3 in the morning and have breakfast with Dr. Davidoff before we take off. You really ought to meet her."

"Sounds like more than a good idea. I'd like to see this woman who might be my competition," she said sarcastically.

"No one can compete with you. Maybe a long trip to Mars will let us relax for awhile. When we get back we'll be refreshed and ready to get to work at full steam. Sam, wake us up at 7:00 if we're not up by then."

"I'll do that."

Sam went back to his chamber to recharge some more while Dick and Kate walked back to the bedroom after taking turns using the toilet. They brushed their teeth, changed into pajamas, and slid under the covers after kissing each other good-night. The next day was going to be a more than interesting day.

CHAPTER 10

Dick was so excited about flying to Mars that he tossed and turned all night. He managed to catch snatches of slumber and dreamed about Dr. Davidoff a few times. In one dream, he was jogging on the runway with the woman toward the end of the strip.

"I'm so glad you were able to join me out here,"she said breathlessly. "It's a bit brisk out here. Maybe we should go back to the hangar and warm up in the shower," he said excitedly. "Sounds good to me."

As what happens in many dreams, the next thing that happened was the fulfillment of a fantasy. Both people were together in the shower enjoying a steamy relaxing cascade of soothing warm water. They stood beside each other lathering up and scrubbing their bodies with sponges.

"This is nice," Dick admitted. "I wish we could spend all day in here. Why are we going to Mars?"

"Because I've been scheduled to fly there. Don't bring your wife. I don't care what they say back here. We can be alone out there and no one needs to know what goes on. To paraphrase an American saying, what goes on in space stays in space."

She turned to Dick and placed her arms around him and began stroking his back with her sponge. He followed suit. They pressed their bodies together and began kissing passionately. The embrace lasted for over a minute. Dick began sucking on her breasts that were still firm as they were when she was much younger. Even her face took on the youthful appearance from her previous life. He was about to put his sponge on her vagina when he heard a familiar voice behind him.

"Now I know why you wanted to go to Mars with her," accused a naked Kate at the entrance of the shower.

"I'm sorry. I'm sorry. This isn't what it looks like."

"That's a lie," said Maria. "This is exactly what it looks like."

Kate marched toward the couple, pushed Maria aside, and embraced her husband. They began making love hot and heavy. After nearly a minute of sex, Maria began rubbing Kate's shoulders before kissing the back of her neck. Maria pulled Kate away from Dick and began kissing her. She was about to place her hands on Kate's breasts when Dick awoke. He smiled broadly as he gazed upon his wife until he drifted off to sleep again. In the second dream, Maria was at the controls of her spaceplane and Dick was sitting beside her. She was wearing the same things she had worn on the treadmill. A look of discomfort was on her face.

"Could you reach down my pants and scratch my vagina?" she asked.

"I...don't know."

"Please? It really itches down there and I'm too busy to scratch." Dick slowly reached his right hand down the front of her pants and began to scratch and feel her vagina. She started to have an orgasm which lasted until the voice of Kate was heard at the back of the cabin.

"Take your hand out of her pants," Kate demanded. Dick immediately pulled his hand out of her pants as Kate stomped toward Maria.

When Kate was near the hatch, Maria flipped a switch and the hatch popped open. Kate was sucked out of the plane and seconds later the hatch closed.

"Now that she's out of here, could you scratch my vagina again?"

Dick was about to place his hand down her pants when the frozen corpse of Kate was seen pounding on the electronic windshield of the plane.

Dick awoke startled. Kate mumbled something before going back to sleep. Dick managed to go back to sleep and dreamed about walking on Mars without a spacesuit on. It was actually hot as if he were walking in the desert in Arizona.

Dick began to sweat and took off his shirt. In the distance he made out two naked women; Maria and Kate. They were both waving at him and urging him to hurry to save them because they were slowly sinking in the sands of the Red Planet. He began to run. By the time he was a couple meters from them, they were up to their necks in sand and desperately reaching out to him. But he could only save one of them.

"You're the only man I have ever loved," cried Maria. "I bore your children," Kate screamed.

Dick hesitated for a moment. He reached out to Kate and she slipped below the surface of Mars. He reached for Maria and she too slipped below the surface of the planet. That was when he began to sink as if he was being dragged under by quicksand. He struggled. But the more he thrashed around the faster he sank. He tried to scream for help, but red sand poured into his mouth. That was when he awoke and accidentally hit his wife.

"What's wrong, honey?" she asked. "I had some weird dreams."

"Oh? Were they about the flight to Mars?"

"They were about the flight and about you and Dr. Davidoff." "Could you tell me about them?"

"They were kind of embarrassing. You and the doctor were naked in two of them."

"Oh really? Did you do the nasty with her?" "Well…uh."

"You did didn't you?" she accused him. "They were only dreams."

"People dream about things they can't have while they're awake.

Is that what was happening?"

"I love you more today than I did the day we were married," he confessed.

"Yeah, yeah."

"I didn't need to invite you along. I didn't want people to think anything was going on up there."

"You were afraid something would."

"To be totally honest, yes I was. She used to be a nude model. She might be a Christian. But she is still a woman. I couldn't trust myself."

"If I were a lesbian I don't think I could trust myself around her either. She's around our age and still a very attractive and sexy woman."

"Maybe I'll need to separate you two if things get out of hand," he jested.

She punched him in the shoulder before telling him to go back to sleep. The rest of the night, Dick slept a bit better. He didn't remember any of the following dreams when Sam woke him in the morning.

Dick and Kate had some Mozart playing over the sound system as they showered and dressed. They also packed some clean clothes, their tooth brushes, a tube of tooth paste, deodorant, mouthwash, and a couple small

EPU recorders that would allow them to experience the trip any time in the future and also allow others to know how a trip to Mars felt like.

They left their apartment a little before 8:00, took the elevator up to the horizontal elevator, and arrived at hangar 3 around 8:10. Maria and her launch team were eating breakfast in the break room. She was wearing a blue jumpsuit that showed off her shape which for her age was fantastic. Everyone greeted the Thurmans and offered them a couple seats at their tables. But they knew that the Thurmans would join the doctor and her two top assistants at their table.

Kate decided to chow down on waffles with syrup, sausages, scrambled eggs, a cinnamon roll, and a big mug of coffee with French vanilla creamer in it. Dick chose to eat like an astronuat and had steak and eggs and black coffee for breakfast. The doctor reached out and grasped their hands after Dick prayed grace over their meal.

"It is so good to meet you, Mrs. Thurman," the doctor said sincerely. "I'm truly glad he invited you to come along."

"Call me Kate."

"All right, Kate. Call me Maria. We are colleagues at the Facility and will hopefully become friends."

"Better than opening the hatch and sucking her out into space," Dick mumbled.

"What did you say?" Maria asked.

"Oh, nothing. I hope all three of us get along well on the trip. I saw how spacious it is inside the cabin. If it were a commercial spaceliner, how many passengers and crew members could be accomodated aboard the plane?"

"Maybe a dozen passengers and three crew members. I have it configured for four with the seats able to recline into beds."

"Is that the reason why you have four spacesuits?"

"Sort of. I have two suits that should fit me and your wife and two suits that are a little larger for men. I've stocked the pantry with two weeks of food and beverages. But we probably won't need all that since it should take no more than three days to reach Mars and three days to get back."

"Will we be weightless at any time?" Kate asked. "There's artificial gravity inside," Maria assured her.

"How does that work exactly? I remember seeing old TV science fiction shows in which the ships used artificial gravity to keep the people from floating around," said Kate.

"Our bodies are drawn toward the floor when we wear ionization footwear and clothes. I am wearing them now. I have some slippers you can place over your shoes that will keep you from floating around the cabin."

"Will I be shocked if I touch anything made from metal?" Kate asked.

"No. The humidity aboard my plane is set at 70% which is comfortable. The floor covering shouldn't generate any static electricity either. So don't worry about being shocked."

"How long will it take for us to fly to Mars?" Dick asked.

"I'm shooting for three days each way. Since I don't think people will want to stay up for a week watching us do mainly nothing, only synthetics will be monitoring the flight. When I arrive on Mars, then the people of the Facility and the rest of the world will see us. I don't want to bore people," said Maria.

"Will you give at least one or two progress reports on the way there?" Kate asked.

"Probably. I might turn the cameras inside the cabin off while we sleep. But the camera that shows Mars getting larger as we approach it will never be turned off. People need to know that nothing bad has happened to the plane during the flight," Maria said.

After breakfast, Maria, Dick, and Kate went to the bathroom first before climbing the steps up into the plane's cabin where Dick and Kate slipped on ionization gravity slippers over their shoes. Dick placed his and his wife's carry-on bags inside lockers at the back of the cabin. There were four lockers beside each other. One of the lockers had Maria's carry-on bag while the fourth one was loaded with boxes of candy, cookies, chips, beef jerky, nuts, and junk food.

There was a refrigerator/freezer in the back of the cabin, a sink, a coffee maker, a beverage machine, cabinets and drawers for food, trays, bowls, plates, cups, utensils, and napkins, a microwave oven, a toaster oven, and a counter large enough to prepare a meal for upwards to six people. There was more food and beverages in the galley than what was in Dick and Kate's apartment.

There was a small bathroom in the back of the cabin that was large enough for a small shower. The computer and the environmental control system were in a closet that was next to the lockers that held the four spacesuits. There was even a treadmill and a magnetic resistance machine in the back of the cabin. Dick could envision the addition of ten more seats and lockers for spacesuits.

Before Maria switched on the engines and wheel motors that would roll the plane onto the runway, she asked Dick to offer a prayer of protection to God. The trio bowed their heads and closed their eyes.

"Dear Heavenly Father, thank-you for this opportunity to enter your heavenly realm and travel to our planetary neighbor Mars. Give us protection during our journey and may we honor you in all that we do. Let nothing go wrong and may this be just one more successful journey to the Red Planet. May the ones who follow us to Mars thank us for what we are about to do. Thank- you for your grace and mercy and let us never think that we don't need you. Bless the Facility. Bless Russia and its President. And bless all our efforts to serve you and the world. I ask this in Christ Jesus' name. Amen."

"Buckle up people," Maria commanded. All three buckled their belts and the plane began rolling out of the hangar and onto the runway. After getting the go ahead, Maria shoved the accelerator levers forward and in seconds, the plane was barreling down the runway at 200 kph. She blew the nose 2/3 of the way down the strip and the plane climbed into the sky.

The plane was 30,000 meters above the earth and doing Mach 15 when Maria closed the intake vents and allowed the compression- field engines to become repulsion-drive engines. By the time the craft was beyond the orbiting obstacles, Maria began discharging the exterior fields and coupled them with the repulsion-drive engines to greatly increase the speed of the craft.

Maria flipped some switches and twisted some dials and within seconds, the craft was doing over 10% of light speed and rapidly accelerating. Within a minute, the craft had shattered the light barrier and continued to accelerate. Seconds later, Maria shut down the engines and the craft began coasting toward Mars at 1.3 times the speed of light. When the craft reached the half way point of the journey, Maria opened the nose vents and flipped on the forward repulsion-drive engines to slow the craft eventually to 5% of the speed of light before they were shut down so the craft could coast at a more controllable speed.

Maria swiveled her seat and told Dick and Kate, "You can unbuckle your belts. We should arrive in Mars orbit within a couple hours."

"Why did you bring so much food and beverages if you were planning on reaching Mars within a few hours?" Dick asked her.

"Call this a supply run. I've heard about the food they have at Mars Base Gagarin. It is slightly better than what the cosmonauts were eating sixty years ago. I brought something all space travelers miss: junk food."

"I was wondering why you packed that locker with so much of it. I guess we won't get a chance to eat any of it," said Dick with some regrets.

"Only if we leave Mars with some. I also brought fruit, pies, cakes, and ice cream."

"They're going to want you to come to Mars more often," said Kate. "Will we have time for me to see my cousin from Volgograd at the base?"

"Who is your cousin?" "Vladimer Premakoff."

"I don't see any reason why not. We can spend a couple or three days on Mars. This plane is so fast that a trip to Mars is like flying from Moscow to Berlin unless I put on more speed. As long as I don't overshoot Mars, I could get there faster than if I took the horizontal elevator from the Facility to Smirnoffgrad."

"What type of reactor are you using?" asked Dick.

"Something that we'll never let President Kursolov know about."

After turning off the cabin cameras she said, "We developed a hyperlight speed reactor. After nearly six months of testing and failing and finally succeeding, sometimes nearly destroying the test facilities, we perfected a reactor that can accelerate charged particles and bundles of energy so far up to 150,000 times the speed of light. The reactors in this spaceplane are no larger than the bathroom at the back of the cabin. I had to dial the reactors back to 0.02% of maximum output. Any more and I was afraid I would fly past Mars and would have to turn around. I was only using the reactors at 0.004% of maximum output yesterday because I didn't want to get to the moon too soon. President Kursolov would have demanded me to design and build fighter planes and bombers that had hyperlight speed reactors. I may love Mother Russia. But I fear what would happen to the rest of the world if Kursolov used hyperlight physics to destroy our enemies and control the world. He might become more evil than the man he looks so much like." "I see why you turned off the cameras. Very smart," said Dick.

"What if they ask what happened back at the Facility?" Kate asked.

"That won't be for another few miniutes. I can lie and say it was technical problems. Or…"

Maria flipped some switches and began some deception. "What did you just do?" Kate asked.

"I began transmitting a recorded cabin feed to go along with the slowed down exterior camera transmission that I began sending back to the Facility before I accelerated to 10% of light speed. Back at the Facility they think I'm about a quarter million kilometers beyond the moon."

"How will you explain arriving at Mars faster than the exterior camera indicates?" Dick asked.

"I'm not going to go directly to Mars. I intend on flying to Pluto, the Kuyper Belt, and maybe to our nearest star system before arriving on Mars. Anyone against that idea?"

"What if something goes wrong and we crash out in the Kuyper Belt? No one will know we are out there and we could die," Kate warned.

Maria considered what Kate said for a few moments before saying, "I guess I didn't think it through enough. It looks like it would be best if I just flew to Mars and forget about being the first person to travel beyond Mars."

Suddenly, the craft came to a stop. Dick and Kate fell out or their seats and Maria nearly fell out of her's.

"What happened?" Kate asked.

"I have no idea," Maria confessed.

Seconds later, the view of space was exchanged for the view of the inside of a landing craft bay where three other landing crafts that looked like smooth turtle shells were parked. Over the sound system came a pleasant baratone voice.

"I'm sorry to stop you so suddenly. I was shifting my ship into your dimension and you ended up in my landing bay. I'm using an energy absorption field to prevent your craft from ripping my ship apart. I could barely fit you in. Turn off your engines and exit your craft."

Chapter 11

Maria shut down the engines and checked the atmosphere outside the craft. There was slightly more oxygen in the landing craft bay than what was on earth (22%) and the temperature was around the same temperature as inside the Facility (75 degrees celsius). Maria opened the hatch and the trio climbed down the ladder to the bay as a man entered the huge room.

"Welcome to the Aremulac," the man said as he extended his right hand in friendship. "Captain George Majors commands the best starship in ACE's fleet."

"ACE?" asked Dick.

"The Alien Cooperation Enterprise. It was started by President McKinley in 1897."

"Why don't the history books mention it?" Kate asked.

"It is one of the oldest best kept serets involving the United States government," the man announced. "Come with me."

The four people left the bay when part of the wall vanished and entered a hallway that led past various rooms to the elevator. A few people, some looking not quite human, passed by the four and nodded at the crewman without saying a word. There was no door on the elevator if you could call it that. What should have been a door dissolved and the four kept walked into the bridge where the captain was sitting at a control console in front of a large screen and two smaller screens on each side of the central 3-D screen. Two crew members were sitting at similar consoles to the right of the captain and two to his left. No one said a word. But there was a lot of nodding.

The captain swiveled his seat around, smiled, and stood to greet Maria, Dick, and Kate.

"Hello. Welcome to the Aremulac. I'm Captain George Majors. For some reason, ACE thought I deserved to command the best ship in the fleet."

"I'm surprised how quiet it is in here," said Kate. "Are you all telepaths?"

"Not all of us. About 30% of the humanoid population and most of the synthetics are telepaths. The rest of us use implants."

"I never knew starships actually existed," Maria said.

"Good. That means ACE is still considered a myth. We can do our job in protecting this solar system without millions of people worrying about evil aliens taking over the world. Best of all, we don't have a bunch of people getting in our way trying to 'help' us or telling us we're not doing our job right. We have a free hand to do what needs to be done when it needs to be done. My crew can handle things up here while I give you three the grand tour of the ship. Thavis, take the com."

As the captain and his guests left the bridge, the man that had met them in the landing craft bay took over the captain's chair. As the wall that should have been the door of the elevator dissolved, the four people walked into the captain's spacious cabin. There was a giant screen on one of the walls, four thin black mats that were standing straight up around a thin black panel that was hovering about a meter above the floor, a silver-colored cube that measured nearly a cubic meter to the left of the entranceway of the kitchen, and a pool table in the middle of the room. There were four pool sticks attached to the side of the table and the balls were racked up in the middle of the table with the cueball atop the rest of the balls. "Sit down," the captain told his guests who stared at the mats.

The man chuckled as he sat on one of the mats that bent into a form fitting chair-like piece of furniture. Maria, Dick, and Kate cautiously sat against the mats that conformed to their bodies and allowed them to sit comfortably with their legs under the levitated panel.

"It takes a bit of getting used to," said the captain. "I know you have a lot of questions, so I'll try to anticipate some of them as I talk. My name is Captain George Majors. I was born in Toledo, Ohio in 1933. Yes, I'm over 106 years old. I was a fighter pilot for the US Air Force in South Korea. I had the nickname of Lightning because I was able to make lightning fast decisions during combat and maneuvered my planes to their limits. I had 15 kills in the first two weeks of combat. I also managed to land two planes that only God knows why I didn't kill myself when I crashed them onto the tarmac. I shouldn't have been able to fly them home because they were breaking up in flight.

"Then one night I was approached by someone dressed in a dark blue jumpsuit as I slept in the barracks. How he got in without being seen was a mystery at the time. But he asked me if I wanted to serve the world defending it from its real enemies and I said sure. He placed his hand on my shoulder after I got out of my bunk and instantly we were shifted to another dimension. The other guys didn't know I was gone because I was replaced by a biosynthetic replicate moments after I left. He was shot down by a ground-to- air missile over North Korea about 100 miles north of the DMZ and killed. I'm sure my parents were crazy with grief. But it had to be done so there would be no turning back from what became my life after that."

"Did any member in your family find out what really happened to you?" Maria asked.

"They went to their graves thinking I was laid to rest in the family plot behind our church. At least I did something Mom and Dad wanted me to do. I married a wonderful woman and had three kids and a dozen grandkids and a couple dozen greats. She is back on her home planet in her home dimension working for ACE as a negotiator for treaties. I go out and come in contact with various races and she talks them into working with ACE."

"What's with the pool table?" Dick asked.

"I love to play pool. Always have. When I learned that as captain of a starship I could have whatever accomodations I wanted in my cabin I jumped at the chance to have a pool table. Then bam, I got my pool table. It helps me relax and think about things. Sure I like to watch TV. And I like the music that I hope you can hear coming from the speakers in the ceiling. But I like to spend my off hours, whenever I get them, playing a few games of pool."

"What is the ratio of humanoids to synthetics aboard this ship?" Dick asked.

"There are over 4,000 people aboard this ship. It's a roughly 12 to 1 ratio of synthetics and robots to organics. As long as the ratio is less than 20 to 1 of synthetics to organics I'll remain the captain. If there were less than 200 organics aboard this ship, one of the synthetics would become the captain. I'd probably go back to being a flyboy or the controller of a drone. Would you like something to eat or drink?"

"We just ate breakfast. So we'll have to pass on that," said Dick. "Maybe an ice tea. Raspberry ice tea," said Kate.

"Sure," said the captain. Instantly, a tall glass of raspberry ice tea appeared on the table in front of her. She nearly knocked it over.

"How about you two?" he asked Maria and Dick.

"I'd like some mint in my ice tea," said Maria. It suddenly appeared in front of her.

"Have you ever heard or Dr. Pepper?" Dick asked.

"I was drinking it before Dick Clark came along," said the captain. It appeared in a tall glass in front of Dick.

Dick took a sip of the beverage and smiled. "This tastes great," Dick praised.

"I programmed the replicator to make it like I remembered it tasting in 1951. Your compliment means I got it right."

"Why don't you look like you're 106?" Kate asked.

"I was rejuvenated in a rejuvenation chamber after I reached 50. I began feeling my age and decided to reverse its effects before I lost my edge too much. I entered the one they've nicknamed the coffin at the Newgate Municipal Hospital which Nicola Tesla used in 1943. He's one of the best engineers ACE has. Those who are rejuvenated have their physical age reversed to their optimum age. You probably thought I was maybe 30."

"Yeah," said Dick.

"I wouldn't mind being rejuvenated," said Kate. "Same here," Maria added.

"Why haven't any of us heard about Newgate, New York?" Dick asked.

"Because that's the way they want it. Have you ever heard of the store Transdimensional Unlimited?"

"Of course not," said Kate. "Is it in Newgate also?"

"Outside of Newgate. It exists in multiple dimensions simultaneously. That's why it's called Transdimensional Unlimited. If you need anything, you can probably find it there."

"Where is this starship going?" Dick asked.

"I'm headed for the Nagarian Empire. My wife has written the treaty of cooperation and a delegation for ACE is in the civilian compound. Since the trip to the empire will take us several days, you'll be able to meet the members after the tour."

"How far away is it?" asked Dick.

"Around 12,000 light years away. It's not too far away."

"I'd be kind of reluctant making nice with an empire," said Dick. "Usually empires want to control as many people and territory as possible. Aren't you and ACE worried that you might be being used?" "ACE has studied the empire for years both in this dimension and adjacent ones. For over half a century we have had watchers observing the empire and actually, ACE is going to use the empire as a buffer between three peaceful sections of the galaxy and a truly evil empire; the Pelorian Empire."

"Why didn't ACE make a treaty of cooperation with the Nagarian Empire sooner?" Maria asked.

"Timing. If ACE had approached it half a century ago when it was starting to expand, the Pelorian Empire which was weak back then would have feared it and kept a closer eye on it as a rival. Also, there is a chance that the Nagarian Empire might have become evil and would have used ACE to take over the Pelorian Empire.

"Twenty years ago when it looked like the Nagarian Empire was going to be invaded by the Pelorian Empire, ACE shifted some weapons systems into an adjacent dimension and the Nagarian Empire 'found' them when they were shifted into this dimension. How the Pelorian Empire became a major power was a mystery back then. ACE now knows they were receiving technical help from a planetary system that was bent on becoming an empire too. ACE used covert interdimensional assistance of the greys which are the mercenaries of the galaxy and some scattered planetary forces to attack the empire in the making and the Pelorian Empire."

"So ACE has been fighting a covert war against the Pelorian Empire for 20 years?" Dick asked.

"Basically. ACE needed the time to allow the Nagarian Empire to become stronger and prove that it was more beneficial than malicious. When ACE realized the Nagarian Empire was ready to work openly with it, negotiations were started and the three people I'm bringing to the signing ceremony will establish a base of operation for ACE on the planet Nagar."

"Won't that mean ACE will be openly at war with the Pelorian Empire?" asked Kate.

"No. It will still be a covert war. But the fear that ACE will make it a full-blown war might keep the Pelorian Empire in check and maybe convince it to reject evil and work with ACE. There's always that hope."

"I'm curious. My wife and I are used to molecular displacement doors like the ones on the elevator and leading out of the landing craft bay. But that wasn't an elevator that took us from wherever we started to the bridge."

"You're right. It was a teleportation device that my first officer you met controlled mentally. He wanted to take you three to the bridge and it happened. I can't teleport from my cabin to any part of the ship. I need to use the access portal down the hall to go anywhere. It is a one-way transporter. Once I arrive at my destination, I can't go back through the transporter to where I came from. There are at least five portals on each of the twelve decks."

"How big is this ship?" Maria asked.

"It's 1.5 kilometers long, 500 meters wide, and 120 meters high at its thickest part. It has six hyperlight speed reactors, four main repulsion-drive engines, and enough firepower to easily destroy a planet as large as Jupiter. If given enough material, it could replicate itself in less than two minutes. I hope that isn't needed because for those two minutes, both the Aremulac and its replicate are vulnerable to attack because the force field needs to be shut down during that time.

"We'll start in the engineering section because that is the heart of the ship if you consider the bridge the brain."

The quartet walked out into the hallway which was a couple steps from the "elevator." They walked through the portal to the engineering section which was abuzz with activity. Maintenance personnel was repairing items in two bays; one for smaller items and the larger one for large items like fighting suits and personal transport devices. In a third bay, fabricators were forming devices of various sizes. Instead of robots assembling the devices, clouds of miniature assemblers like swarms of bees were assembling the devices in less than a minute. As soon as a device was fully formed, it would disappear.

"What is happening to the devices?" Dick asked.

"They're being shifted into one of three interdimensional companion ships. When this ship was constructed, three other ships in three different dimensions were constructed and linked together. Each ship is as powerful as this one but they are occupied by skeleton crews of 300 synthetics. Each has a working bridge, engines, the works. But I control all four ships. They're mainly used to store devices and take care of personnel of this ship if they need medical care that would burden our medical facilities too much.

If for some reason a squadron of soldiers were injured in a ground battle, they would be teleported here and shifted to one of the other ships for care. If, God forbid, this ship was about to be destroyed, we would use one of the ships as an escape vessel. This ship could be vaporized, but no one would die in the explosion. We would all be safe and the only effect felt by the other three ships would be a sharp jolt. But since they are in other dimensions, they wouldn't be damaged."

"So if the enemy thought it had destroyed this ship, you would remain in another dimension to fool the enemy," said Kate.

"That's right. Thank God we haven't need to resort to such a measure. But we have that option if we need it."

"What about the force field? Are there four different force fields around the ships?" asked Maria.

"Yes. But they are transdimensional. They make our integrated force field system stronger and more protective. They also distribute the destructive force of an energy weapon to weaken its effect on the ships. So if, let's say, a Pelorian starship were to unleash a powerful energy projectile and it slammed into our field, the energy would be shifted to the other fields and distributed. It would be as if the enemy ship were going up against four ships. So far, none of our enemies have attacked us transdimensionally. But I fear that day is coming. I hope we are capable of surviving such an attack." Toward the back of the engineering section was where the engines, force field, reactors, and main weapons were monitored. The main computer was also back there which controlled the ship and its systems. There were 30 synthetic recharging chambers with over 20 occupied by synthetics and robots of various sizes and capabilities. As the quartet passed by the bay, an android and a large robot vanished and a synthetic occupied one of the empty chambers after the other two units disappeared.

The quartet stopped in the back of the section and looked at the monitors and the personnel controlling the systems. "These people keep the ship fuctioning at peak performance. Can you read the monitor designations?"

His guests tried but failed to read the words.

"We can guess which monitor indicates a function without being able to read the designations," said Dick.

"I don't need to be able to read minds to know you don't want to admit you feel like an idiot back here. This is a setup to fool possible spies. The words are basically nonsensical combinations of letters and symbols. The people watching the monitors are using a hive system that allows them to see more than one monitor at a time and respond to the information presented. That's one of the reasons why information is switching monitors every few seconds. The person monitoring the reactors is not at the controls of the monitor indicating the functions of the reactors right now. But that person is paying attention to the functions even as the information changes monitors. By the way, the reactors are accelerating particles and fields at—"

"Between 250 and 375,000 times the speed of light," Maria interupted.

"Yeah. How did you know?" the captain asked Maria.

"I have similar reactors in my spaceplane. They're no doubt not as advanced as yours are. But they do the job," said Maria confidently. "Did you design and build your reactors and ship or are you just a glorified driver?" the captain said to prompt a reaction.

"I had the help of a team of engineers, a fabricator, and robots to build my ship and its reactors. But the basic designs are 90% mine inluding the reactors."

"If ever you decide to leave where you are, make sure at least one watcher knows your intentions and tells ACE. You might be able to meet Tesla. He's workng in every dimension ACE has access to and loves it. You should try to cross paths with him. Just do it before you're rejuvenated because he is often distracted by beautiful women. And I have a feeling you were a stunner when you were at your optimum age."

"If you can read minds, you know what I was when I was much younger," Maria said, embarrassed.

"Even I'm aroused and my wife is gorgeous. I would never cheat on her. Basically I'm afraid of her relatives. I had a good friend back in South Korea at the base who was Sicilian and he told me about some of his relatives in the Mafia. If one of them was offended, a vendetta would be carried out against the offender. But at least the offender had the chance to escape. I couldn't escape because her family employs watchers to keep track of me."

"Really?" asked Kate.

He smiled and said, "I'm joking. There's no one on one of the other ships watching me who could tell my wife I'm thinking of either of you women naked."

"Really?" asked Dick.

"In this case I'm not joking. But I blame both of you women and you," he told Dick pointedly. "What are you three; a trio of perverts?"

His guests stood silently and stared at each other until the captain began to laugh. The others laughed nervously.

"I'm sorry for embarrassing you three. But if you could read minds like everyone on this ship can, when an unprotected mind can be read, wouldn't you do it?"

"Yeah," admitted Dick. "How does one protect his mind from being read?"

"Aboard this ship we have mind blocks and what they call in Newgate, New York double minds. If an enemy had the ability to read minds, he might read our vulnerable alternate mind and think he is reading our authentic thoughts. Back at where you come from I would advise that you develop what they have had in Newgate for decades."

"Maybe when we get back we could go to Newgate and they could help us out," said Kate.

"That might be a good idea as long as you teleport there since they still like to remain mostly a secret to the rest of the world," said the captain. "A watcher could tell ACE your intentions and arrange transport to the city. Maybe in a few years they'll be able to remove the cloaking field and let people see the city from the air and out in space. But until then, teleportation and ground travel will be basically the only ways to enter the city unless you know where it is and the city's defenses don't shift you into another dimension. They don't want another incident like what happened a decade ago when terrorists penetrated the field and tried to destroy the city with a nuclear device."

"What is your fuel usage rate?" Maria asked.

"It varies depending on how much material we come in contact with that we can change into fuel. Right now we have enough fuel material to allow us to fly to the furthest point in the universe and back three times. Most of the material is stored on two of the other ships and being collected by the fourth ship as we go along. I had just collected the material from a pulverized asteroid when we caught your ship accidentally. You were in the right place at the right time when we came along."

Suddenly, the ship was rocked by an explosion. One of the people at the monitors announced, "We've got seven ships in a hexagon formation firing upon us from the central ship."

"Return fire," the captain demanded.

"They shifted out of this dimension," said the crew member before another explosion rocked the ship.

"They're firing from behind us."

"Grab them before they shift," he ordered. "Missed," the person said.

The ship was rocked a third time a bit harder. "Got 'em," the person shouted.

"Have at it," the captain told his weapons controller.

Multiple explosions occured and the first person managed to snag a few of the formations of ships and destroyed them. But most of the ships shifted away to fire upon the ship again.

"Grab a chair or sit on the floor, people. This is going to be rough," the captain said as he grabbed the back of one of the chairs.

CHAPTER 12

"**S**end out the suicide drones," the captain demanded as another explosion rocked the ship. "All the drones."

Two of the people at the controls pushed buttons and within seconds, swarms of motorcycle-sized drones were spit out of their compartments in all four dimensions the ships existed in. But the enemy ships kept coming as if there was an unlimited supply of ships. But they were no match it seemed for the Aremulac that kept destroying ships as if it were whack-a-mole. Often the ship's weapons would destroy a formation the moment it appeared in this dimension.

"We lost a ship," yelled one of the crew members who was monitoring the other three ships.

"We lost another," yelled another crew member.

"Shift this ship out of here," the captain demanded a split second before the most violent explosion rocked the ship.

The ship shifted into a dimension where hundreds of smaller ships began firing upon it. Suicide drones took out a third of the ships and the Aremulac took out another third. The last third shifted to other dimensions before they could be destroyed.

After a few seconds of peace, the captain told the crew member who monitored the engines, "I want a tunnel field around both ships for two minutes out to a light year and then accelerate to 2 million times light speed."

Rings of drones were expelled from the ships in both dimensions and exit drones were shot out to a light year in front of the ships. They were joined by electromagnetic beams that were generated by reactors that were sacrificed as were the first drones. Once the beams were generated, the drones began to travel in a circle fast enough to make it appear tunnels of energy had been formed in two dimensions. In ten seconds they were hurtling through space at 2 million times the speed of light and out of danger for the moment.

The exit drones were also left behind and kept traveling in circles. Enemy ships converged on the field-like beams and fired upon them in case the ships that had shot out of them without being seen were hiding inside the tunnels. To add to the deception, projection spheres the size of wrecking balls were discharged from the ships to project the image of starships that moved constantly inside the tunnels. By the time the enemy ships discovered they were being fooled, the Aremulac and its partner ship were light years away. Instead of easing back on the speed, the captain had the ships go to 4.5 million times light speed.

The captain's guests stood as the captain released the back of the chair he was holding on to.

"We're going to arrive a bit earlier than expected. I just hope Aremulac 3 can collect enough material to turn into fuel to allow us to continue to shift dimensions every 1/10 of a second until we arrive at Nagar."

"What if we enter a region full of material that can be collected for fuel and construction material long enough to replicate ships to replace the two you lost?" asked Maria.

"The ships and the non-organic objects can be replicated in a little over five minutes," said the captain.

"I thought you said it would take less than two minutes," protested Kate. "Two ships. Two replicates."

"Only the original ship can replicate. The other ships that are joined to this one don't have that ability. Why? I don't know."

"Maybe if somehow a ship were to fall into enemy hands it could be replicated to form a fleet of 1,000 ships within 20 minutes if each ship could replicate," Dick suggested.

"At least the crews of the ships we lost teleported to the Aremulac 3."

"Captain, they couldn't all teleport to safety from the ships that were destroyed. Only 15 survived," said the crew member that monitored the ships.

"I'll distribute robots and synthetics from this ship to the replicated ones if I go along with your suggestion and become vulnerable to attack for over five minutes. I know what I'll do. I'll divert my course away from Nagar and replicate wherever I can find an abundance of material to use."

"There's several regions you can choose from?" said a crew member. "The closes one is 150 light years away. If we change course in ten seconds there is another region 210 light years away. But ACE doesn't have a cooperation treaty with the region."

"If we need to give the people there a replicated ship or two, do it. We'll be vulnerable a little longer though."

Seconds later, the ships changed course and in less than three hours would be in the region. The captain and his guests continued the tour.

"I was afraid some enemy would discover how to attack us interdimensionally," the captain complained.

"Were they enemies you have confronted in the past?"asked Dick. "Yes. They were the Salorians, Havenales, and some attackers I don't recall encountering in the past. They are vicious fighters. But in the past they remained in the dimension you three and I come from."

"Could they have received help from the Pelorians?" asked Maria. "I don't know. The Pelorians aren't normally advanced enough to allow others to have that level of technology. Double our speed," demanded the captain. Minutes later, the ships achieved a speed 9 million times light speed.

"We've got five hours until we arrive at the region where we'll replicate this ship. As long as we aren't attacked again, we should be able to complete the tour."

"I have a suggestion about how to protect this ship while it is being replicated," said Maria. "You were able to use projection spheres to fool those enemy ships in thinking your ships were in the tunnels. Why not replicate around 1,000 ships that look like this ship and have them shift into our dimension while this one is shifting? Would they have working weapons?"

"Not as potent as the ones we have. But yeah. They will have weapons. Each sphere will have a small hyperlight speed reactor in its center. There is a degree of AI in each sphere to form the projections and make them seem like the objects they're duplicating. That should work. Thanks. I wish I had thought of it. Maybe when you leave where you're at, ACE will make you a starship captain. Just as long as they don't replace me with you. I would miss my pool table."

"You could always take it with you," Maria joked. "I'd hate to deprive some man of what brings him pleasure."

"Didn't you do that when you left the former life?" Dick kidded. "I hate to admit it, but you're right," Maria said, cringing.

"By the way. Are you a Christian?" Kate asked the captain. "Next year I will be 100 years old as a Christian. It was the best decision I've ever made; even better than the one I made to join ACE. You would be amazed to find out how many Christians there are in the universe and how many know about and trust in God. Back on earth, Newgate, New York has no atheists because they know where Heaven and Hell are located. Let me show you the two most popular places on the ship. They should be a great time waster."

As the quartet was passing the replication bay, the captain told the crew members, "We need 1,000 large projection spheres to duplicate this ship within the next five hours. Put them in the other ship until we are about to shift. If there's any trouble where we shift to, we need to present a sign of overwhelming force. Just as long as any enemy thinks we can't be defeated while we're replicating and teleporting crew members aboard the new ships, we'll be fine. I need at least six minutes. Can I have all that?"

"We'll do our best," said five of the crew members as they began programming in the instructions into their fabricators.

The quartet walked through the portal and into the simulation chamber that was similar to those that had been seen on "Star Trek" programs.

Nobody was in it which relieved the captain.

"I know you know what this is. They got pretty close back in our dimension on 'Star Trek: the Next Generation.' The big difference between this chamber and the fake ones is that we have self-contained dimensions that people can shift to. The chamber is proteted so well that it can be used as an escape chamber if the ship is destroyed. The crew members that survived the destruction of their ships might have entered chambers like this one and shifted to safety."

"How many people can occupy this chamber in all the dimensions contained in it?" Kate asked.

"Twice as many as what are on this ship as long as they don't mind being packed in like sardines. As long as we stick together we'll have no problems. With four people there are physical limitations. If I were to stand here and all three of you were to run as fast as you can in three different directions, you'd run into the walls and probably smash your faces. That is why it is advisable to shift individually into different dimensions. You could then run naked on a California beach for hours and nothing bad will happen unless you want it to happen."

"Do you use the chamber for training purposes?" Kate asked.

"There are crew members in the chamber everyday just for that reason. I don't know how often I've used it. Probably a couple thousand times. Do you want to stay together or do you want to split up? I would advise splitting up so you can enjoy yourself more. This will be like your mind trips, Kate."

"As long as they're good trips. How did you…Oh that's right.

You read my mind." "like a book. Well?"

"I'd like to fly a Yak against the Luftwaffe back in 1941," said Maria. "My great-grandfather was a tank commander and fantasized about flying against the Nazis during the Great Patriotic War."

"The program will be based mainly on your imagination because the computer doesn't have as many earth-based programs as I'd like. Definitely not WW II in Russia. But it will do its best to satisfy you."

"Great. My Yak will be a nuke with power rays and a compression-field engine."

"I don't remember Russia having flying saucers back then," said the captain. "Maybe they were flown by its alien allies," the captain said sarcastically. "This chamber is like the ones back in the real world. It has to be technically possible during the time represented."

Maria shifted from the chamber to another dimension where her fighter pilot program existed.

"How about you two?"

"I'd like to hang glide over the Pacific off the coast of the Big Island of Hawaii," said Kate.

"Naked?" the captain asked.

"Heavens no. I don't want my boobs to be flapping like bean bags in the wind."

"You can imagine being in a tight flight suit to cut down on flapping."

Kate shifted from the chamber to another dimension to hang glide.

"I'd like to fight aliens in a star fighter," Dick proclaimed. "Fancy yourself as another Luke Skywalker?"

"Did you see the 'Star Wars Saga'?" Dick asked, surprised.

"I might spend most of my time in other dimensions and even less on earth. But I've got all the movies downloaded in my mind link system back in my cabin and into the chamber's program computer. Which reminds me. I need to see if the projection sphere idea to protect this ship while it's replicating will work in the worst case scenario. Go have some fun fighting against the Empire. Hey. How about using ACE's best stuff? I bet it could take on a death star by itself. The controls will be seen in English so you shouldn't have any problem with the controls and monitors."

"Sounds good."

Dick was shifted to another dimension to fight against the Empire while the captain remained in the original dimension to test out the strategy that was about to transpire in less than five hours.

CHAPTER 13

The deeply tanned shirtless islander was harnessed to his hang glider and Kate was harnessed to hers. They were standing on a plateau several meters back from the edge of a cliff with the wind attempting to lift the gliders. "Hold down on the right side of the bar to bank right and the left side to bank left. Push the bar forward to go up and pull toward you to go down. If the wind dies down, which I doubt it will do, flip on the motors under the glider. You can fly for around an hour with them on. just don't be too far away from here if that happens.

Got it?"

"Yeah. Don't we need a crash helmet?" "Do you intend on crashing?" "No."

"Then don't worry about it. Enjoy yourself. We're out here to have fun. So have fun. That's an order. Follow me."

The man ran toward the edge of the cliff and was lifted into the air. He and Kate had headsets on to allow them to talk to each other while in flight. Kate followed her instructor seconds later. The view of the island and ocean below was spectacular. The only sound heard was the wind uplifting the gliders.

"How you doing back there?" the instructor asked. "Fantastic. I could stay up here all day."

"Let's go up higher and toward the interior of the island. The view is spectacular," the instructor suggested.

"Sure."

The flyers tilted the leading edges of the gliders up and soared to a couple thousand meters into the air. The upper half of the Inouye stratotower in Honolulu was seen to the north west. Its red laser beams that accompanied the support beams reminded Kate of the light saber Darth Vader used in the "Star Wars Saga."

Kate followed her instructor and in seconds was over the mountains of the Big Island of Hawaii. The pair was high enough over the peaks that they were in no danger of crashing.

Kate noticed some huge birds ahead of her and her instructor. When he lifted higher into the air, she followed suit. In less than a minute, the pair was over 3,000 meters above the island, but the winged beasts ascended to meet them. The closer they came, the more recognizable they became. They were pteranodons straight out of movies about dinosaurs.

"For God sake, fly higher," the instructor shouted seconds before a creature from one's nightmares slammed its body into his glider. The fabric was ripped and the talons of the monster latched onto the flyer. He tried to punch the beast to make it let go of him. But he couldn't touch it because the talons dug into his shoulders.

Instead of gaining altitude, Kate dove her glider toward the ground with one of the creatures in pursuit. She wished she could have power rays on the bar to fire upon her attacker. Instantly they appeared as well as two ray weapons on her hips. She flipped on the motors and lifted back into the air a split second before the creature crashed to the ground.

As Kate was ascending, two more pteranodons descended toward her. She squeezed the triggers and charged particle beams ripped into the creatures that screamed in pain. The one on the right was sliced in half while the one on the left had a wing sliced off. Both fell to the ground with a thud.

A pteranodon below Kate ascended toward her. She whipped out the power ray on her right hip and nailed the creature in the head between its eyes. It crumpled and fell to the ground. As her attention was drawn to the attacker below her, another pteranodon grabbed her glider and tore it apart. She fired her right hand power ray at the beast and ripped its stomach open. She also tore the rest of her glider and plunged like a leaf to the ground. She twirled as she descended and almost became dizzy. The glider motors slowed the descent as they tried to lift Kate and the remnants of the glider. Kate slammed hard onto the ground, but she didn't break any bones or damage any muscles. Two pteranodons descended;

talons extended. Kate fired both power rays and sliced their heads off. If she hadn't started running, one of the corpses would have landed on her.

A wonderful day was turning into a nightmare as Kate ran for her life from three winged monsters that were screaming defiantly at her. One of them dived upon her. She wheeled around and fired both power rays at it. She sliced off its head and a wing. It fluttered less gracefully than she did to the ground. The remaining two pteranodons flew off so they wouldn't be killed.

Kate trudged through the tall grass and heard all manner of creatures screaming, grunting, whistling, and roaring in the distance. There were no pleasant aromas wafting on the breeze. Instead, it smelled like a farm and she was nearing the manure pit. She looked down to make sure she didn't step in a pile of excrement.

The sun was blocked by clouds and the humidity was oppressive. What was worst were the clouds of insects that bedeviled the woman. She used her power rays to incinerate the critters which caused the grass to ignite when their remains fell to the ground. Kate started to run for her life again.

She was barely in front of the blaze when she spotted a cave in front of her. But there was a creek between her and possible safety and she didn't know how deep it was. To her relief it was shallow. But it looked like worms were swimming through the water. She ran as fast as she could, but slipped on a flat rock and landed face down in the water. The worms converged on her and planted their suction mouths on any portion of skin they came in contact with.

She desperately grabbed their wiggling bodies and tore them off of her arms, legs, and face leaving behind some bloody heads.

Kate entered the cave a meter in front of the raging inferno. As the flame neared the entrance, Kate edged away and backed deeper into the cave. She had an uneasy feeling. But the heat of the flames drove her to enter more darkness and increase her nervousness.

The low rumble of a creature was heard behind her. She drew out her weapons and saw a few meters deeper in the cave glowing yellow eyes.

"Nice kitty. You don't want to hurt me," she said softly. "You don't want to die. I don't want to kill you."

The rumbling growl grew louder until it became a roar. The creature sprang toward Kate. She shot it between the eyes and it dropped a few centimeters from her with its claws reaching out toward her. It was a sabertooth cat that was nearly as large as a tiger. Its claws would have ripped her apart as would the fangs.

How could prehistoric creatures exist in 21st century Hawaii? Then she realized she wasn't on earth. She was on a starship in a simulation chamber in another dimension. She just didn't know how to exit the program.

After the fire swept through the area, Kate left the cave and headed back to the beach she had flown over. If she could have power rays appear, maybe she could have a boat appear on the beach and she could either row or motor to Honolulu which looked like it was existing in the 21st century.

Kate was 100 meters from the beach when she saw a pirate ship flying the skull and crossbones flag come out from behind the high rocks and a long boat with pirates aboard near the beach. There was nothing to hide her and the men began to shout at her. A couple fired their muskets at her, but the balls missed her by a few meters. When the boat reached the beach, the men piled out and ran toward Kate. Instead of running, Kate stood her ground and fired upon the pirates. They were all killed in a matter of seconds. Kate walked past the smouldering bodies of her victims and stepped into the boat which had a wooden chest in the middle. She opened it and saw enough gold and jewels to make her a wealthy woman. It was something she hadn't imagined, but she appreciated having it in the program.

Kate pushed away from the beach and in seconds was rowing away from the island toward Honolulu which was a few hundred kilometers away. Before she could make a water jet engine latch onto the bow of the boat, a cannon ball was fired from the pirate ship toward her. The ball splashed down a meter to her right and drenched her with water. She pulled out her guns and fired back at the ship. A few ray sweeps demasted the ship. The next cannon ball rocked the boat as it splashed less than a meter to her left. She aimed her weapons a couple meters below the waterline and slashed at the prow furiously. The ship plunged below the waves and the crew members on the deck were forced to swim.

Kate had the water jet engine appear and seconds later was zipping through the water at 150 kph. In around two hours she would be safe. At least she thought she would be safe.

She was south of Molokai staring at the Inouye stratotower when a pod of killer whales surfaced. The boat skimmed over the back of one whale and slammed onto the back of another whale; breaking the boat in half. A whale opened its mouth and tried to chomp down on her legs and lower torso. But she managed to nail the predator with a power ray beam in the mouth. Blood gushed from the wound and the creature swam away in a hurry. The other whales followed suit which relieved Kate. But she wasn't out of hot water; literally.

A red glow from the bottom of the ocean appeared and a low rumble was heard. Hot bubbles of water surfaced and sulphur fumes from the burst bubbles sickened Kate. The red glow became brighter and enlarged as the water became hot tub hot and then boiling hot. Kate screamed in pain as she was scalded by the superhot water.

"Why can't there be an iceberg when you need one?" she cried out.

Suddenly, a platform of ice lifted the woman out of the water. The snow on the surface of the iceberg provided soothing relief. But the lava was still ascending and the ice was quickly melting. Within a few minutes the ice would be gone and death would be imminent. "Where's a surfacing submarine when you need one?" she said in desperation.

The conning tower of a surfacing submarine appeared several meters away and the side hatch opened.

"Swim or die," the man at the hatch cried out. Kate plunged into the ocean and swam toward the submarine. The man pulled the desperate woman out of the water and took her aboard the boat which proceeded toward Honolulu at 50 knots once Kate was safely below.

"You're lucky we came along, ma'am," said the submariner. "Why were you on that chunk of ice?"

"A volcano is about to surface and I needed that chunk of ice to appear just like I needed this sub to appear. I feel like a jinx. I start out hang gliding and wind up fighting off pteranodons. Then I start a fire which drives me to seek shelter in a cave that evidently was the home of a sabertooth cat. After killing it and heading for the beach I had to kill a boat load of pirates and sink their ship. Then I smash into a pod of killer whales, swim in boiling water, find relief on an iceberg, and finally I'm rescued by you guys."

"You're safe now. Ensign, take this woman to the galley and get her a warm mug of good navy coffee."

One of the young submariners led Kate down a hall toward the galley when something collided with the boat. Kate and the submariner were knocked off their feet and the red warning lights started to spin. The warning horns sounded and the captain came on the speaker.

"People, a giant squid has just grabbed us. Unlike the Nautilus, we don't have an electrified hull and there is no way in Hell I'm going to send guys with harpoons topside to fight it off."

Kate and the ensign got to their feet and hurried to the galley.

"I told you I was a jinx," said Kate.

"My grampa had to serve with women in the Persian Gulf. He said some were as good as any sailor on the ship. But there were some that made men think maybe having a woman aboard a warship brought bad luck. Then again, my dad wouldn't be here and neither would I if Grampa hadn't knocked up one of his shipmates."

The boat was rocked again only harder.

"Another God damn giant squid is pulling at our bow near the engine intake. Suck that sucker into the engine."

The engine ionized the creature and tried to suck it by linear induction through the water jet. But it was too large and clogged the engine.

"Captain, it's stuck," said the engine man.

"When the first sucker is in front of a torpedo tube, fire. Tank, turn the rear sucker into calamari," demanded the captain.

The sound of bubbling was heard coming from the engine as the electromagnetic field was turned up to a full boil. Bloody pieces of squid were spit out the exhaust. Seconds later, a torpedo was fired which took the front squid with it.

"This can't get any worst," said the captain.

"Yes it can. We've got a megladon coming up from the depths and its about to crash with us," cried another submariner.

"Brace for impact."

The prehistoric fish nearly broke the boat apart. Submariners were knocked out of their seats and bunks.

"Is the rear sucker out?" screamed the captain. "The engine is clear," yelled the engine man.

"Gun it and get us the Hell out of here," the captain demanded.

The boat gained speed and a minute later was plying through the ocean at 100 knots.

"We're going to make it," said the captain. "Nothing can stop us now."

He didn't realize until it was too late that his boat was lifted by a giant tsunami wave as if the boat were a surfer riding a curl. The speed was over 200 knots.

"Captain, our altitude is 110 meters," said the navigator. "Altitude? What the Hell are you talking about?"

"We're surfing to Honolulu," said the navigator. "We're at the front of a tsunami wave and it's going to slam into downtown Honolulu. We're higher than the Japs that attacked Pearl Harbor." The boat passed over Pearl Harbor and slammed into the Inouye stratotower at the tenth story. An eletromagnetic support beam sliced open the sub as if it were a slab of baloney on a meat cutter. The only good thing was that the three kilometer high tower remained standing despite the fact that a few floors were missing.

The support beams kept the building standing as designed.

It was a miracle Kate and most of the crew survived the impact. She found a stairway and descended to the ground. She was happy to be alive until she felt the heat of exposed nuclear fuel radiating from one of the reactors that had been sliced open by the support beam. She felt the effects of radiation and became weak. She started to vomit and dropped to her hands and knees. Blood started oozing out of her nose, mouth, ears, and eyes. She closed her eyes, laid down on the wet pavement beside a couple flopping fish, and awoke back in the simulation chamber she had entered first.

CHAPTER 14

Russian music that could put fire in the soul of a Cossack was blaring over the loud speakers shortly after dawn.

"Man your planes. Man your planes," commanded the air marshal in Russian over the loud speakers.

Pilots piled out of the dining hall and out onto the field. Some headed for the Yaks. Some headed for the Bell Air Cobras. Maria was decked out in a flight suit and climbed the steps up to the cockpit of her Yak and after the wheel chocks were removed, rolled out onto the tarmac. She gunned her engine and less than a minute later was in the air and flying toward German bombers and fighters that were intent on doing as much carnage as possible.

"Take the bomber on the left and I'll take the one on the right," said a woman to Kate.

Kate dived to the level of her target and flew straight at the Blom Voss; guns blazing. She only had a couple seconds but blasted open the cockpit before pulling up after sending the plane to the ground. Her wingman dived upon a Heinkel and tore the starboard main wing off. Both women were about to attack a couple more bombers. That was when German fighters dived out of the clouds toward the two women. Maria and her wingman climbed toward the aggressors and fired upon the cockpits; shattering the glass and sending the Focke Wolfs to the ground where they exploded.

For the next few minutes, Maria and her wingman took on fighters and bombers like demons. They smiled as they blasted away at the invaders and sent the pilots and bomber crews to Hell. Bomb loads left craters in the fields below as they exploded on impact. But it was better to lose livestock and crops than people in the cities and factories the dealers of death wanted to exterminate. After the Luftwaffe was blown out of the sky, Maria and the other pilots strafed German troops that were following tanks into a field of wheat. The pilots took pleasure in tearing bodies apart and setting the field on fire with missiles. The cannons of the Air Cobras ripped the tops of the tanks open like 20 mm can openers. Ground fire caught a couple planes, but they managed to limp back to base. The rest of the pilots landed safely and congratulated each other on the ground. Maria hugged her wingman who was as beautiful as she was. In the simulation, both women were in their 20's and more than worthy of being pin-up girls.

A photographer rushed out of the air marshal's office and out onto the field with his camera in his hand.

"Ladies. Ladies. Stand beside Maria's plane. I want to take your picture for Pravda. You two are more than heroes. Your pictures will inspire hot blooded Soviets to fight for Mother Russia. So show some skin."

Maria was reluctant to unsnap her flight suit. But when the other woman nearly bared her breasts for the camera, Maria followed suit. It wasn't as if she was naked. But she felt a little embarrassed. "The sows in Germany think they're beautiful. I say they are indeed fit for the hog pin compared to you two stunners," the photographer said as he snapped the women posing around the plane. "A little more skin, please."

Maria's wingman tore open her blouse to expose her bra and tore open Maria's blouse. The photographer kept snapping pictures.

"Two more, please," he demanded.

Maria's wingman grabbed her bra and pulled it over her head to expose her breasts and Maria followed suit. The photographer nearly dropped his camera and the other pilots on the field whooped and yelled and applauded the exhibition. Maria's wingman jiggled her breasts to excite the pilots more while Maria wrapped her flight suit jacket over her breasts and ran into the women's barracks to change.

After crying for a couple minutes, Maria's wingman and the other three women who were mechanics entered the barracks. Maria wiped her tears with the sleave of her blouse and tried to smile. But she was still shook up.

"Why did you leave so fast?" her wingman asked.

"Don't you know he was using us out there?" Maria protested. "Of course he was using us. If he had been Stalin, he could have raped me and I would have screamed in ecstasy."

"That's sick. Rape isn't a demonstration of love. It's violence against women."

"If our leader wants something and it benefits the Motherland, he could rape me everyday and I could give him 100 kids and I would consider it my duty as a good party member."

"I don't care if he promised me 100 medals and a million rubles. I wouldn't have sex with that...I don't want to say what I think of him because you might turn me in. Isn't it enough to kill Nazis and save the Motherland that way from the invaders?"

"I will do anything that benefits the Motherland and the party."

"You're a whore. An absolute degenerate whore."

"You showed your breasts too. Are you a whore too?" she accused her.

Maria lunged at her wingman and knocked her to the floor as the mechanics watched. She began flailing away with her fists on the woman's face. Her wingman used her right knee to punch Maria in the gut and push her away. They grabbed each other's blouse and tore them down to their belly buttons exposing their breasts. They grabbed each other's breasts and twisted their tits. Both women screamed in both pain and anger. They continued punching each other in the face, stomach, and breasts. The wingman bit down hard on Maria's left breast and nearly bit off her tit. Maria kicked her in the vagina and kept punching her.

The fight attracted the attention of some of the pilots who stood at the door to watch. They yelled their support for one of the women and that the fight should continue. The commotion attracted the attention of the air marshal who shoved his way past the men at the door. His assistant followed him in and they each grabbed a woman and pulled them apart.

"Why are you two fighting?" the air marshal demanded.

"She thinks I'm a whore because I showed my breasts," Maria complained.

"You called me a whore too," her wingman added.

"Ladies, this is no way to act as pilots. You're two of the best and you've been friends since before the war. When you two showed your breasts, we all thought you two were acting like whores. We've got invaders out there that are the real enemy. I don't need you two to be at each other's throat. We need to be unified. I want you two to apologize to each other right now," the air marshal insisted.

Both women stared at each other for several seconds not wanting to make up.

"If you don't say you're sorry I'm going to have to ground you two. I can't afford to lose you."

"I'm sorry for attacking you," Maria admitted. "I was out of line.

I just felt used out there and didn't like it."

"I'm sorry too. We do need to concentrate on defeating the enemy and you are not my enemy."

Maria extended her hand in friendship and her wingman embraced her. They both began to cry and everyone started to applaud.

"That's the way I want my best pilots to act. You both need each other out there because it's either work together or die. As I said, I can't afford to lose you two. Go take a shower and calm down some more. I need you two ready to fight Nazis. As for you other ladies, gas up the planes and make them ready for battle."

The air marshal, his assistant, and the three mechanics left the barracks while Maria and her wingman removed their clothes and entered the shower room to take a warm relaxing shower.

As they were scrubbing up they said ouch more than once because both were battered and brusied. The bite on Maria's breast was still tender and black and blue. The teeth marks were very evident. At least her wingman didn't draw blood.

"We were acting like jealous school girls fighting over a boyfriend," Maria pointed out. "I truly am sorry for beating you up. As a Christian I should act better than most people do."

"You're a Christian? How long have you been a Christian?" "For years. When I was younger, a lot of people thought I was a whore because of what I was doing." "What was that?"

"I used to pose naked for money. I'm so ashamed of myself."

"I really was a whore in Leningrad before the war. I used to have sex with sailors that came into port. The money was good and I actually liked what I was doing. One of my clients taught me how to fly. I really liked flying. When the war began, I entered the air corps and was accepted immediately. They wanted me to be a trainer. But I wanted to kill invaders. So they sent me here to do what I wanted to do for the Motherland. What is your story? Why are you here?"

"I have loved flying all my life and when I got the chance to join the war effort, I knew exactly what I wanted to do. I wanted to fly a Yak against those that wanted me and my relatives dead. Also, I like to tear Nazis apart with my machine guns. Each time I see a plane explode that I shot down I have a little orgasm. It's better than sex." "You're right. I also don't need to worry about getting pregnant.

I get the thrills without being penalized with having kids. You say you're a Christian? I thought only weak-minded people were Christians."

"Far from it. God gives me a reason to live. He also gives me the courage to face my enemies because I know He is with me to help me no matter how bad things look. I may not like our leaders as much as you do. But I love Mother Russia and respect our leaders enough to give my life in sevice to it. If I do my best to serve my nation, I also honor God because He wants His people to be the best citizens of their homelands possible. Would you like to become a Christian?"

"My grandmother was a Godly person who attented church services faithfully all her life. But she died poor and suffered from consumption. Her God didn't do much for her. I think she was a fool."

"The Bible says the preaching of the gospel is to them that perish foolishnes. So you can call me a fool and I won't be at your throat. I expect it. We could be dead before tonight. Are you ready to meet your maker?"

"I don't believe in God or Heaven. When I die I die. There is no afterlife."

"What if I'm right and you have to stand before God who will be your judge? Do you want to go to Hell?"

"It is as much a myth as Heaven is. I can't see God, or Heaven, or Hell. That is because they don't exist."

"You love to fly don't you?" "It's my life at the moment." "Have you ever seen air?" "Of course not."

"Then why do you believe in something you can't see?" "God and air are two different things."

"We need both in order to live. You may not want to admit it. God is going to help us defeat the invaders because their evil leader, Adolf

Hitler, is a Godless infidel. He hates the Jews and those that hate the Jews, according to the Bible, are hated by God and will be cursed. Do you have Jewish friends?"

"I knew a few in the profession in Leningrad. They were all right."

"Hitler wants them to die because they are considered little more than animals. I have Jewish friends that I love a lot. That's how God wants it. Do you worry about dying?"

"I try not to. A pilot loses their edge if they worry about dying while in the cockpit."

"I'm not afraid to die because I know that after I die I will go to Heaven. I pray that you will give your heart and life to God before it's too late."

"I'll think about it. I'm not going to promise you anything. But I'll think about it."

Russian folk music was heard blaring from the loud speakers. "Man your planes. Man your planes. The enemy is minutes away from being on us. Man your planes now," demanded the air marshal. Maria and her wingman ran out of the shower and only had time to put on their boots before rushing to their planes. The other pilots were too busy getting ready to take off to notice two naked women running out to their Yaks to take on the enemy. Maria's seat was a bit wetter than her wingman's seat because she needed to go to the bathroom while she was showering and thought she would have time to reieve herself after drying off. Instead, she urinated while she took off.

"Are you ready to meet the enemy?" her wingman asked her. "I am now. I just peed in my seat."

"Do you feel better?" "Much. How about you?"

"I want to kill Nazis," she said excitedly. "Here they come."

In the distance were bombers coming in at about 1,000 meters. Maria and her wingman flew nearly straight up because they knew fighter planes would be hiding in the clouds. They weren't visible yet. But Maria knew they had to be close to protect the bombers. As expected, once Maria flew above the clouds, enemy fighters were spotted.

Maria's wingman entered a cloud and ascended blindly. A split second later, a cross on the side of a Messerschmitt was spotted in the cloud. But before she could warn her wingman, both planes collided and exploded. Maria screamed in anguish and gunned her engine to full throttle.

Her rage heightened her hatred for the Nazis. She sprayed two fighter planes with bullets and pulled up as they were exploding.

She banked hard when she saw a plane below her and nailed the cockpit with a deadly spray of bullets. When she saw a trio if bombers below her, she dived toward them; guns blazing. She ignited wing tanks of one plane and blasted the cockpit of another. A gunner on the third bomber buried a slug in her engine which started a fire. But there were two fighters diving out of a cloud toward her. She pulled up and took both of them on. She nailed one. But the guns of the second fighter shattered her windshield and blinded her in one eye. As she screamed in pain and blood splurted from the wound, a fighter she hadn't seen came out of another cloud and tore her chest apart with slugs. She died instantly and suddenly found herself back at the original simulation chamber.

Chapter 15

Dick found himself at the controls of a craft that was similar to what he wanted to design and construct back in Siberia. It was oval shaped and had an electronic windshield like what Maria's spaceplane had. It felt like he was inside a craft made of glass because it was crystal clear beside, in front, and above him. The craft was able to read his mind and responded instantly to his thoughts.

He wanted to know what was ahead of him and instantly it showed three battle cruisers that were the size of small cities in front of him 300,000 kilometers. At his speed he'd be on them in less than a minute.

"Guys, the enemy is seconds away from me," he said.

"Thanks, Dick. What do you want us to do?" asked a man who was in a star fighter that was flying in formation with six other star fighters that were behind him.

"Let me go in and attack them from the front and you guys can hit them from behind. I've draw all their fire."

"Either you're the bravest man in the Resistance or an idiot. You sure you can take them on by yourself? Maybe I could accompany you."

"I'm the idiot who wants them to shoot at me. They'll be too busy concentrating on me to pay attention to you guys. I see them in front of me, so go wide right and I'll make sure they are as vulnerable as possible. They probably won't fire on me at the start because they will consider me more a nuisance than a threat. But when I unload on them, they'll concentrate their fire on me. Wait until then before staging your attack. Here I go."

Dick flew his craft straight at the bridge of one of the battle cruisers and opened fire. A hyperlight speed beam of energy punctured the bridge of the battle cruiser and the front portion of a second battle cruiser. As

Dick's fighter craft turned, the beam tore open the bridge and the front section of the other battle cruiser.

The ships opened fire on Dick and launched both missiles and fighter crafts against him. His AI-controlled weapons fired upon individual targets and when a beam would hit his force field, a beam that was many times more powerful would follow the first beam back to the weapon and destroy the craft that fired the initial beam. If a craft came within ten meters of Dick's craft, a field discharge would slam into it and either knock it off course or split it apart.

A tractor beam was projected from the third battle cruiser that latched onto Dick's craft. That was a huge mistake because a potent energy projectile was discharged at hyperlight speed back at the cruiser. The ship was blown apart. The star fighters arrived and took on the remaining enemy fighter crafts as did Dick. He received blast after blast from the plasma cannons. But his force field absorbed the energy of the blasts and used it against the weapons that fired them. Escape crafts were ejected from the dying ships and not followed or harassed because Dick thought the humiliation of being defeated by mainly a single fighter craft was punishment enough because the crew members aboard the powerful battle cruisers, some able to tear small moons apart, would most likely be executed and news of the skirmish would be squelched.

The fighter crafts landed at a base on a small rocky world that had little importance to an empire. Few people lived there because there was no agricultural area because the soil couldn't sustain crops. The only things that grew were mainly underground fungi and something called leech plants that stuck like glue to rocks and the ground and could be eaten if you didn't mind eating something that tasted like dirt. It was surprisingly nourishing and could be made into a mush if you didn't mind eating mush that tasted like dirt. The fungi could be eaten too and had a nutty taste when it was dried and roasted. Most people ate that instead of the leech plant. But if they were starving or deathly sick, they would eat leech plant because it absorbed the nutrients and minerals from the rocks and ground and had medicinal uses. It was able to draw infections and toxic substances out of the blood and aided in healing. Just as long as one removed a poultice made from the plant after they were healed and it were thoroughly cleaned off of the skin, the leech plant wouldn't be able to start living off of the person.

The base was underground and a cloaking field kept it from being detected by the Empire. The fighter crafts penetrated a hologram and landed near the entrance to a huge cavern which was large enough for over 1,000 people to live and work. The fighter crafts that had followed Dick had to be wheeled into the base while Dick levitated his craft and glided inside. After the crafts were inside, giant rock doors were slid into place to seal the cavern. It was dusk and the outside temperature was 10 degrees celsius and dropping.

After the cockpit of Dick's fighter craft opened, a man that looked to be twenty years older than Dick approached him.

"As expected, you were your old cocky yet lucky self," said the old man as he stood a couple meters in front of the craft.

"And hello yourself."

"You're going to have to let the others get their share of fighting in. You are making them lazy. What if you weren't around? They are too dependent on you. They wouldn't last a second out there if you weren't out there with them," the man complained.

"I don't mind doing my part in the resistance."

"You're playing too much of a part. You're a one-man rebel squadron. Someday you'll be out there flying into the jaws of death and the jaws will close around you and eat you alive."

"What do you want me to do?" he asked as he left his craft and followed the man toward the command center deeper in the cavern.

"Don't do everything by yourself. If somene wants to join you in an attack, let them. They are tough and capable fighters. They don't need their dad there protecting them when they can do that themselves. They may not admit it, but they want to prove themselves and may in fact resent having you fight their battles. They have wives and sweethearts that they want to impress. Your do-it-myself-with-no-one's-help attitude makes them look weak in the eyes of those they love."

"Should I maybe hang back during an attack and let them strike first?"

"They'll know I told you to do that if that happens. When you attack, tell them you can't do it all by yourself. It might be a lie since your fighter craft is the best we have. But include them as equals and not like children who need their daddy to be there with them. As I asked. What if you weren't around?"

"I see your point. If they depended on me all the time, they would become too dependent and the rebellion might end with the resistance being crushed. I suspect that isn't the main reason why you're out here talking with me."

"No it is not. I just received alarming news from one of our outposts in the Cacksarian System. The Empire is running tests on a weapon that has the capability of destroying a world, changing the molecular structure of the debris into usable materials, and then forming whatever it needs. It might be a fleet of 10,000 battle cruisers or even another world eater as it's being called. I need you to lead your men and maybe all the squadrons of this base to where it is at and destroy it. You can't do it all by yourself. When we enter the conference room I'll fill you and the other squadron leaders in on more details."

The men entered the conference room where the nine other squadron leaders were seated around the conference table that had a holographic projector in the middle. Dick sat next to the base leader.

"Ladies and gentlemen, our next mission will be the most dangerous one you have ever been on," said the base commander.

A sphere that had five spikes, one in the middle and four surrounding it pointed in the same direction, appeared suspended above the projector.

"This is a world eater. Agents in an adjacent dimension in the Cacksarian System transmitted information about it to this base. They couldn't shift into the thing because it has a shift guard that prevents that from happening. All we know about it is that it is nearly the size of this planet. It could probably consume us and turn everything into another world eater. And it wouldn't take years to do that. This world eater went from planet to rubble to world eater in 12 days."

The men and women looked at each other and grumbled. "I find it hard to believe," scoffed one of the women.

"Our agents have never been wrong. They saw it when it was the planet Cacksar 2 before it became rubble when three destruction bases tore that planet apart. Afterwards, a core unit that looked like this thing minus the ray weapons came in and the rubble was turned into material for the world eater around the core. It took a few hours to destroy Cacksar 2 and reduce the initial rubble into managable chunks. When the core came in, rubble was ground up and molecularly changed by the core and added to the core. The world eater grew and couldn't be stopped. Here's why."

The projection of the world eater became smaller and hundreds of battle cruisers were projected around it. "The Empire made sure no rebel force, no matter how large, could get close to the world eater to attack it. The battle cruisers are out to a million kilometers from the world eater and spaced close enough that no rebel fighter, even if it were the size of a small drone, could get by them. That is also because each battle cruiser has upwards to 300 fighter craft patroling the region out to two million kilometerts from the world eater."

"What if we shift to adjacent dimensions to get close to the world eater?" asked one of the men.

"The Empire has thousands of battle cruisers in over 20 different dimensions and over a million fighter crafts in three times that many. Even if we could shift to the dimension where Hell exists we couldn't get past the layers of protection the Empire has around its world eater. We need to approach and destroy it in this dimension." "That will be suicidal," said another woman. "We'll never stop the thing."

"How many crafts do we need to get by to get to the world eater?" Dick asked.

"At least a quarter million fighter crafts and maybe 900 battle cruisers in this dimension alone. I have no idea how many they have in other dimensions," said the base commander.

"How many fighter crafts and light cruisers do we have?" Dick asked.

"Not enough to go against such as overwhelming force," said another man.

"We have 1,200 fighter crafts, 70 light cruisers, and 15,000 battle drones in seven different dimensions," said the base commander.

"How many projection spheres do we have?" Dick asked. "Millions of them," said the base commander. "I think I know what you are suggesting. You want to flood the region with millions of projections and make the enemy crafts concentrate their fire on them as well as the real attack crafts and light cruisers. But that will only last so long and then there will just be the real crafts."

"Generate thousands of field tunnels to the world eater and send projection spheres along with real crafts and missiles to it. The Empire crafts can only slice through so many in the time it takes to hit the world eater," said a third man.

"I don't know how difficult it would be to destroy the thing even if a dozen or more hit it," said the base commander.

"Even at high hyperlight speed?" Dick asked. "How high?" asked the first woman.

"Over 100,000 times light speed," said Dick. "I could blast my way through the thing in a split second with a projection sphere. The tunnel could be a billion kilometers long and it would take around three hundreths of a second to go through the thing. I don't think the world eater's defenses are fast enough to prevent penetration."

"You might be right. I know the energy mass would be incredible," said the base commander. "A bomb could be sent in to explode in the middle of the world eater and we wouldn't need to risk one attack craft. Let's do it."

The plan was set in motion and within three hours the attack crafts, light cruisers, field generators, and bombs were assembled and sent out to the Cacksarian System which was 5 light years away. At a speed of a million times light speed it would take almost three miniutes to get in position.

The rebel crafts spread out to surround the area around the world eater and the battle cruisers plus their fighter crafts. The tunnels had to thread the needle between enemy ships, hit the world eater, and bombs had to be sent in to explode inside the thing. Before the enemy ships could react, the tunnels were produced and the bombs and the energy projectiles were sent through the tunnels to explode inside the world eater.

The explosion was seen about an hour later. Everyone celebrated wildly for a couple minutes before they headed back toward the base at a "leisurely" 100,000 times light speed. Dick and the others expected the base to be jubilant after the victory.

Dick transmitted back to the base, "Mission accomplished. The world eater is destroyed. We'll be back in around an hour."

The reply was supposed to take no more than 25 seconds to get to him since it was transmitted as a hyperlight speed information bundle at a speed of a 10 million times light speed. Twenty-five seconds passed. Nothing. Dick retransmitted his message and waited 25 seconds. Still nothing.

A bad feeling plagued his mind. Could it be the Empire had intercepted his message? Worst yet. Could it be the base was destroyed while the rebel forces were on the mission?

Dick accelerated to a million times light speed and went ahead of everyone else. In 2 minutes, Dick saw something that made him heartsick. The sun of the system where the planet that had the rebel base was located expanded rapidly and just as quickly contracted. The only way that could be possible would be if the sun were exploded and then the energy were absorbed. Dick magnified the view and saw battle cruisers ahead and a world eater pounding away at the planet he was headed for. Shining tongues of energy were emitted by the five main weapons of the world eater that shattered the small planet below it and then withdrawn. It reminded Dick of five frogs flicking out their tongues to capture insects.

Dick didn't wait to see the entire planet turned into rubble. He transmitted a message back to the squadrons that were intending on being celebrated as heroes at a base on a planet that no longer existed.

"People, our base is gone. A world eater is devouring the planet. Either the one we destroyed was a diversion to draw us away from our base or there could be a bunch of them. I'll come back to join you or we can assemble above the planet between here and where you're at."

Dick waited around a minute for a reply.

"Meet us over Thingula Four. Better yet, go to Thingula Three. We have an old base there that can accomodate all of us. There may still be food and water there and food and beverage replicators unless they were all moved to the base that was destroyed. We can be there in half an hour."

"See you there."

Dick flew to the old base that still had food replicators minutes before the rest of the squadrons arrived. He loaded them with rocks and debris and turned on the water which came out red due to rust in the pipes. He replicated enough food for thousands of hungry people because they had brought no food or water with them for the mission.

The fighters and light cruisers descended and landed near the main building of the base. The people were surprised to see tables loaded with food and beverages as they entered the main building. They were grateful and chowed down. Many headed for the toilets or relieved themselves outside. When everyone was in the assembly room, Dick stood on a chair to talk to everyone after he got their attention by whistling.

"Listen up, people. This is our base now since the one we left is gone. I don't know what happened exactly. But there is a world eater finishing up our homes and when it is done, it might head here. We can try our tactic against the thing that destroyed our homes. It might work again. But if it doesn't, we'll need a backup plan. Anyone with any ideas?"

"Why don't we scatter and find some safe places to go to?" asked one of the men in the crowd.

"And let the Empire destroy another planet and its people.

That's the coward's way out."

"But at least we'll survive to fight another day," said another man. "That world eater destroyed our children and my mother," a woman complained. "Did they die in vain?" There was some grumbling.

"My family is gone. The deaths need to be avenged," said another man. "I'd rather try to destroy that evil thing and be killed by it than be 1,000 light years away and know that billions are dying because of it."

Most of the people agreed.

"Okay," said Dick. "Since we have nothing to lose and if God wants it, an empire to defeat, we'll try something desperate. We'll create more tunnels—"

"We used all our beam generators and target units," said another man.

"Plan B. We'll destroy as many battle cruisers we can to carve out a path to the world eater and then head straight at the thing as fast as we can push our fighter crafts. We'll need to be as far away from the thing as possible so we can reach maximum speed when we go through the thing. If my learning about hyperlight physics worth the effort, we should be able to go through the thing and not be destroyed. But if they are using technology I don't know about, it could be a suicide run," Dick warned.

"I'd rather die as long as we can spare the lives of billions. If that isn't possible, why should our lives be considered more valuable than all the other victims?" asked another woman.

"After we have eaten our fill, let's get back up there and do the job that needs to be done. If you think your life isn't long enough and you want to live a few more decades, you can go your own way. You'll just have to try and live with yourself and remember there was a time when suicide was preferable to life as a coward."

There was a precious time of eating, crying, hugging, and saying good-bye to people that might be gone in less than a day. Food and beverages were placed in the fighter crafts to be consumed before the final conflict or after the victory.

The squadrons headed for the region that was missing a sun and a planet. At maximum magnification, Dick saw the world eater do something he wasn't expecting. It split open and the core that looked like the one in the projection back at the base was about to leave the world eater and have debris from the planet that had been destroyed applied to it so it could become another world eater.

Dick told the computer that controlled his craft to travel straight ahead at maximum speed. Within seconds, the fighter craft was doing 500 million times light speed. In a split second he would hopefully destroy the core of the world eater and maybe prevent the destruction of another planet.

The plunge through the core also included a field discharge that caused a hyperlight energy expansion that destroyed the two halves of the world eater that had separated from each other. The warning the base commander had given him hadn't been obeyed and he was able to survive the jaws of death. He was instantly removed from the program and shifted back to the simulation chamber he had first entered. His hyperlight physics instructions on the Internet had paid off.

CHAPTER 16

Captain Majors flew toward the system with both starships in the same dimension. He was joined by 1,000 projections of starships as he shifted into this dimension which to an enemy would look overwhelming. As long as the enemy didn't find out the projections were more like hard to pop balloons, the captain could maintain the deception.

As the long-range sensors indicated, there was ample material to replicate over 500 starships. But the captain only needed two starships to replace the two that had been destroyed and integrate them with the remaining pair.

The ships were barely in the system when hundreds of enemy ships shifted into this dimension and began firing upon them. The projections were able to take out some of the smaller ships. But the weapons that were a part of the projections weren't as potent as the ones of the primary starships. When the enemy ships realized the primary ships were the ones they should concentrate their fire on, they began firing beam weapons and missiles at the Aremulac 1 and 3 more intensely.

The size of the Aremulacs compared to the opponents was like comparing two grizzly bears to a pack of vicious dogs. At the start, the larger ships were swatting at the smaller ones and destroying them right and left. But the smaller ships learned how to dodge the ray weapons and field discharges and inflicted damage here and there until attack strategies managed to allow the smaller ships to disable the Aremulac 3 first. With it out of the way, most of the ships became like angry bees as they tore into the Aremulac 1 and inflicted deadly wounds that eventually destroyed the ship.

Captain Majors tried the simulation again. This time he didn't shift into this dimension; only the projections. They engaged the enemy ships and drew them away from the area where the asteroid field was located. Several bodies were shifted into the other dimension and pulverized before the material was transformed into construction material. During the first replication there was no problem. But half way through the replication of the second ship, enemy ships shifted into the other dimension and attacked the Aremulac 1 while it was vulnerable and converged on it. The Aremulac 1 was able to hit back hard. But with no field protection, beam weapons were able to rip it apart and destroyed the other ships with ease except for the Aremulac 3 which was fully shielded. But after the Armeulac 1 and its replicates were destroyed, the remaining Aremulac was pounded mercilessly until it was destroyed. In the third simulation, Captain Majors shifted the projections into this dimension like he did in the second simulation to take on the enemy ships and shifted asteroids into 30 different dimensions where projections of the Aremulac 1 and 3 were produced. Only the two Aremulacs were real in one of the dimensions. Both replicates were produced in five minutes. After they generated their force fields, each ship was grabbed by a tractor beam and shifted into a different dimension where it was attacked until each ship was demolished. The fields were gapped and beam weapons tore the ships apart.

In the fourth simulation, Captain Majors replaced asteroids with projections of the asteroids and shifted the real ones into an adjacent dimension so rapidly that no one in this dimension detected the switch. Instead of replicating the Aremulac 1 twice, the captain replicated his ship five times to make the integrated ships more powerful. After the captain was ready to shift back into this dimension, he sent the projections in first and then shifted in along with two of the replicated ones. The other four remained in adjacent dimensions but integrated their force fields to strengthen them.

That was when the ships were surrounded by a dozen enormous ships that were five times larger than the Aremulacs. They created a multiple-layer force field around the ships and began circulating the force fields away from the Aremulacs to strip them bare of their energy protection. The Aremulacs tried to fire upon the huge ships. But the energy of the beams was absorbed by the enemy ships. The beams, even if they were being emitted at hyperlight speed, were absorbed. The energy contained in the reactors was sucked out. Afterwards, the ships were crumpled as if they were made of paper. In the fifth simulation, Captain Majors did the asteroid swap without being noticed. He replicated ten Aremulacs. Four remained with the Aremulac 1 and formed a square around the ship. They bonded their force fields and integrated them with the fields of the other seven Aremulacs. With the Aremulac 1 in the center, the intensity of the beams fired by the central ship was increased four-fold.

Since the ships were replicated without being noticed, when they shifted into this dimension they used a cloaking field to make themselves invisible to any enemy so they could leave the area undetected. At least that is what Captain Majors hoped.

One thing he evidently forgot was that the repulsive energy bundles that were expelled from the exhausts of the ships were detectable. All an enemy needed to do was observe the exhausts and the ships had to be in front of the energy being expelled. The fields were latched onto by the giant enemy ships and the same outcome happened.

In the sixth simulation, Captain Majors did the right things he had done during the fifth simulation. But instead of twelve Aremulacs there were 36. Six pentagons were formed with ships in the center of the formations. Three formations remained in adjacent dimensions while three cloaked ones shifted into this dimension. Instead of keeping their engines on, they got up to 100,000 times light speed and coasted through space after they shifted into this dimension. When the ships were a couple light years past the enemy ships, they turned on their engines and proceeded to Nagar at 10 million times light speed.

The captain felt confident that everything would have a happy ending since his ships had gotten past a powerful enemy. But the simulation computer wasn't done tormenting him. When he was about to enter the system, Pelorian battle cruisers stood between him and the planet that was surrounded by more Pelorian battle cruisers and a "porcupine." The hundreds of ray weapons were aimed at the planet; ready to unleash destruction that would turn the planet into rubble within a minute.

On the main screens on the bridge appeared a Pelorian commander who said, "Leave now and we will spare Nagar. We know that ACE is responsible for the war we have been fighting for too long because you want to add the Nagarian Empire to your federation. You think that it can join you and destroy our empire. As you see, we have the upper hand. If you care about the lives of over 10 billion people, you will leave this system within the next five minutes or we will unleash Hell fire."

The man's image left the screen and a countdown began.

"He doesn't know about our ships in adjacent dimensions. I'm glad I left so many replicates there," said the captain, relieved.

"There are too many ships and that porcupine around the planet," mentioned one of the crew members on the bridge. "Even if the porcupine were destroyed along with half of the battle cruisers, there would still be enough ships to inflict major damage to that world. I suggest we leave and return with overwhelming force in this and many other dimensions."

"That means the people of that planet may have to endure oppression they weren't counting on," the captain pointed out. "But it looks like we'll have to do what they want and come back later when we can overwhelm them with a force that is at least three or four times larger than the one we have."

The Pelorian commander came on thr screens again and asked, "Have you considered my offer?"

"Yes we have," said Captain Majors. "I don't want needless bloodshed. We will be leaving the system immediately. Maybe our logical actions will convince you that you should pursue peace and live with your neighbors as a civilized federation of planets. ACE has a lot of good things to offer your empire."

"Be a salesman elsewhere. Leave now or witness devastation that will haunt you forever."

After the man's image left the screens, the captain ordered his ships to leave the system and shift into another dimension half a light year away. With thousands of real and projection ships assembled in a region full of small planetoids, the captain devised a strategy that he hoped would free the Nagarian Empire of Pelorian domination.

"We have enough material around us to replicate hundreds of ships like this one and a million attack crafts. I counted around 3,000 battle cruisers and that hideous porcupine. The Pelorians know we will return. But I don't think they're counting on us coming back so soon. I wish we had known about this region before we spent time in that other one first. I want to spend the next day in this region pulverizing the surrounding planetoids and turning the rubble into construction material for 700 replicates and at least 10,000 attack crafts. The attack crafts can be replicated in the fabrication chambers. They only need to be a few meters long. But they should have enough weapontry that is potent enough to take on a battle cruiser."

"Captain, I did a long-range probe of the porcupine and it has shift guards to prevent us from shifting a bomb into the thing," said another crew member.

"What about the battle cruisers?" the captain asked.

"Same with them. We'll have to take them on in our home dimension."

"We will shift back into our home dimension as close to the ships and the porcupine as possible and do as much damage as possible as long as we prevent the destruction of the planet. Let's get started," the captain commanded.

The Aremulac 1 began the replication process immediately after one of the planetoids was turned into rubble and then into construction material. For three hours, starships and fighter crafts were replicated and fabricated. It looked like the planet would be rescued within a day and the Pelorian Empire would be dealt a deadly blow that might end its dreams of conquest.

Suddenly, the Pelorian battle cruisers and two porcupines shifted into the dimension where the replication process was going on A full-blown battle happened. Captain Majors stopped the replication of another Aremulac and had his ship regenerate a force field to protect it as it battled the attackers.

During the battle, disturbing images appeared on the screens on the bridge. The porcupine over Nagar pounded the planet into rubble. Battle cruisers rained destruction upon other inhabited worlds in the system. The Pelorian commander came on the screen after the demonstration of total destruction.

"You are at fault for the deaths of over 10 billion people on three different worlds. You should have been a man who honored his word," the commander accused the captain.

"We did, you bastard. Their deaths are your fault; not mine."

"I didn't ask you to be in the neighborhood of this system. I wanted you totally gone. It's too late now. Deal with the consequences for your arrogance."

In the seventh simulation, the captain decided to go to the region rich in construction material and build up his forces before heading for the Nagarian Empire. For two days, replicates and fighter crafts were produced to contend with the Pelorians. But a couple hours into the third day, the Pelorian commander was seen on the screens on the bridge.

"My spies in 20 dimensions and on Nagar knew you were coming with overwhelming force. Strange that a federation supposedly desiring peace would use weapons of war to push its agenda. And ACE considers us evil? It wages a war through those it can use because it wants to present a false face of love, compassion, and understanding. ACE wants to use the Nagarians to conquer us. We know about your cooperation treaty. I am about to nullify it before it is signed because yes, we are evil. But ACE made us that way. Here's proof."

On the screens appeared Nagar surrounded by hundreds of Pelorian battle cruisers and a porcupine that turned the planet into rubble before moving on to the other occupied worlds and doing the same. The commander came on again.

"If ACE had never interfered with the progress of the Nagarian Empire and the Pelorian Empire, our empires might have formed an alliance rivaling that of ACE eventually. Now ACE will never know. Instead, your foolish actions compounded by an unwanted war will steel our resolve to oppose your federation and expand our empire until we destroy you. And that minor world you call Earth will become another victim of a device you amusingly call a porcupine. Leave now and return to the safety of your region far from our empire and maybe we will slow our expansion. But that depends on ACE. Tell your handlers that. If you don't leave the region immediately, you will be set upon by our superior force and we will show no mercy."

In the eighth simulation, the captain tried an entirely different tactic that was more dangerous than any of the previous strategies. He flew his ship to the Pelorian system without the Aremulac 3 in an adjacent dimension to act like a lifeboat. If his ship was attacked, it could be destroyed and everyone would die. The simulation of the Pelorian commander reminded him of one of the reasons why ACE existed. Yes, it was supposed to show overwhelming strength before its enemies. But a more legitimate reason for its existence was to promote peace and progress for those it was allied with. The covert war against the Pelorian Empire was wrong and should have never been waged. How he was going to handle that situation was still unknown.

The captain approached the Pelorian Empire's main planet Pelor 2 in another dimension and sent 1,000 microdroids down to the planet to find the leader of the empire. It was discovered that the empire had seven emperors that had equal power. Four of them were on the planet in four different locations and the other three were on the three other inhabited worlds in the Pelorian system. It could be to prevent the death of a single emperor causing the empire to collapse. The six replacements would make sure that wouldn't happen.

The captain sent 1,000 more microdroids to each of the other inhabited worlds to find the emperors. Once all the emperors were discovered, they were "tagged" by microdroids that shifted into this dimension a split second before they were teleported to the Aremulac. The captain was waiting in the transporter room for them to appear. Once they were in the ship, they complained loudly about being kidnapped. After they stopped yelling, the captain began talking with them.

"I'm sorry for the intrusion on your lives. But I thought I had to beam you aboard to try and correct an enormous mistake on ACE's part. The war that has been waged against you for too long is the fault of ACE because it didn't want to directly fight against you. I'm sorry. Please accept my apology on the behalf of ACE for something that could be considered unforgivable."

"You better believe it can't be forgiven," said one of the emperors. "Can you bring back to life the dead that ACE through its sarogates murdered?"

"I'm sorry—"

"No you can't. When our people find you, they will kill you and your people on your ships."

"Ship. There is only one ship." The men began to laugh.

"One ship?" asked another emperor. "You dare take us without a fleet to support your actions? You are a fool."

"You might be right. I intend on bringing you men to the Nagarian Empire to be signatories to a cooperation treaty with that empire." The men laughed even harder.

"Ask us to become children again," said a third emperor. "That would be easier than making an alliance with the Nagarian Empire. ACE must think we are still children willing to obey our elders. You are not our father. You're not even a sadistic uncle. You are one of our enemies who talks peace while in your heart seeks our destruction."

"My heart may not be pure at all times. But my intentions are pure. I sincerely want your empire to form an alliance with the Nagarian Empire and with ACE. The past iniquities can never be forgotten or fully forgiven. But our mutual future of peace and progress can begin today if you are willing to do what is logical. It is not logical to resist an offer from someone who has the power to take your lives from you," he warned.

"And if we decide not to sign our names to a damnable document, you might as well kill us now."

"You need not be so melodramatic. You're not signing your names in blood to a contract requiring the forfeiture of your souls. It is a simple agreement that will bring an abundance of benefits to your empire. Just the fact that we will no longer be at war with your empire will be a blessing among a host of blessings that will follow. ACE can provide protection from your enemies."

"Why should we trust you?" asked the first emperor.

"If I wanted you dead, you wouldn't be standing in front of me. I could have left your lifeless bodies floating in space. Instead, all seven of you are my guests. As guests, you will be treated graciously and with respect. I have a guest area I hope you will find more than adequate. There are food and beverage replicators, entertainment systems, and comfortable surroundings. You will meet the representatives of ACE that will co-sign the treaty of cooperation with you and the representatives of the Nagarian Empire. I hope and pray you will enjoy their company during the journey."

The captain had three of his crew members escourt the men to the guest facilities where they stayed during the trip to Nagar. It could have been a quick one hour flight; enough time for a meal and some introductions. But Captain Majors decided to slow the trip down so the seven emperors would realize it was in the best interest of the Pelorian Empire to be a part of ACE as the Nagarian Empire was going to become. They were eventually convinced they were better off being partners and not enemies of ACE.

The signing ceremony had all the pomp and prestige expected of treaty signings. And the celebration afterwards which lasted three days convinced the emperors they had made the right choice to join ACE. It also helped to have scores of beautiful Nagarian women surround the emperors and the wine and spirits loosened them up enough to allow them to enjoy their time on the planet. The communal bath was also a real pleasure and allowed the emperors to get to know how friendly Nagarians could be; especially the women who were there to serve them any way they desired.

That simulation looked like something the captain wanted to experience often in the future and helped him in making the right decisions when there were no do-overs.

CHAPTER 17

Due to time compression, Maria returned to the simulation chamber first about 8 seconds after leaving it.

Dick followed a second later. Kate kissed the floor of the chamber 15 seconds after leaving it. She was so relieved to be alive. "That felt so real," said Maria. "I felt like I was actually back in time about a century. It was incredible. How were your simulations?"

she asked the Thurmans.

"I felt like I was in the biggest disaster film ever made," Kate complained. "All I wanted to do was have a fun time in Hawaii hang gliding. I was attacked by pteranodons, had to outrun a wild fire, kill a sabertooth cat, take on pirates, nearly boiled alive by an undersea volcano, survived an attack by giant squids and a megladon on the sub I was on, and smashed into a stratotower after being thrown there by a tsunami. I thought I finally was experiencing some good fortune. Wrong. I suffered radiation poisoning and died in the simulation. It was a nightmare of a nightmare. At least I was able to have power rays appear so I could take on the monsters. If that hadn't happened, I probably would have been eaten alive. I probably would have smelled like poop if I came out of the pteranodon from the end."

Dick laughed at the joke. Maria gave him a nasty look not realizing Kate's comment was sarcasm.

"How was your time fighting the Empire" Kate asked.

"Fantastic. At least I survived the program. I guess that Rick Badman guy was right when he wrote about hyperlight physics on the Internet 30 years ago. If he had been wrong about being able to go through things and not dying I would have ended up dead like you two. I guess I lucked out.

"In my program I was able to chow down. But my stomach is complaining. Since we don't know when the captain is going to come back, maybe we should eat some lunch."

"How will he know where we are?" Kate asked.

The AI voice of the simulation chamber said in a pleasant female voice, "I will tell him where you three are. Think where you want to go and step through the portal. Captain Majors will be with you as soon as the simulation he is in is over. That might be within the next couple minutes."

The trio stepped through the wall into the chamber and into the main dining room. There were about 100 crew members eating, talking, laughing, and having a generally good time enjoying their meals. Pleasant music was being piped into the room slightly below conversation level. The trio walked up to the bank of food and beverage replicators and thought about what they wanted to eat and drink after they were prompted telepathically to make their food and drink orders. In a matter of seconds, savory meats and vegetables and delicious desserts appeared on plates on the trays the three had placed in front of the replicators. A couple seconds later, tall glasses of cold beverages appeared. Dick sampled his and smiled broadly.

"I think this is better than the Dr. Pepper I had in the captain's cabin," complimented Dick. "I wish we had these things back at the Facility."

"Then what would the cooks do back there?" asked Maria.

"I don't know. Maybe they could learn how to master the art of food replication delivery and be employed at restaurants," said Dick. "You mean become glorified waiters," said Kate. "I'm glad our jobs haven't been done away with due to AI." "Give them time and it will," said Dick.

Shortly after the trio sat at one of the tables, the captain entered the dining room. After replicating a foot-long sub piled high with ham, roast beef, salami, and some meat the three had never seen before, the captain replicated a Dr. Pepper and headed for the table where his guests were seated.

"Sorry it took so long. I appologize."

"I guess you survived your simulation," Dick mentioned.

"I almost didn't. I'm just glad the simulation of a Pelorian commander knocked some sense into my head. But I'm still going to have a Plan B in case everything goes to Hell out there."

"What is Plan A?" Dick asked.

"I'm going to shift into an adjacent dimension where the Aremulac 3 is at along with the projections and replicate an overwhelming force in case the Pelorians are waiting for us near Nagar. We'll stay in that dimension and I will fly this ship to the Pelorian system to kidnap the emperors to take them to the signing ceremony."

"Whoa. Whoa. Kidnap the emperors?" Dick asked. "How many emperors do they have in the Pelorian Empire?"

"Seven. Four live on Pelor 2 and the other three live on the other three inhabited worlds."

"How do you know that? It was only a simulation program," Dick pointed out.

"We have had spies in adjacent dimensions for years."

"Have they had spies in adjacent dimensions keeping an eye on ACE?" Maria asked.

"Probably. That's why we have shift guards to prevent dimensional shifts into this ship and the other Aremulac. If we didn't, an enemy could shift a bomb into one of our reactors and destroy the ship from the inside. If the Pentagon had known about interdimensional travel when it was built nearly a century ago, WW II could have ended mighty fast and millions of lives would have been spared. But ACE couldn't allow its people to help the Allied forces back then no matter how evil people like Hitler and Tojo were. And Maria, I hope you're not offended when I say the world would have been a whole lot better off if Stalin had been taken out."

"My grandparents would have complained. But I think my parents would have said it was for the best if the Soviet Union had become Russia and everyone would have done better," Maria admitted. "When the Soviet Union dissolved and became Russia, we still had a lot of problems."

"I know," said Dick. "That's why I proposed the Russian Madhouse to President Kursolov. If Kate and I hadn't gone to Russia a few years ago, I wouldn't have been inspired to propose it to your President."

"I can't thank you enough for that," said Maria. "Captain, where are we headed for?"

"There are areas where there is enough material to replicate thousands of Aremulacs. It's sometimes too bad the replicates can't replicate more ships. We'd have over 2 billion Aremulacs in an hour. But if one of our enemies seized one, they could have trillions of starships. ACE was wise to make only one ship able to replicate in a starship formation."

"So if an enemy were to seize this ship, ACE would be overwhelmed," said Kate.

"Only if they could override the self-destruct system," the captain said. "Each primary starship has that in case it's taken by an enemy. The captain wears a ring that is called the dead man's switch."

He showed the trio a ring that was flesh colored that was around the finger on his left hand near his pinky finger. It looked almost like a callus.

"I sometimes forget I have it on. But if it were removed, this ship would dissolve into atomic particles after an explosion ten seconds later. If I am killed, the ring would signal the self-destruct system to destroy the ship."

"So we better make sure you don't die on us," said Dick.

"How long do you want to spend replicating this ship?" Maria asked.

"About a day. I'll be able to replicate around 700 Aremulacs and produce maybe 10,000 fighter crafts. It depends on how much material is in the region."

"I've got an idea," said Maria. "What if I design a replication vessel that will replicate small cruisers that can replicate other small cruisers. It could be the size of the Aremulac and able to replicate itself. It would be a warship; just not as powerful as this one. The technology to produce a replcator that can replicate itself shouldn't be that difficult to master."

"You would think so. But every time I've tried to replicate a replicator, the device has refused to be replicated," said the captain. "Yet you can replicate fabricators that can fabricate fabricators," said Maria. "A replicator is like a fabricator only more elaborate. As the Aremulac is replicating more Aremulacs, the replication vessel can replicate more replication vessels that are forming fabricators that act like replicators in small cruisers. Each cruiser would be able to replicate another cruiser because the replicator is actually a fabricator."

"That could be an end around to make a multitude of ships. Just as long as an enemy doesn't get their hand on a cruiser and start multiplying it geometrically."

"I could design it to have a self-destruct system in case an enemy gets their hands on one," said Maria who looked like a brilliant idea was percolating in her brain. "I could do all the designing and developing in a simulation chamber at accelerated speed. Once I'm done, I could have the computer in the simulation chamber transfer that information to the fabricators and begin the process of replication."

"Each cruiser might be inaccessible to intruders," said the captain. "AI could control each cruiser when humans aren't in control of them. We might have only 700 Aremulacs after a day of replication. But we could have over a billion cruisers possibly. It just depends on how much material there is in the region."

"Since the technology possessed by ACE is far superior to what we have back on earth, maybe I could have access to it to fully design the ships we need," said Maria in anticipation.

The captain had a pained look on his face.

"I'm sorry. From the beginning of ACE it was decided that no one that didn't belong to ACE would be able to use the advanced technology to help others that didn't belong to ACE. It didn't want advanced weapons technology to fall into the wrong hands and be used to potentially destroy the world. You might be another Albert Einstein who was a man of peace. But others around you wouldn't be and the technology is beyond what most people on earth can be allowed to have. You can do basic design work. But only our human and synthetic technicians will be allowed to work on the more advanced systems. I hope you understand."

"If that's the way it has to be, that's the way it has to be. I'd like to get to work on the ships as soon as I'm done with lunch." "I'd like to work on some things too," said Dick.

"Same here," said Kate.

"All right. You can go ahead and use the simulation chamber for your work. Afterwards, you can download the information into portable fabricators I'll let you take back to Siberia. It won't technically be ACE allowing illegal advanced technology being made available to non-ACE associates except for what Maria will be working on. Anything that isn't produced by her will not be allowed to be downloaded into memory units of the fabricators. Other than that, knock yourselves out."

After the meal, Dick, Kate, and Maria entered simulation programs in three different dimensions in the chamber. Maria's cruiser that could fabricate other cruisers as if they were being replicated was ready before the Aremulacs were in the region where replication would take place.

Fabrication took a bit longer than replication; about 15 minutes to fabricate a cruiser. But since each cruiser could fabricate another cruiser, after a billion were fabricated, the captain stopped before there was no more material in the region to turn into construction material. An entire world that was incapable of being occupied was used primarily to turn into construction material.

Once the ships were replicated, they shifted into another dimension and followed the Aremulacs to the Pelorian Empire where the microdroids were sent in to tag the emperors after the droids shifted into this dimension so they could be teleported to the Aremulac 1 for the three seconds it was in this dimension before shifting back to an adjacent dimension for the trip to Nagar. The simulation program the captain had experienced was programmed for worst case scenarios. In the real universe, the seven emperors were more cowardly than men to be feared. Two fainted, three wet themselves, and the last two were shaking and crying. They were brought to the guest quarters for the trip to Nagar and treated with more respect than they probably deserved since they acted more like children than adults. In the mind of the captain and his crew the Pelorian emperors before they were kidnapped seemed like tigers. But they turned out to be more like kittens willing to do whatever Captain Majors wanted them to do. They would gladly sign a cooperation treaty if it meant the war would be over and they could be allied with ACE.

There was a wonderful signing ceremony and a three-day celebration. Since there were hundreds of extra Aremulacs and a billion cruisers available, the captain decided to allow the Nagarian Empire and the Pelorian Empire to have fleets of Aremulacs and cruisers. But to make sure the empires couldn't replicate billions or trillions of ships, the replicators or fabricators programed to fabricate more ships were removed. The rest of the ships were sent to a storage region in another dimension where they would be available for future use. The trip back to this solar system was a lot faster than the trip to the Pelorian and Nagarian Empires. Dick, Kate, and Maria entered their ship about 100 million kilometers away from Mars on the side opposite of earth so the Aremulac 1 couldn't be seen by sensors or observers on earth. The trio continued their trip to Mars which seemed like an anticlimax after days of traveling to farflung worlds and back.

CHAPTER 18

Dick, Kate, and Maria flew out of the landing craft bay seconds before the Aremulac shifted to another dimension and flew away to who knows where. The plane was on the other side of Mars and the trio couldn't tell anyone the whole truth about where they had been for a few days when everyone thought they were possibly dead. The portable fabricators were evidence that the trip had been in contact with people that possessed advanced technology. They couldn't be explained away too easily unless they were hidden in some lockers aboard the plane and never allowed to be seen by anyone back in Siberia. Then again, the information contained in the devices was too valuable to not use. And if they could be integrated into the fabricators at the Facility, they would increase the speed of fabrication.

As the plane was flying toward Mars at half the speed of light to give the occupants time to devise a story, the fabricators were placed in lockers underneath the space suits stored inside. The trio sat and looked at each other as they discussed what they were going to do.

"I suggest that we tell everyone a Barney and Betty Hill story," said Dick. "We were picked up by an alien craft which isn't totally false since ACE stands for Alien Cooperation Enterprise. We were given the devices like Betty Hill was given the map and they just happen to be more advanced. It's very believable."

"Sounds reasonable. But our fabricators have English writing and not alien symbols. How can we explain that?" asked Maria.

"And what about the telepathic brain implants I did work on out there?" asked Kate. "The fabricators are much more advanced than anything we have back at the Facility. Just add construction material and they form what is programmed into them. You saw what happened in the simulation chamber."

"I thought it was part of the simulation," Dick said in amazemenmt. "You mean it can actually make what is programmed into its memory recorder?"

"Yeah. Here, I'll show you."

Kate turned on her fabricator and projected the image of a telepathic brain implant above the unit. It was magnified 1,000 times normal size to show the details. She pushed a button marked with a C and seconds later, a tray similar to that of a CD or DVD player slid out of the unit with a yellow capsule similar to one of the micromachine capsules in the tech lab on it. The trio stared at it.

"Do you think there is a telepathic brain implant in that capsule?" Dick asked Kate.

"I think there is. The only way to find out is to swallow it," said Kate confidently a second before she grabbed it with two fingers and swallowed it.

Maria and Dick stared at her, concerned. A couple minutes later, Kate smniled and spoke to them.

"Yes, the thing works. In fact, there were enough micromachines and construction material in the capsule to implant a series of implants. Even the capsule material was used for construction material. And yes, it tasted like banana. But I think it's because I was thinking of a banana. Of course you can. And you too. Why should I be the only telepath in the plane?"

Dick and Kate looked at each other in bewilderment because it looked like Kate had actually read their minds. Kate tried to produce two more capsules, but the device required more construction material. Kate walked back to the galley and pulled out a drawer. She removed a spoon and shut the drawer before coming back to the device.

"What are you going to do with that?" Maria asked her. "It needs construction material."

She opened a bin in the back of the fabricator and dropped in the spoon. The bin slid back into the device and a green light came on which showed that there was enough material to make the capsules that were requested. Seconds later, two capsules appeared on the tray when it slid out. Dick and Maria swallowed them and a couple minutes later tried an experiment.

Without speaking, Dick said to both women, "I wonder if this is how aliens communicate with humans."

"They don't need implants," thought Kate to the other two. "Dick!" Maria said mentally when she saw herself naked in a shower which was what was on Dick's mind.

"I didn't go all the way," Dick thought defensively.

"Dick," Kate thought while she smiled knowing her husband was now thinking of both of them in the shower shortly before they had their first day on the job at the Russian Madhouse.

"Ladies," Dick thought to them as he saw them making love as lesbians in the shower. Both women laughed.

Dick spoke out loud, "So the implants work; probably too well. I hope this doesn't mean we'll be in each other's mind constantly." "Not if they work like I designed them to," said Kate. "They also have a way to block others from reading your mind. Think of a blocking image and the implant will prevent others from reading your mind. Try it."

The trio stared at each other intently for nearly a minute. "All I see is a brick wall in your mind," he said to Kate.

"All I see in your mind is a dark brown wooden door," he said to Maria.

"Your blocking image looks like a shower curtain," Kate said to Dick. "I bet you're thinking of me and Maria doing the nasty behind that curtain."

Dick smiled and couldn't contain himself. He began laughing and nearly cried.

"I'm glad you two couldn't see what I was thinking. It's sick. I was getting it on hot and heavy with President Kursolov in the shower."

"I'm glad we couldn't," said Maria as she grimaced.

"If your's can make telepathic implants, I wonder if mine can make the flying suit I was working on," said Dick expectantly.

Dick projected a full-sized image of a flying suit he was working on in the simulation chamber and pushed the button with a C on it. The device indicated that the bin wasn't large enough to hold enough material to change into construction material to make the suit. But if another bin that dumped material into the smaller bin was used, the flying suit could be fabricated.

"I guess I'm going to have to wait until I return to the Facility before I can have my flying suit," Dick said with some regrets.

"I'll have to wait until I return to hanger 3 before I can have my small battle cruiser," said Maria.

As the spaceplane neared Mars, Maria slowed the craft to give herself and the others time to hide the fabricators. They were the size of an old-fashioned family Bible and a bit hard to conceal. Maybe they could be explained away. That was when Dick noticed something he should have expected. On the side of each fabricator was a tab that looked a little like a key. Dick pulled the tab out of his fabricator and it disappeared as it shifted into another dimension. Dick went through the motions of inserting the key into his device and it appeared again.

"I guess we'll have to save our Barney and Betty Hill story for the Facility when we get back," said Dick, relieved.

Kate and Maria placed their devices in the space suit lockers and pulled out their keys. They also shifted to another dimension. All three placed their keys in their pockets.

"We better not lose our keys," warned Kate.

Maria went back to the pilot seat and strapped in while Dick and Kate fastened their seat belts as the plane neared Mars. Below them was Mars Base Gagarin with the Chinese and American bases in the distance. Since the plane was coming in slow and easy, the protective force field around the plane didn't need to be as potent because there wasn't as much atmospheric friction. With a level landing area free of debris, Maria opened the landing gear bays and extended the wheels. Even though the atmosphere was thin, the plane landed softly and stopped in a short distance in front of the main structure.

Before Maria and the others put on space suits, she radioed to the base in Russian, "I'm sorry for taking so long. We had an unexpected side trip that kept us away longer than we were counting on."

"At least you three are here and not a moment too soon. Did you see that dust storm coming our way?"

"I thought I saw something bad in the distance. How long do we have before it gets here?"

"We predict that it will be on us in half an hour. Did you bring the goodies with you?"

"Send about a dozen guys out here and once we're suited up, we'll be able to transfer the food and drink to them. They'll be using levitation carts, won't they?"

"Sure. They'll also be driving some big American pickups trucks," he said sarcastically. "We've got handtrucks and wheelbarrows. That'll have to do."

"Send them out now. I'll open the hatch when we're ready."

The trio donned their suits as quickly as possible and by the time the hatch was opened, the men were waiting to be loaded up with boxes of food and beverages. There were even a couple cases of Russian Madhouse vodka, traditional and cherry-flavored, stowed away in the reactor/computer room. At least the trio had small levitation carts they could load up with food and beverages and glide to the hatch. The most important cargo on the plane (the junk food and the vodka) was removed from the plane first and brought to the main building of the base. The last of the food and beverages except for what the trio thought they would require during the trip back to earth was brought into the building by the trio on levitation carts as the dust was kicking up. Maria hoped the wind wouldn't be strong enough to catch the wings of her plane and flip the craft over.

The base commander, Ivan Gashenko, hugged Maria and kissed her on both cheeks.

"Welcome to Mars Base Gagarin. What you brought for us is more appreciated than you'll ever know."

"At least I was able to give you something you probably haven't had for a long time."

"You mean the vodka?"

"That and some delicious American chocolate bars."

The man chuckled a bit and said, "Even the American base doesn't have that."

"We've got Twinkies too," said one of the men excitedly.

"The Americans think they have it good over there with the best food on the planet. But they don't have Twinkies," said the base commander with glee.

"I can have my people make vodka and Twinkie runs every couple weeks if you want," Maria said confidently.

The crew members rejoiced.

"I've heard about Russian Madhouse vodka. They say it goes down like fire, but you can drink a case of it and not get drunk. That sort of takes the fun out of drinking vodka if you can't get drunk. But as long as it tastes like vodka, I won't complain all that much." One of the men opened the case holding the traditional vodka and brought a bottle over for the base commander to sample. He opened the screwtop stopper and downed a fourth of the bottle. "They were right. It goes down like fire. That's the most important thing. Thank the distiller for me when you get back." "I will."

Kate interrupted, "I have a cousin from Volgograd, Vladimer Premakoff, who is somewhere on the base. Do you know where he is?"

The base commander twitched his right eye a few times before saying, "He's outside driving to our nuclear power plant that supplies much of our power. He's inspecting the power line we buried."

Dick, Kate, and Maria knew he was lying, but they didn't dare say they knew. He was actually at a site where an interesting find had been made. There actualy had been a race of people who lived on Mars and neither the Americans or Chinese knew that fact.

"I'll wait for him to come back," said Kate.

"With the storm out there, I don't know when he'll be back," said the base commander.

"Don't risk personnel going out there to bring him back," said Kate a bit dejected. "I can see him the next time I'm back."

"You aren't in a hurry to leave are you?"asked the base commander. "It's Hell out there. It's nearly dinner time. Join us. Let's celebrate. At least spend the night with us."

"Sure," agreed Maria. "We won't be a burden will we?"

"If you could bring us as much food and drink every time, you'd be welcomed to stay a week."

Joyous Russian music was piped into the dining area where the trio were honored guests. They feasted, sang, danced, and really enjoyed themselves into the night. Kate put on a happy face even though she was concerned about her cousin being out in the storm. She was still worried when she and Dick went to bed in one of the guest rooms.

"Honey, you know the base commander was lying about Vladimer," said Kate.

"Yeah. Finding proof that Mars was at one time inhabited by people would be a monumental discovery. I can see why the Russians wouldn't want the Americans and Chinese to find out. It would be hard for Washington and Beijing to admit the supermarket tabloids have been right for years and the people once considered whacky were right. The world would demand disclosure about aliens; at least more than it does now."

"I think it's beyond that. I have a feeling that there might be inhabitants still alive below the surface of Mars."

"After all I've seen and experienced, I wouldn't be surprised. That would be more a reason to not be straight forward about the discovery. If an advanced race of people was still living below the surface of Mars, imagine how much of a boost to technology they could give the Russians."

"Like when we met Captain Majors and found out about ACE." "If there are any inhabitants of Mars living below the surface, they might know about ACE for all I know."

"If that is the case, maybe the rest of the world will find out about ACE and will benefit from the advanced technology they are using. I know the Facility would benefit greatly if it were partnered with ACE."

Dick prayed, "Dear Heavenly Father, thank-you for allowing us to have such a great experience these last few days and letting us arrive on Mars safely. Protect Vladimer wherever he is and if he is dealing with people who inhabit this world, help him be successful. "Back at the Facility, let everything run well. Help the people there do their jobs to the best of their ability. May we help the world and the people of the world to make it better. Thank-you for not allowing us to destroy the world you created. Give us wisdom to preserve it and may we never think we know better than you how it should be. For too long, people thought man was more powerful than you and able to decide the future of the world. Thank-you for not allowing us to go too far. May we always seek your guidance to do what is right. I ask this in Christ Jesus' name. Amen."

CHAPTER 19

Near Olympus Mons over a kilometer below the surface of Mars, Vladimer had met with a five-man committee in the underground city of Janvuor earlier in the day. A big-breasted woman wearing a glistening green jumpsuit that was skin tight sat between the Russian and the Martians as the mediator who was able to discern the thoughts of all the men to determine if they were lying or telling the truth. The Martians had for over a century learned a lot about the people of earth from the radio and TV broadcasts emitted from the planet.

The first contact with humans during the modern era happened during the late 18th century when men from Newgate, New York flew a GSLP projectile which landed in the area. They came in peace but were armed with potent weapons in case first contact turned into a conflict. Everything turned out well and gifts were exchanged as a sign of friendship. The Martians thought they could form an alliance with the people of earth. But when no one returned, three spaceships traveled to earth years later to see if an alliance could be formed with some of the heads of state of the most powerful nations. They had shifted into an adjacent dimension to observe people without being detected.

But the year was 1812. The British had invaded America and the French had invaded Russia. England was at war with the French in Spain and multitudes were being enslaved in Africa. Japan and China had little contact with European nations and the British Empire ruled large portions of the world. The Martians thought the people of Earth were too violent and too superstitious to form an alliance with.

The only place the Martians felt welcome was in Newgate, New York; the city that had sent men to Mars years before. Since the citizens of the small city were used to people from other dimensions and worlds, they didn't feel out of place there. People from Mars visited Newgate several times between 1812 and 1870.

Unfortunately, there was war on Mars between two tribes in 1870. It was a short war because the most powerful tribe used a thermal nuclear device to destroy the capitol of the other tribe. But it was too powerful. It not only destroyed the city and its suburbs, it also destroyed much of the atmosphere. The survivors went below the surface of Mars and avoided going topside as much as possible. The city of Janvuor had once been a community of over 500,000. But the population of survivors plunged to 5,000 who managed to go underground. They used technology to retain a breathable atmosphere and synthesize food.

With the surface of Mars being so cold and the atmosphere so thin, a truce was signed and the people of both tribes decided surviving together was preferable to dying together. The 15 remaining cities, Janvuor, Shartang, Vavanese, Norgun, Calofrene, Baybor, Noganese, Chrevu, Laquavor, Mornganstene, Hovas Tortenus, Reevane, Tralon, Servosnang, and Druse were connected by a tube system that circled the planet. The population had been over a billion people in 285 cities in 1870. But after the war, the population plunged to fewer than 375,000 in 1872. Since then, the population steadily declined until it stabilized at around 80,000 people in 2000. A few thousand even came to earth and blended in with the people of the planet. The rest of the people who left the planet went to numerous other worlds in the galaxy. As Dick suspected, more people joined ACE than what settled on Earth. Due to synthetic skin and physical reconfiguration, the Martians looked just like humans wherever they settled. They tried not to bring attention to themselves and were successful to some extent.

The radio and TV signals coming from Earth were considered anti-Martian. The Orson Wells broadcast of "War Of the Worlds" convinced most Martians that they wouldn't be welcome in most places of the world. The brave ones that left Mars for Earth were at times considered foolish. They weren't expected to return to Mars and most didn't.

Vladimer had no knowledge of the history of Mars. He also didn't know that two of his ancestors had come from Mars. They settled in Russia before it became the Soviet Union. When he came to Mars, the committee was aware of his presence due to a genetic marker that triggerd a response from microsensors that were launched when the first Russian cosmonauts landed. Vladimer was one of seven that established Mars Base Gagarin. He didn't realize one of the microsensors put the thought in his mind to travel to Olympus Mon. He was accompanied by two other cosmonauts and they discovered evidence of what they thought was an extinct race of people. That was a year ago.

Mars Base Gagarin in 2040 had 15 people. By then, America and China had established bases on Mars. A tube system was being bored out by plasma moles designed and developed by the Madhouse in Arizona and built by various heavy equipment companies. Vladimer and the cosmonauts that had worked the site for a year didn't realize much of the evidence of a long-dead civilization had been planted by the living inhabitants of Janvuor until one day early in the morning, Vladimer and his team members saw someone near the site.

Vladimer and the others ran after the person and followed him into a cave where he ran through what looked like a rock wall. When they came up to the wall they reached out to feel it. Vladimer's team mates felt cold hard stone. But when Vladimer reached out, his hand went through the wall which startled him and almost caused him to fall. He walked through the wall which was impenetrable for the others. Since they had no tools that would allow them to break through the rock, they headed back to the base and told the base commander what had happened. They arrived back about 15 minutes before Dick, Kate, and Maria landed. With the dust storm almost upon them, the base commander thought it was wiser to wait until after the storm passed to go out after him. They rehearsed the story they would tell the trio and it was decided that since they actually had a nuclear power plant that supplimented their solar and wind systems, the story of why he was gone was that he needed to check the reactor and the underground power line for problems.

Vladimer was more curious than scared. He walked a few steps when the person he had run after appeard in front of him after walking through another rock wall. In perfect Russian, the person who was wearing a face mask spoke to Vladimer.

"Welcome, brother. We knew that one day someone like you would return to Kerian."

"Kerian?"

"That is the true name of this planet which you know as Mars.

We know your planet as Vorion which you know as Earth." "How did I walk through the wall? Where am I anyways?"

"You are genetically capable as all Kerianites are of passing through barrier entrances. I need to bring you before the committee to discuss a treaty of cooperation between your people and my people. Do you have the authority to finalize such a treaty?"

"I…don't know. I'm a nobody. How could I be a Kerianite?" "Two of your ancestors left this planet and landed on your planet to live life as humans. They left this planet in the Vorionite year of 1887. The original members of the committee decided that if a Vorionite of Kerianite ancestory ever returned to the planet, he or she would be contacted and brought to the committee room to talk with the committee members. Consider it a great honor. Follow me."

Vladimer followed the totally bald man through a wall into a cavity in the stone onto a flat slab of rock. The slab began to descend rapidly until it slowed before coming to stop st the bottom of the shaft. The Kerianite removed his face mask as he walked into a dimly lit city with Vladimer.

The city was nestled inside a cavern that was large enough to hold a couple dozen football stadiums. The tallest building was ten stories tall and was within twenty meters of touching the ceiling. Most of the buildings were no more than four stories tall.

There were no vehicles on the streets. Instead, the people traveled via high-speed levitated plates which they stood on or walked on the sidewalks. It was eerily silent.

"Step onto that plate with me," the Kerianite told Vladimer as they approached the street. "And don't worry about falling down. Once we're on the move, a gravitational pad will hold you in place. Don't worry about your feet and legs feeling heavy. That's the way they're supposed to feel."

Both men stepped onto a plate that was a meter long and 1.5 meters wide. Once they were standing beside each other, the Kerianite thought about his destination and the plate read his mind. A couple seconds later, the plate was zipping over the street at 50 kph. Minutes later, the pair was walking into a light grey building that had no door or windows. The men entered it like they had walked through the stone wall at the surface.

Inside the building, the wall facing the street became transparent. The floor was the same shade of grey as the building and reflected the soft lighting emitted by the ceiling. A stunning black-haired beauty sat behind a computer screen that was connected to the floor by a thin curved metal bar. Two arms of her chair that were as wide as her elbows where they were joined to the back cushion of the chair spread out to 30 centimeters where she rested her hands. She wore a tight shiney red jumpsuit that showed off her curves well without being too revealing.

She looked at the men and asked, "May I help you?"

"This man is here to see the committee. He is the one we have been waiting for for so long," said the Kerianite with a degree of urgency.

"Go in," she said after she touched the arm rest with her right index finger.

The men walked through the wall and stood in front of five chairs against the wall and a chair between them and the other chairs. It was dark inside the room except for the lights that were shining down upon the chairs. Seconds later, the committee members and the mediator appeared seated before them. A light from the ceiling beamed down upon the pair.

"Gentlemen, this is the one we have been waiting for since the committee was instituted," said the Kerianite.

"Are you willing to be questioned?" asked the committee head who was sitting in the center chair.

"Sure. Go ahead. I have nothing to hide," Vladimer said confidently.

"I know you never expected to be talking with a living… Martian. I can tell by your thoughts our appearance is different from what you thought we would look like. Little green men? Really?" asked the committee member at the far left.

"I'm sorry," Vladimer apologized.

"Don't be sorry. We're just curious why your people would think of us that way. We've seen your electronic media portray us as a race of small green people and have no idea how your people got the impression that we could look like that. Personally, I think we look more like American aboriginals and Asian races. Only the males lose their hair by the time they are adults. That could be because an alien race known as the Ortasians came here and to your planet over 40,000 years ago. They interbred with our peoples and then, for some reason, left to go back to their home planet.

But we aren't here to talk about history. We need to find out if you would be an appropriate representative on behalf of your people."

"I…don't know. We have a president, President Kursolov, who really should be talking with you. Why me?"

"For one thing, your ancestors, most likely one set of great- great-great-great grandparents, genetically gave you the genetic markers that alerted us to your presense on the planet. Besides.

Your president supports violence if it helps him achieve his goals. I can tell by your thoughts that you are a man of peace," said the man who sat to the right of him.

"You can read my mind?"

"Of course. We aren't actually speaking Russian. You perceive our words as sounding like Russian. To make sure your words match what you are thinking, the mediator breaks down any mental barriers you might have to conceal your true thoughts and intentions."

"Do you know about the American and Chinese bases? Do they have any people who had Martian ancestors?"

"No," said the committee member to the right of the committee head. "We sent microsensors to both bases when their people landed and none of the people had genetic markers."

"Why is that important?"

"We can trust someone more who has Kerianite ancestors than someone who doesn't," said the committee head. "Call it empathy. Call it what you want. Your ancestors evidently were accepted by the people they lived around. Since that is the case. It is the case, isn't it?"

"My great-grandmother used to talk about great-great-great- great grandmother and grandfather Irena and Sasha who lived east of the Ural Mountains. She thought it was strange that they had no baptismal certificates that the Russian Orthodox Church often issued. But the government was anti-God for so long that it was no big deal to her. There were no census records either. She thought maybe the records were lost. Now I know why they weren't counted since they weren't on Earth until 1887."

"How do you feel about having ancestors from this planet?" asked the committee member on the far right.

"I remember when I was a child in Kazan watching a program titled 'Ancient Aliens.' It came from America. When it dealt with people coming from Mars to Earth, I sometimes wondered if my ancestors might have come from here. I didn't know why back then. Now I know. If you consider me an ambassador of Earth suited to make any treaty between your planet and mine, I accept your proposition. I just hope the governments of my planet will accept me as an ambassador in good standing. But I think when they find out there are people living here and there has been for millions of years, they will want to send their own people up here to make agreements with your people. Are you willing to let that happen?" "Are you married?" asked the committee member to the left of the committee head. "No. Why?"

"Would you like to be married?" he asked.

"I've had a lot of girlfriends. But I couldn't commit to any of them to be their husband. For the last few years I never gave it much thought. Is it important?"

"If you married a woman like the mediator, she could determine who is appropriate to make treaties between our peoples," said the committee head. "She could be with you reading the minds of the representatives of the various governments because I know they will feel obligated to come to you first before appearing before this committee."

"If they knew she was a full-blooded Martian, wouldn't they want to deal with just her?"

"We know that some nations of your world have female leaders of their governments. On Kerian, we have had a long tradition of male leadership. Our female population is more compliant to our traditions and do not seek to overthrow the status quo. If you marry a Kerianite, she will be compliant to your desires up to a point. If you were to attempt to rape her, she will fight you and could injure you. Sexual purity is taught to Kerianites from an early age. We aren't promiscuous like many of your people are. We enjoy sex like your people do. But fidelity is important. A female, once joined to a male, will not have relations with another male. A male will not have relations with another female either. It is a means of controlling the population. Also, females only give birth to no more than four children; two males and two females. That also controls our population."

"Living underground doesn't leave you much choice either." "Since the war, couples have limited themselves to no more than two children. If for some reason the surface became habitable again, we might rebuild our surface communities and our people might have larger families. But until that time, we will do what we feel is best."

"You know, being married to someone who looks as fine as the receptionist outside this room or the mediator wouldn't be all that bad. Would I be allowed to go back home with her to show her off to my parents and my other relatives?"

"Of course. If we expect appropriate people to deal with us, she will have to be by your side to determine their suitability. Would you object to having us present some females that you might want to marry?"

"This is so fast that my head is spinning. An hour ago I was excited about the archeological find at the surface I was about to examine and now I'm thinking about marrying a Martian. If I didn't know this was real I would think I was dreaming."

"I know you are familiar with the technology that allows you to experience simulations of reality. We have such technology that can allow you to experience various females to determine which one is most desirable to you."

"That's a relief. I thought you might present them naked to me to see which one aroused me the most."

"That can be done," said the man on the far left.

"No, that won't be necessary. My mother taught me to respect women and choosing someone because they make you horny is not how one should choose their mate for life."

"Your mother is a wise woman," said the committee head. "Our representative who came here with you will take you to the electronic simulation gallery for you to experience various available females in various situations and settings. If you discover one who is compatable with you, the marriage ceremony can be performed after you two physically meet."

"Will the women also be experiencing the simulations while I experience them?"

"Yes. There is a mating service which has a contract with 15 available females that are willing to marry you to serve this committee."

"It almost sounds like an arranged marriage." "It will be. Are you offended?"

"I don't know. It might be fun."

"Consider it serving your people and our people for the greater good of both planets. You may leave now and have some fun, if you want to consider it being that."

The committee members and the mediator vanished and Vladimer and his host left the room to walk to the gallery. That building was 100 meters away near a busy area where people were shopping. As they entered the light brown building through the wall, Vladimer wasn't surprised to see almost all the simulation chambers occupied. The pair approached the counter where another beautiful black-haired woman dressed in glistening blue from the neck to the tip of her toes was seated. Behind her was a panel with 185 out of 200 lights lit. In front of her was a counter that was around three meters wide that had 200 small screens on it. "May I help you?" she asked the men as they stepped up to the counter.

"Yes you can," said the Kerianite. "This is the one we have been waiting for from Vorion. He has been convinced by the committee that he needs to be married to a mediator. Are any of them in a simulation anywhere?"

"Four of them are in simulations in this gallery, two are in Vavanese, three are in Norgun, one is in Calofrene, two are in Noganese, one is in Chrevu, one is in Mornganstene, and the last one is in Hovas Tortenus. Most are at their jobs while a few are in recreational simulations. Does it matter who you meet at the start?" she asked Vladimer.

"I don't want to interrupt any of them while they are busy. Just put me into one of the simulations where I can be integrated easily into the program. I don't want to be anyone special because that might make the women act out of character to impress me. So just slip me into one of the simulations which will allow me to meet the first one naturally."

"One is in this gallery. I'll integrate you into the simulation she is experiencing. Go to an empty chamber and lie down in it. Once the lid closes, you'll be in the simulation within seconds. I hope you can find the right woman today."

"Same here," Vladimer said with some uncertainty.

Vladimer walked to one of the empty chambers and laid down in it. He took a deep breath, let it out, and waited for the lid to close. He had no idea what to expect since he didn't choose the simulation he was going to experience.

CHAPTER 20

Vladimer found himself in a simulation of life in a huge city with stratotowers, moving sidewalks, levitated vehicles, and the sky crowded with aircraft of various sizes and configurations. The suns were shining brightly with one about to set as the other was coming up over slick black buildings.

Vladimer was coming up to a restaurant which had an outdoor dining area with tables large enough for couples. Most of the tables were fully occupied except for one where a stunning black-haired beauty was sitting reading an electronic book as she sipped a dark drink in a tall glass. He stepped off of the sidewalk next to the table. "Is that all you could afford or are you waiting for someone?"

Vladimer asked.

The woman looked up at him and said, "I enjoy their sparkling crem de cocoa negra. Would you like one?"

"Sure. May I sit down?"

She nodded yes. Vladimer sat as a hologram of a waiter appeared. "May I get you something to drink or eat?" the projection asked. "I'll have what she is drinking. Oh, and I hope you make bacon cheeseburgers here. I haven't had one since I left Earth." "How would you like your burger cooked?"

"Well-done"

The projection vanished. The woman gave Vladimer a puzzled stare. "You're from Earth?"

"Yes. I'm from Russia. I came to Mars awhile back to find some answers. One I wasn't expecting was where my great-great-great- great-grandparents came from."

"Are you saying you're the one we have been waiting for?" she asked excitedly.

"That's what they keep telling me. Why is having ancestors from Mars so important? And don't give me that we can only trust someone with Martian ancestory garbage."

"Garbage? You are privileged to have Kerianite ancestors. Why would you say that?"

"I wanted to see your reaction. Actually, I think it's kind of great knowing my ancestors came from Mars. I've heard some stories about my great-great-great-great-grandparents. They were salt- of-the-earth people that lived off the land. He used to hunt for food and furs while his wife tended the garden and hunted for mushrooms. She also painted and sold some of her works. Her husband made more money selling furs though. They didn't have many children; only four. But they all survived childhood to live long lives just like their parents."

"Kerianites often live to be 150. How long did your ancestors live?"

"My Martian ancestors lived until 1970. Since there's no birth records of either one, no one knows how old they were when they died. But great-great-great-grandmother Olga lived from 1890 until 2001. I wish I could have met her. She could have told me about her parents."

"I'm curious. How is living on Vorion compared to living on Kerian?"

"I call it Earth. But I should have figured a person living all their life on a planet they call Kerian and not Mars would have another name for my home planet. At least we can go outside and see the sun. The sky is blue and not redish. We also have plenty of water outside. Yours is mainly underground. There are also over 9 billion people on my planet. But in some places in Siberia you can travel for over an hour and not see another soul."

The bacon cheeseburger and glass of a sparkling dark chocolate beverage appeared on the table in front of Vladimer. After the first bite he smiled and took a sip of his beverage.

"This reminds me of what someone in New York City might have; a bacon cheeseburger and a Yoo Hoo. They probably don't have cows on Mars."

"Never have. I've never tasted meat. Could I try it?"

"I don't know if your digestive system can digest hamburger. Wait a minute. How would they know about hamburgers on an alien world? Do they have cows?"

"In simulations, the program takes from your memory what it needs to construct a believable experience. It tastes like it should because that is how you remember it all tasting like. If you reach into your pants pocket you will find something to hold money. Your meal will cost what you expect it to cost."

"About 200 rubles."

Vladimer reached into his hip pocket and pulled out a billfold. He found 20,000 rubles in currency and 5,000 rubles of gold and platinum coins.

"It looks like I can afford this meal. Would it be all right if I paid for your drink?"

Suddenly, a salad and a piece of pie appeared in front of her. "Will you pay for this too?"

"Of course. It looks like we're going to be here for awhile."

For the next half hour, Vladimer and the woman talked about themselves and had a pleasant meal. He offered to take her shopping, but she told him maybe later if she was the one he chose to marry. But they hit it off real well. He made sure before he left the simulation he learned her name and how to contact her later.

Vladimer left the simulation and the chamber and walked back to the counter to enter another simulation. Around 45 minutes passed for Vladimer in the simulation, but only 15 minutes had transpired.

When he returned to the counter, his host wasn't there. "Is he experiencing a simulation?"

"Yes he is. Are you ready to experience another simulation?"

"Yes. By the way, do these simulations cost me anything to experience?"

"In your case, no. You're—'

"The one you've been waiting for. Yeah, yeah. I feel kind of pressured. It's as if the survival of Mars relies on me."

"There are three bases on the surface of this planet and if they are linked by an underground transportation system, one or more of the bases will discover our cities. We've seen what happens to people your people consider a hinderance to progress on our electronic media systems. We do indeed depend on you succeeding to help us survive. We don't want to be treated like the American aboriginals were treated over 150 years ago."

"So I guess the sooner I get married, the sooner I can start the job of saving the Martian race."

"I can integrate you into another simulation being experienced by another woman in another city. I have access to all the galleries." "I'll go back to the chamber I left when you tell me you have a simulation ready for me to enter."

The woman pushed some buttons and seconds later she said there was a simulation available for integration. Vladimer walkwd back to the chamber he left and entered it. Seconds later, Vladimer found himself on a battlefield with soldiers in fighting suits. The commander was standing in front of his troops as planes were fighting it out above them.

"The enemy troops are in the mountains waiting to engage us in battle. Their fighter droids are going up against ours as you see. Once their droids are destroyed, ours will join us in the mountains. Ready to join our droids?"

Everyone gave a shout and pumped their mechanical arms in agreement. The commander turned and ran toward the enemy and the other troops followed him. On the lower part of the heads-up display, the woman Vladimer was supposed to meet was seen.

"Who are you, soldier?" she asked. "Vladimer. I'm from Earth."

"Earth? How did you get in this simulation?"

"I'm the one your people have been waiting for. My ancestors came from Mars. So you're stuck with me whether you like it or not."

"Are you a trained soldier or just a wannabe?"

"I've flown fighter planes and fired a rifle on the practice range. I'm considered a marksman."

"Have you fought with a suit on?"

"No. But how tough can it be? You point the weapons at the enemy and fire. I see this suit can fly."

"Don't do it unless we all do it. I've seen some soldiers who thought they were hot stuff, as you Vorionites say, get shot down because they made themselves targets. So stay grounded until you're told to go up."

The enemy droids were fairly easy to destroy. You first cut off their legs and when they were down on the ground you blasted them with your weapons. The attack strategy was called slash and smash. After the battlefield was littered with mangled droids, the troops were ready to assault the enemy in the mountains.

When they neared the mountain trails that led up to the caves, the enemy fired upon them with ray weapons and missiles. Vladimer and the others returned fire. But Vladimer didn't want to fire directly at the enemy troops in the caves. He fired at overhanging rocks above the cave entrances and blocked the caves with boulders that prevented the enemy troops from firing at the troops he was with. Once the caves were blocked up, Vladimer and the others flew toward the caves to finish off the enemy.

"Whoever you are, follow me to the top," said Vladimer. "I have a feeling the enemy is waiting for us to spend our time on the caves and not the ones that might be over the top."

Vladimer and the woman flew above the mountain and confirmed his fear. Enemy droids that were the size of rhinos that had four legs and four arms that had ray and projectile weapons instead of hands were climbing the mountain and nearly at the summit. The pair began firing upon the droids that tumbled backward down the mountain.

The other droids concentrated their fire upon the pair that dropped to the summit behind some boulders to make themselves harder targets to hit. Enemy planes were seen in the distance coming toward the mountain.

"I'll take on the planes and you take on the droids," Vladimer told the woman.

He was joined in the air by three of his comrades while the others joined the woman to fight the droids that were ascending the mountain. The planes had intended on hitting ground targets. But now they had to contend with Vladimer and the other three who were wearing fighting suits.

Vladimer shot straight up to draw fire away from the other three who were able to blast away at the planes they took on. A pair of fighters went up to take Vladimer on. They fired their missiles and ray weapons at the Russian, but he had seen the Ironman movies and maneuvered his suit as if it were a fighter plane. His feet and legs determined his speed, direction, and altitude. He performed like a gymnast as he flipped and rolled as he fired at the enemy. The first pair that took him on were easily destroyed as were the second pair. His franetic fighting style confused the enemy so much that two of the planes accidentally fired upon each other while another plane collided with another plane and exploded. The planes that remained fled the scene.

After the droids on the mountain were destroyed, Vladimer and the other three with him descended to the summit of the mountain. None of the troops had been killed, but three of the suits were a bit damaged. This included the commander's suit that had the left arm sliced off.

"People, I'm proud of you. This battle went better than I expected. All we have left to do is finish the assault on the caves," said the commander. His image came upon Vladimer's heads-up display. "Nice job, whoever you are. Do you have any suggestions on how to assault the caves?"

"Bury the enemy. Tear open the top of this mountain and collapse the caves. Make sure this mountain becomes a mass grave."

"I like it. Okay people, lets do it."

The troops flew about 100 meters above the mountain and bombarded it with ray fire and projectiles that tore open the mountain down to the caves. The enemy troops inside weren't wearing fighting suits and were easily killed even though they used potent weapons against Vladimer and the others. But eventually the enemy was totally defeated and the troops flew back to the base which was a couple kilometers behind where Vladimer had joined them.

The image of the woman appeared on Vladimer's heads-up display as they flew back to the base.

"I guess you knew what you were doing," she told him. "Could you tell me who you are?"

"I'm Sharinda. You said you are the one we have been waiting for." "That's what they tell me. It's kind of strange meeting someone I might marry on the battlefield. Do you enjoy this type of simulations?"

"Very much. Does that disqualify me as a prospective bride?" "Not at all. I think it's great. I enjoy battle simulations too. But I've got a bunch of other women to meet. By the way. What will we be doing when we get back to the base?"

"I don't know. I usually go into another simulation when I get back to the bases in the programs. I'm going to fight out in space after this simulation. Want to join me?"

"I'll have to pass on that. I've got more women to meet. But I'll keep you in mind."

"I'd be honored to be your wife."

Vladimer left the simulation and the chamber to approach the woman at the counter again.

"Did you enjoy yourself in the simulation?" she asked.

"Very much. I could really go for a woman like Sharinda. She was into war games like I am."

"Should I bring her here for the ceremony?" "Not right now. By the way. Are you available?"

"Oh no. I've been joined to my mate for years and we're very happy together."

"Joined to your mate. I assume that is the same as being married.

But it has to be different here on Mars."

"When two people are joined, a minister of physical conjunction administers an implant into the arm of each participant which joins both people in a psychic and mental conjunction. The implants go to the brains to permanently bond the partners. Only the death of one of the partners can break the bond."

"So once married always married."

"That's pretty much it. I have no interest in any other man and my partner is only interested in me."

"So if I tried to have sex with you—"

"I'd hurt you. No offense. You're an attractive man, for a Vorionite. But the implants are too powerful. I wouldn't think of having sexual relations with another man."

"So if my wife turns out to be a bitch I have no choice but to kill her in order to leave her," he said sarcastically.

"Are all Vorionites as sarcastic as you?"

"Thank goodness no. Back on earth the wedding vows state until death parts you. Here on Mars it's taken litterally. Do you love your partner?"

"Yes I do. He would do anything for me and I would do anything for him, within reason."

"I guess I better choose wisely since I'll be stuck with her for the rest of my life."

"Pretty much. But the moment you are bonded to your partner, you will be totally devoted to her and she will be totally devoted to you."

"That's good to know because you Martian women look fantastic. I mean supermodel gorgeous. Are all Martian women as beautiful as you and the others I've seen?"

"I guess so. I never really noticed."

"So I should only worry about men wanting to kill me so they can have my wife."

"That's an advantage to being mentally and psychically bonded. If someone were to try and have sexual relations with either one of you, both of you will know it. Heightened emotions are easier to read. It's almost like the person is shouting at you. I hope you aren't the jealous type."

"If I know she's going to deck someone if they get fresh with her, why should I be jealous? What if I were into pornography and like looking at pictures and videos of naked women? Will being joined to my partner change all that?"

"Interesting that you should say that. Kerianite men and women can sexually stimulate a member of the opposite sex more intensely than Vorionite men and women can. But we are physically incapable of having consummation unless we are joined. That means you could have sex with a Kerianite woman and she won't become pregnant." "Do you have any sexually explicit simulations I could experience to see for myself if a Martian woman really can stimulate me more than a woman from Earth can?"

"Not in this gallery. You would have to go to another gallery that is down the street from here. But none of the women you want to meet are there. So you would be better off staying here. Are you ready to experience another simulation?"

"Sure."

Vladimer headed back to the chamber as the woman pushed some buttons. By the time he got back, the woman was ready to integrate him into another simulation.

He found himself walking into a concert hall with a ticket in his hand. His seat was in the orchestra section of the theater. After excusing himself as he made his way to his seat, he found a gorgeous woman wearing a black evening gown sitting to the left of him. She was reading her program when he sat down. The performers were warming up on many instruments he had never seen before.

"Hi," he said politely. "Is the orchestra good?"

She gave him a strange look and said, "They are some of the finest instrumentalists in this simulation. I've never seen you here before."

"That's because I'm from Earth."

"Earth? Oh, you mean Vorion. How did you get in here?" "They say I'm the one they've been waiting for. I don't feel all that specal. But if they say I am, I guess I am. Are you interested in getting joined today?"

"Can that wait until after the concert? They're going to play one of my favorite symphonies"

"Actually, I have a few more women I need to meet. But I have time for a concert. I hope I enjoy the music."

"I think you will."

The conductor walked out onto the stage amidst applause and stepped upon the podium. He raised his hands and started the concert. The music sounded like technopop music from late 20th century Earth. It made him tap his feet, but he didn't feel like dancing.

After the last note was played, the woman Vladimer was sitting beside stood and applauded while he sat in his seat and clapped politely. She looked down at him and glared at him. He left the concert hall as soon as he could and entered another simulation.

In the next simulation, Vladimer found himself walking down a shopping boulevard where people were window shopping. He pulled out his billfold and found it stuffed with high denomination rubles. He came upon a gorgeous woman dressed from her neck to her toes in red. She was staring at a fur coat in the window. He had a feeling that she wanted someone who could buy her affection, so he walked past her and out of the simulation.

In the fifth simulation, Vladimer found himself walking down a forest trail toward a cabin that was beside a peaceful lake. It was early afternoon in the simulation and sunny. He stepped upon the front porch and knocked on the door. It was opened by another gorgeous woman with large breasts who was wearing just a white apron. He couldn't help but stare at her breasts.

"May I help you?" she asked.

"Uh, yeah. Forgive me for staring at you."

"Usually I'm naked. But I was baking some cookies and didn't want to burn myself if I bumped into the trays. Come in."

Vladimer entered the cabin and saw a couple dozen cookies cooling on a white cloth on the table. They smelled delicious. The woman walked over to the stove where a tea kettle was whistling. He smiled as he gazed upon her shapely butt and dancer's legs.

"I was brewing some tea I made from berries I gathered the other day. I dried and crushed them and mixed them with tea leaves. Would you like some?"

"Sure. I like my tea sweet."

"I have some honey in the cupboard."

She placed two tea cups on saucers and spooned out some honey into both cups before pouring the tea. She set one cup and saucer in front of Vladimer as he sampled a cookie. He shook his head and smiled.

"Great cookies. Do you bake these things all the time?" "Sometimes I bake cakes or pies when I'm here in the cabin.

Most of the time I read, or fish, or gather nuts and berries, or play the keyboard in the living room. After I finish my tea I will remove this apron and take a swim in the lake. Would you like to join me?"

"Sure," he said excitedly.

"By the way you're looking at me, I sort of expected you did." "I hope I don't offend you."

"Hey, I spent years working out at the gym and helping others develop their bodies. Your staring proves I wasn't wasting my effort." "I thought that Martian women were sort of prudish. At least I was led to believe that."

"If you tried to have your way with me I'd have to deck you. By the way. Who are you?"

"My name is Vladimer Premakoff. I'm from Earth. My great- great-great-great-grandparents came from Mars. The committee said—"

"You met the committee?"

"Yeah. They advised me to get married so I would have a mediator as my wife to read the minds of those who want to deal with your people."

"Makes a lot of sense. I've seen TV shows transmitted from your planet and your people lie a lot. I trust you're not a liar, are you?"

"If I told you I'd give up pornography if I could marry you, would you believe me?"

"No. But that is because we aren't joined as partners yet. The implant will change you."

"If I have to spend the rest of my life looking at you, I wouldn't complain."

"That is the truth."

"This is a beautiful location. It definitely doesn't look like Mars." "It's supposed to be a place called Canada. Do you know of it?" "Yes. It is almost like Russia in some areas. Do you have bears in your simulation?"

"No way. They're dangerous and I hate guns. Deer are about the only dangerous animals I have in the simulation and they sometimes eat out of my hand."

"Beside not having bears, you got the location down pretty good. I could spend all day here with you. But I have a couple more women to check out yet."

"Do you have time for a swim?"

He thought for a moment before saying yes. They spent the next hour eating cookies, drinking tea, talking, and swimming naked in the lake. Vladimer caressed her body and kissed her a few times without being slugged. He respected her too much to go any further. There would be plenty of time for that if they became partners.

Before leaving the simulation, he hugged her and gave her a long kiss which proved that Martian women could stimulate a man better than Earth women could.

In the sixth simulation, Vladimer found himself in a temple that reminded him of a Christian cathedral. There was a minister speaking from a pulpit a lively message that excited the congregation. He sat in a pew toward the back of the sanctuary beside a gorgeous woman who was wearing a long blue jumpsuit that was covered by a black jacket. He could see she was listening intently and didn't speak to her. He feared she might be too religous for him, so he left without saying a word to her.

In the seventh simulation, Vladimer found himself in a military camp that reminded him of medievel times. He was wearing a full suit of armor and had a sturdy broadsword in a sheath on his left hip. Knights in full suits of armor were walking around or riding horses. Most men were dressed in leather and had swords by their sides. Vladimer walked into a tent with two guards wearing armor standing at attention with pikes in their hands outside. They let Vladimer enter without challenging him.

Inside the tent was a bearded commander who was wearing a suit of armor except for the helmet talking to other armored knights. They were studying a map and discussing a strategy.

"The king is offering a chest of gold and jewels for her return. But the bastard usurper has surrounded his castle with hundreds of his best knights and on the castle walls are nearly a hundred deadly archers," said the commander.

The commander looked up from the map and said to Vladimer, "We've been waiting a long time for you. Do you have any ideas on how to rescue the princess"

"Is this simulation set in its period or is it a freestyle program?" The men stared at each other for a moment before the commander said, "You speak strange words. Who are you and where do you come from?"

"I'm Vladimer Premakoff. I'm from Earth. I guess the princess is the one experiencing this simulation as the person in control."

"She is being held prisoner in a high tower of the castle we need to attack. I would say that is far from being in control."

"For a simulation, this is pretty elaborate. It's as if I'm back in time about six or seven centuries."

"Again with the strange words," the commander protested. "Our situation is life or death. Why do you jest?"

"Hey, I'd like to rescue her like all of you would like to do. But I need to know the rules."

"The rules?"

"Can I chuck all this heavy steel and step into a fighting suit with ray and projectile weapons?"

"You're wearing the suit you will fight in. Are you afraid to face our enemies?" the commander asked as an accusation.

"This is a simulation. If I die in battle, I'll just be pulled out of the simulation. No big deal. But if I can advance the technology a few centuries, I could handle the bastard usurper as you call him all by myself as a one-man army."

The men looked at each other and laughed. To see if he could have what he wanted, he stretched out his right hand and seconds later had a power ray pistol in his grasp. The men gasped in amazement.

"You are a powerful wizard," said the commander.

"If you think that's something, watch what I do to your fire in the middle of the tent."

Vladimer aimed his weapon at the wood in the fire pot and nearly melted the pot when his plasma beam vaporized the wood. The men were visibly shaken by the demonstration.

"Are you a god?" the commander asked, shaking nervously. "You might say that. I'm a guy who knows how to work these simulations if they're freestyle programs in which anything goes." "Then lead us to victory, sir. If you can conjure miracle weapons like the one in your hand, we can not be defeated." "Let me see if the simulation will cooperate."

Vladimer stepped outside and awaiting him was a two and a half meter tall fighting suit similar to the one he wore in the second simultion. He was glad he had remembered it. His sword and suit of armor vanished. He opened the back of the fighting suit and stepped inside. He was ready to make his enemies think he was a wrathful god.

He flew up to 100 meters as horses reared in fear and threw their riders to the ground. Men scattered in fear. Field displacement allowed him to soar over the field silently. The fear and confusion below caused Vladimer to chuckle.

A couple kilometers away was the castle where the princess was being held prisoner. He flew swiftly toward his objective and within a minute was slashing knights in half and clearing the ramparts of archers who tried to shoot him out of the sky. But the arrows that reached him bounced off the suit harmlessly.

Out of the window of the tower came shouts of joy. Moments later, a beautiful woman wearing a gold gown waved at Vladimer who flew to her. He reached out his arms and she let him hold her as he carried her back to the camp.

"Thank-you for rescuing me. You are indeed the one we have been waiting for. I can help you rule your world as the partner of a powerful god."

"Are you serious?"

"Very. Anyone who can imagine an indestuctable suit that can fly must possess wonders and wealth few can imagine."

Vladimer realized she was more of a dreamer of fantasies than someone he would feel comfortable marrying. He set her down on the ground when he returned to camp amidst shouts of joy and took off to get as far away as possible. He left the simulation soon afterwards and went back to the counter.

"I've made up my mind. I'd like to become the partner of the woman in the fifth simulation. How soon can she get here?"

"That was Lonayha Muns. She lives in Calofrene. Once she is contacted, it will take about half an hour to get her here. While you're waiting, you can enjoy more simulations. We have a wide selection for people with various interests and abilities. Would you like to experience any?"

"No. I'm kind of tired. Is there anywhere I can take a nap for half an hour?"

"You can go back to the chamber and I won't give you any simulation to experience."

"Thanks. Wake me when she arrives along with the guy who will perform the ceremony."

"I'll do that. And congratulation for making your choice. You two are fortunate you found each other."

"The big thing that sold me were her cookies. They were fantastic. I'm sure she'll bake thousands of batches of them for me for years to come." Vladimer walked back to the chamber and took a nap for over half an hour and had a nice dream about his future bride walking hand-in-hand through the woods; not naked, but wearing hiking clothes. The deer would come up to the couple and Lonayha would reach into her backpack and pull out a loaf of bread she would feed them. Vladimer was able to pet the animals and they wouldn't flinch.

"We're ready," the counter woman said as she stood over the chamber.

Vladimer left the chamber and walked over to the counter where Lanayha, the counter woman, and a minister of physical conjunction stood. He was relieved to see his bride fully clothed in a white gown that was like a traditional wedding gown he was familiar with. The minister was dressed in black like a minister in a church on Earth. He wasn't holding a Bible. Instead, it was a golden box in his hands. "Are both of you ready to be joined?" the minister asked.

They both said yes. The minister placed the box on the counter, opened it, and removed something that looked like a tube of lipstick. "As is our tradition, any couple that desires to be bonded mentally and psychically must be injected with implants that will integrate their lives in a physical conjunction which can not be broken except during the death of one or both partners. Such a partnership must not be entered into casually. Are you sure beyond all doubt that you are willing to be conjoined to one another?"

"I am," said Vladimer. "This is one of the best decisions I have ever made."

"I have wanted to be joined to a man who respected me all of my life. I wish my parents were here to see me being joined—"

"We weren't going to miss this blessed occasion for anything," said a man who entered the room with a beautiful woman who didn't look much older than Lonayha. They hugged and kissed their daughter and cried for joy. They also thanked the counter woman for alerting them to the upcoming blessed event.

The minister opened the end of the implantation device and placed it against Vladimer's right arm. He pushed the back of the device and for a few seconds, Vladimer felt a tingle coming from his arm. The minister did the same thing to Lonayha and a few seconds later placed the device back in its box and closed the top. "I've been joined to my partner for over a century and I thank the Creator of the universe for such a joyous relationship," said the minister. "I have a feeling you two, even though one of you is a Vorionite and the other is a Kerianite, will have a long and happy relationship. Trust me."

"Thank-you, sir," said Vladimer. "Do I owe you anything for the ceremony?"

"You owe me nothing. Seeing how you're the one we have been waiting for since before my parents were born, it is my honor to administer the implants. You two will have to be registered at the Office of Conjunctive Partnership before you can be recognized as a couple by the government. They're the ones that will require payment for the service."

Slight panic struck Vladimer. But the minister pressed a couple coins into Vladimer's hand.

"That should cover the cost of registration with enough left over for the traditional conjunction meal which is served at the government facilities. The office is just down the street. It's the tallest building in Janvuor. The office is on the third floor and the meal is served on the second floor. Since I know you can't read Kerianite, your partner will help you."

"I don't know how I'm going to explain what has happened to me when I get back to Mars Base Gagarin with my new wife."

"Tell them the truth no matter if they believe you or not. We're counting on you to create a successful parnership between Kerian and Vorion. May the Creator of the universe bless and guide you forever."

The minister shook the hands of Vladimer and Lonayha, her parents, and the counter woman. It was too bad Vladimer's host had missed the ceremony. He had left the gallery while Vladimer was taking his nap. But he left a video message before leaving which the happy couple and her parents viewed before going to the registration office. The counter woman projected the full-body image of the man in front of the counter.

"Congratulation, brother. I'm sure the woman you chose to be your partner will give you years of happiness and at least two healthy children that will make you two proud of their accomplishments. I hope and pray our two planets will become good partners. It's going to be quite a shock to your people that we have always been here. Another shock will be that we look so much alike. The Creator of this world and its people is the same Creator of your world and its people. I hope and pray we can have a bright and successful future together. We're counting on you. May your descendants consider themselves fortunate that you two were their ancestors."

After his image disappeared, Vladimer, Lonayha, and her parents left the gallery and took levitated plates to the registration office where the new partners registered to be considered conjunctive partners. After paying the fee and getting change, the quartet went down one floor to enjoy the meal of replicated food and beverages. Instead of a traditional wedding cake Vladimer was used to, there was a sweet pastry given to the couple. They held onto the pastry that was 20 centimeters long and started eating at each end toward one another. When they finished the pastry they kissed.

The parents and onlookers applauded. The couple were given a sparkling clear beverage that had the kick of champagne in fluted glasses that they drank quickly. They kissed again as everyone applauded.

The quartet ate multi-layered meat dishes, fruits, nuts, and a crunchy sweet dessert that had a caramel center and a fruity frosting that reminded Vladimer of strawberries. The people got along so well that Vladimer felt sorry to see Lonayha's parents leave.

How was Vladimer and Lonayha going to travel to Mars Base Gagarin? Janvuor was close to the base. But the wind storm was still raging and they had no means of transportation to use to get there. The American base, Bradbury Station, was within 100 meters of Reevane's access to the surface. There would be a lot of explaining to do. But if the couple wanted to go to Mars Base Gagarin safely, they would need the help of Americans.

CHAPTER 21

Before going to Reevane via the tube system, the couple traveled to Calofrene to the house Lonayha had shared with two old women who were widows who couldn't afford to stay by themselves. Their government pensions helped pay the rent. But the income Lonayha made from her work as a trainer provided food, money for entertainment, and emergency money. It also helped that the young woman owned the house and wouldn't have thrown the women out if they couldn't pay her the rent they owed her. They were more like great-grandmothers to Lonayha.

As Vladimer and Lonayha entered the house, the elderly women were in the living room watching TV and drinking tea. It was a Martian drama similar to an afternoon drama viewed on American TV. Since the actors weren't communicating telepathically, Vladimer couldn't understand a word they were saying.

The pair put their tea cups down on saucers on the coffee table between them and looked thrilled to see Lonayha. Their hair was silver and their faces were tight; not wrinkled. They smiled as they looked up at the couple and recognized the wedding garment Lonayha was wearing.

"Congratulation you two," said one of the women. "We know you were waiting to be joined to… You're the one we have been waiting for, aren't you?"

"That's what they keep telling me. My great-great-great-great-grandparents came from Mars and settled in Russia."

"I knew you looked familiar," said the other woman. "You almost look like Dronon after he had his appearance changed to look more like a Vorionite."

"Did he also change his name to Sasha before he left?" Vladimer asked.

"Yes, yes," said the woman. "And his partner changed her name from Sushia to Irena. If he hadn't had his heart set on making a new life for himself on Vorion and hadn't met his partner who also wanted to go there, he might have been joined to me."

"You mean to me," the other woman protested.

"He wanted me more than he wanted you," the first woman replied.

"Ladies, if he didn't do what he did, I wouldn't be standing before you right now," Vladimr reminded them.

"Why don't you two sit down on the couch?" suggested the first woman. They complied.

"We are so proud of our little Lonayha. She has been like a great-granddaughter to us for…how many years now?" asked the second woman.

"Fifteen," said Lonayha. "I guess now you two are going to own the place and won't need to pay me any more rent."

Suddenly, the projection of a man appeared between the quartet and the TV.

"I have come to tell you two women that your housemate has been joined to the one we have been waiting for. From now on, you two will each receive an extra 10,000 units of currency each year until both of you die. I am honored to give you this information. Expect to see it added to your accounts immediately. Since she will be with her partner from this day forward, her income will cease to come in to cover living and entertainment expenses. The extra 20,000 units should br more than sufficient to allow you to remain in your dwelling for the rest of your lives. This has been an announcement from the Kerianite government."

The projection disappeared.

Vladimer again didn't understand a word he had said since he wasn't communicating telepathically. But he could tell by the thrilled looks on the faces of the three women that it was good news. "If you two knew my ancestors, how old are you two?" Vladimer asked suspiciously.

"I'm 192 in Vorionite years," said the woman near Vladimer. "And I'm 190," said the other woman.

"So both of you were in love with Sasha. That's quite a coincidence seeing how he was one of many who traveled from Mars to Earth. Do you have any pictures of them before they left Mars?"

One of the women left her recliner and walked over to a book case where plates Vladimer assumed were picture albums were neatly shelved. She rummaged through the plates with something that looked like a level bubble by sliding it in front of the shelf. A projection which revealed the contents of each plate was flashed above the device. She finally found the right plate and pulled it from the shelf. She walked over to the TV and inserted the plate into the front of the set. She walked back to her recliner and picked up the remote from off of the coffee table.

"We have many decades of memories recorded on our plates.

Would you like to see how Kerian looked before the war?" asked the woman who had placed the plate into the set.

"Yeah," said Vladimer.

A few seconds later, on the TV appeared a 3-D presentation of what Mars looked like before the war in 1870. The city of Calofrene was a pleasant looking community similar to ones in desert regions. There were few trees and patches of grass where low-rise buildings dotted the landscape. There was a small stream running through the community which ran to a huge lake. Levitated plates were gliding over the roads as people walked upon the sidewalks. It seemed incredible that there was no evidence of Calofrene in 2040. The war came suddenly and the warning of impending doom came too late for most people of the city. Sirens sounded and people fled for their lives. The last images of the city was of buildings crumbling and trees on fire. That was when the person remembering the disaster escaped to the underground portion of the city. Field barriers were activated and disguised as rock walls like the one Vladimer had penetrated. According to atmospheric monitors, the air temperature was over 2000 degrees celsius. The atmosphere was literally burning away.

The woman skipped many years of memories of friends and relatives until she came upon Dronon. He had no hair on his head just like the men he had seen earlier. He almost looked Chinese. But after he was genetically altered and his appearance was changed, Vladimer stared at him wide-eyed in amazement. He looked so much like him that people might have thought they were brothers. When Dronon talked before he was altered, Valdimer couldn't understand a word he said. But days before he left for Earth, he was with his wife who had also been altered. She was the woman Vladimer knew as Irena and he was the Sasha he had seen in old photographs. He spoke in perfect Russian.

"How old were they back then?" Vladimer asked.

"He had to be 50, maybe 51 Vorion years old. He was a little older than me and Stalia."

"Vangra told me that it was kind of tough learning to live underground without being able to go to the surface," Lonayha said. "We had three choices," said Vangra. "We could learn to live underground, or move away from Kerian as thousands did, or commit suicide by going to the surface without a breathing mask or an environmental suit for the first several years. Radiation killed many people for the first several years while suffocation did it after the radiation levels lowered to safe levels."

"So that's why there is little evidence of people living on the surface," said Vladimer. "The evidence literally melted away. I'm amazed anyone survived the destrution let alone to live over 190 years. I thought you people didn't live beyond 150."

"That's normally the case," said Stalia. "But we think we have lived this long so we could see our little Lonayha find the man she would spend the rest of her life with."

"Don't forget the children," Vangra mentioned. "What?" Lonayha asked in amazement.

"We're not going to live forever except where the Creator of the universe exists. We want to see a little one in the arms of our little one. You two better get busy."

"Ladies, I'll do my part. It's up to her to do her part. We've only been joioned for less than an hour."

"Come back to visit us as often as you can," Stalia insisted. "We're going to be on Earth quite a lot. It won't be like getting in the car and driving back to see you."

Stalia left her recliner and walked to a desk where a computer was located. She pulled out a drawer and picked up something that looked like an old-fashioned flip phone. She handed it to Lonayha. The young woman flipped open the device.

"What is that thing?" Vladimer asked.

"It is called a transdimensional chamber access controller," said Lonayha. "Everyone who intends on leaving Kerian is given such a device.

It is how they can keep in touch with this planet no matter how far away they are. It is part teleportation control and part transdimensional chamber access system."

"We have it set on your area of the house and the teleportation receiver chamber," said Stalia. "We also have it set on the public teleportation receiver chambers of Janvuor, Vavanese, Hovas Tortenus, Reevane, and Druse."

"We'll be going to Reevane after we leave here," said Lonayha. "We won't need to use the tube to get there."

"Is there a device like that for me?" Vladimer asked.

"All you need to do is stand beside her and touch her," Stalia said. "A containment field will be generated around you two."

"Uh, what if a fly were on my shoulder when we teleported?" All three women smiled and began to chuckle.

"What's so funny?" he asked.

"You think you'll turn into part fly like in that silly movie 'The Fly.' Am I right?" asked Lonayha.

"Yeah. So I won't turn into a guy with a giant fly head?"

"If a fly were on your shoulder when we teleport, the fly will still be there when we arrive at our destination," said Lonayha.

"I remember the first time when I saw that movie on TV I laughed so hard that I almost wet my underwear," said Stalia. "Your people think they understand more than they do. I hope your people have seen how silly they were less than a century ago believing that such a thing could happen. They have developed teleportation by now haven't they?"

"I don't know. I heard there are at least a couple places on my planet that might be working on teleportation. One opened up in Siberia after I came to Mars. They call it the Facility. But I heard it started out being called the Russian Madhouse, similar to the Madhouse in Arizona, America. If it's being developed it has to be at those places."

"Are you two in a hurry to leave?" Vangra asked.

"Do you know how the conditions are topside?" Vladimer asked. "I'll check," said Vangra. She clicked the TV controller and changed the channel to one showing Martian weather topside.

It was like watching the weather channel. The storm was still raging near Mars Base Gagarin which, to Vladimer's surprise, was listed as a

Vorionite base as were the American and Chinese bases. At least Vladimer assumed that because the location of the bases were where he knew they were. Their designation was in the Martian language as were the locations of American, Russian, and Chinese landers and robots.

It was evening on Mars and people at the bases were asleep. Vladimer was getting used to the extraordinary becoming commonplace, so when he saw inside Mars Base Gagarin and heard crewmates talking about the new arrivals to the base, he wasn't shocked. He wasn't surprised to hear the voice of Lonayha in his head saying cameras in an adjacent dimension had access to all the Vorionite bases on Kerian. When he heard that his cousin from America, Kate Thurman, was at the base, he was overjoyed. He was disappointed to have the coverage change to inside the American base for several minutes and lastly at the Chinese base for several minutes.

Something occured to him. Maybe his discovery of the surface evidence of Janvuor wasn't coincidental. Maybe he was meant to find it and the man he followed to the underground city of Janvuor was assigned to lure him below because his ancestors had come from Mars and he was supposed to be an ambassador for Earth which was known as Vorion to these people. Seeing his ancestors in 3-D on TV made them seem more real than all the stories his great-grandmother had told him about them.

Since it was getting late, Vladimer suggested to Lonayha that they spend their last night in the underground portion of Mars eating dinner with Stalia and Vangra, talking about things, watching memories, and finally going to bed. Since the portion of the house Lonayha owned was going to follow them everywhere, if he wanted a good meal made by his partner, they could enter her home away from home.

Lonayha's bed was large enough for her. But if Vladimer wanted to sleep with her, one of them was almost certain to fall off. So he agreed to sleep in the recliner which was nearly as comfortable as a bed.

The next morning, Vladimer turned on the TV and turned to the weather channel to see how conditions were topside. The dust storm had moved out of the area and people were having breakfast in all three bases. His pulse quickened when he saw his cousin sitting at a table eating breakfast with her husband and the base commander. What they were eating surprised him. They were eating waffles drenched in syrup. That had never been served at the base before because food was considered only a necessity to keep you alive and not something to be enjoyed. That was more of a reason to return to the base.

He still had to go to the American base with his wife because it was closes to one of the cities. He and his wife ate breakfast, hugged and kissed Stalia and Vangra good-bye, and teleported to Reevane. The public teleportation center wasn't too busy. But there was some exciting news that excited Lonayha which caused her to believe the center would be much busier in the near future.

"Looks like we won't need masks when we leave," she told him. "The Americans with the help of the Chinese are testing their field atmospheric containment system. They finished erecting the field towers yesterday and established the field to keep an atmosphere contained inside of it. It only covers the area between the American and Chinese bases plus some of the areas they are working at. The oxygen level is now at 5% of the atmosphere. But if we wait another hour or so, the level might be 10%."

"We could always hold our breaths when we run to the American base," Vladimer suggested. "Does field containment cover the area we will be entering when we are topside?"

"Yes," she said as she tucked the teleportation control device in her hip pouch.

"To be on the safe side, do you have a mask back at your place and an extra one for me?"

"Yes I do. I have one for me and I can replicate one for you."

"I saw the food replicator in the kitchen beside the stove. Where is the other replicator?"

"In my bedroom. It looks like a closet cabinet with a mirrored door. I use it so often that I forgot to mention what it was when I gave you a tour of my place."

"Speaking of your place. Since you have continual access to it with your controller, does that mean a big hole will be left behind at your house?"

"No. It is being replicated as we stand here. Everything in the house is stored in the household memory system. Even Stalia and Vangra. So if in the future our children want to meet those two dear old ladies and they've been dead for awhile, they'll be able to meet their replicates."

"Are you sure they haven't been dead for awhile already? If a replicate is so much like the real person, wouldn't it be hard to tell each apart?"

"Replicates have memories only up to the time they were replicated. Then again, replicates can eat and interact with people. But there are a few things replicates don't have that people do have. They don't have souls and they don't have auras. Those two old ladies had souls and I could sense their physoelectrical fields. They were very much alive. I just don't know how much longer they will be alive."

"If after they die, will their replicates receive the government money?"

"Yes. But it will be reduced to minimal levels. Eventually the government will own the house and everything in it; even the old ladies. It might be set up as a museum in honor of me being the partner to you since we will be so important in the future for Kerian."

"So there will be replicates of us back there too?"

"Yes. It's just that your replicate won't be as authentic as mine since there is so little information about you stored in memory."

"How could that problem be solved so my replicate will seem authentic?"

"Down the hall after we leave the reception area you will see the door to the replication generation and storage area. You won't be able to read the sign above the door since it will be in Kerianite. But as long as you go down the hall and don't stop until you have reached the door, you'll arrive at your destination."

After leaving the teleportation reception area, Vladimer left his wife after giving her a kiss and walked down the hall to the replication generation and storage area. The door slid open and he entered a small room where a gorgeous woman was seated behind a desk and monitor.

"May I help you? Oh wow! You're the one we have been waiting for."

"You too? Why do you people always call me that?" "Because that is what you are."

"How did you know? It's not like I have a glow around me or angel wings. Oh, that's right. I have hair on my head."

"After you were joined to your partner, you received the implant which enhanced your telepathic abilities. It also allowed regular people like me to read your mind. You really need to go to the Office of Mental Enhancement and Protection to receive more implants which will prevent unauthorized people from reading your mind and allow you to understand the Kerianite language."

"I can't read—"

"I know you can't read our language. After you are finished with the replication process, leave through the exit to your left and walk down the hall to the office. The injections will take no time and you'll be all set."

The door to his left slid open and Vladimer walked into another room that was a bit larger. Another absolutely gorgeous woman was sitting behind a desk and monitor.

"Enter the next room and stand on the platform. Don't try to move when the replication chamber comes up and closes around you. You'll be electronically put to sleep and several minutes later you'll be able to go about your day."

The door slid open and Vladimer entered a room smaller than the reception area. There was a silver platform in front of him with a red arrow pointing away from him. He stepped upon the platform and suddenly, four concave plates ascended from the floor. They closed around him and seconds after being electronically anesthetized, the process of replication began. Minutes later, the plates moved away as Vladimer was electronically stimulated awake. He nearly fell to the platform. But he managed to stay standing.

The door in front of him opened and he entered a small area with two doors. He walked through the left exit and proceeded down the hall to the Office of Mental Enhancement and Protection. A bald man wearing a brilliant white jumpsuit sat behind a counter.

"Yeah, yeah, I know why you're here. Do you want the basic package or the deluxe one?"

"What is the deluxe package?"

"If I were you, I'd go for it since the committee is paying for everything. The deluxe package not only protects your mind from telepathic intrusion and allows you to understand our language completely, you will be able to manipulate most minds, gain wireless connection to most computer systems, and understand the language and communicate in the language of any person you scan the mind of. Synthetics are a bit harder to scan since they have scan protection. But those without protection are fair game. Since your people aren't as advanced technically as my people, most synthetics will be vulnerable to your enhanced mental abilities. I know the Asimov three laws of robotics don't work in the real universe. You'll be able to prove me right because with the deluxe package, you'll be able to turn a normally peaceful service synthetic into a killing machine. Personally, I wouldn't do that because I've known of people who have done that and the synthetics had to be destroyed because they couldn't be deprogrammed. So be careful what you do once you receive your enhanced abilities."

"I'll try to be careful."

"Don't just try. You better be careful because the only way the implants will be able to be removed will be if you either have portions of your brain removed or you die and those portions are removed afterwards. Do you still want the deluxe package? Of course you want it. You'd be an idiot if you turned it down."

Another door opened and Vladimer entered another small room where something that looked like an aluminum fish bowl was hanging from the ceiling. He stepped under it and it slowly descended upon his shoulders. For the next minute, Vladimer's head felt numb as the electronic pain bypass prevented pain from being felt and the implants were injected directly into his brain. The holes in the skull were filled with biodegradable bone cement and the skin was joined by cellular fusion which left no scars.

The bowl ascended and Vladimer walked into another small room. There were three doors to consider. To prove that he could read Kerianite, two signs were nonsense words and one sign read in Russian EXIT. Since he also understood English and Mandarin, the sign would alternate between Russian, English, and Mandarin.

After going through the exit, Vladimer walked down some hallways as if by instinct back to Lonayha. She was sitting at a small table in a snack shop next to the teleportation reception area.

"How'd it go?" she asked.

"Quite well. I was replicated and then mentally enhanced. I guess I have homing pigeon instincts too. I found you even though you didn't tell me you would be here.

"I'm impressed. Can you read that sign over the counter?"

Vladimer glanced at the sign and said, "It lists the sandwiches offered here, the desserts, the types of coffees, the teas, and something similar to energy drinks that are popular back on Earth. I saw you put some money in your pouch. I believe you have enough to pay for anything you order. Have you ordered anything yet?"

"Yeah. It should be coming in a couple minutes."

"Let me see if I truly have the ability to manipulate minds."

Vladimer stared at one of the counter people and placed an order for a dessert and a flavored hot tea. She walked over to where a particular pie was located and cut out a slice and placed it on a small plate. She also dispensed some tea in a cup and placed an ice cube into the cup as Vladimer had telepathically ordered. She placed both orders on a tray and brought them to the table along with the check.

She placed the tray on the table and walked back to the counter. "Now I really am impressed. But you didn't make the meal free."

Vladimer flipped the check over and saw the price was very reasonable.

"I didn't want to get her fired for giving us free food and beverages."

Vladimer dug into the pie and took a bite. It reminded him of cherry pie.

"You don't have trees. At least I didn't see any. How could they have cherries?"

"It's replicated. Over a century and a half ago we sent people to your planet to gather food and beverage samples and bring them back to Kerian so we could replicate them. The pie you are eating is the same as the cherry pie they used to eat in America in 1890.

The same with the tea. It also helped to have people moving to your planet teleporting food and beverages to Kerian for nearly two and a half centuries."

"Why didn't your people try to make treaties with the people of Earth back then?"

"Wars. Your people can be so violent. Of course my people haven't been blessed ones all along either. That's why we are underground thanks to the war. But with the atmosphere containment system being erected by people from your planet, it's only a matter of time before we'll be able to reconstruct our surface cities. I'm getting excited about the future of my planet."

"Same here. I better negotiate well to make some really good treaties which help both of our peoples."

"You can manipulate minds. If they don't agree with you at the start, make them agree."

"I'll have to be careful. How do you think it would look if someone who wanted to take Martian property from Martians suddenly agreed with me and what your people wanted?"

"It would look like he came to his senses."

"I need to make it look like he came to the right position due to my verbal persuasion and not by my manipulation of their mind. At least with a gorgeous woman beside me reading their minds and wanting to please you, things should go pretty good. If I confront a woman who is anti-male, you could negotiate some treaties. We will become sort of a tag team negotiation team. I'm looking forward to forming my first treaty as soon as possible."

After the snack, Vladimer and Lonayha headed for the surface. By the time they reached the rock barrier similar to the one Vladimer had penetrated, the oxygen content of the atmosphere was up to 12%. It was like being on a high mountain on Earth. Both people had forgotten about having air masks on. But it didn't matter. The air was breathable and as long as they didn't exert themselves, they could walk slowly to the American base and be fine.

Three astronauts wearing insulated jackets were about to enter a construction vehicle that had tower material on a long trailor behind another trailor that had heavy equipment on it when they saw the couple approaching them.

"Hey, where did you two come from?" one of the men asked. "We came up from the city of Reevane," said Vladimer in perfect English but with a Russian accent.

"Reevane?" asked the man. "Never heard of it."

"Of course you haven't heard of it. It's one of several cities underground."

"You mean there are people underground?" asked one of the other astronauts.

Vladimer and Lonayha looked at each other and began to chuckle.

"Well duh. She isn't a mirage."

"You're Russian, aren't you?" asked the third astronaut.

"So? I also happen to be part Martian thanks to my great- great-great-great-grandparents. Because of that I got the chance to marry one of the hottest women I've ever seen. Where are you guys going?"

"We're heading out to some erection sites to put up atmospheric containment towers. Once we power them up, we'll extend the atmosphere out another 50%. By next week we might be down to your base. It depends on how much material they send up by GSLP projectiles from America," said the first astronaut who looked to the north at a similar erection set-up being driven to another erection site.

"The Chinese are helping expand the atmosphere and we're helping them since Beijing isn't. As long as the Madhouse keeps sending up what we need, we'll keep expanding the atmosphere," said the first astronaut who Vladimer assumed was the foreman of the work team.

"Maybe the Facility in Siberia will use its GSLP system to send up what we need," said the second astronaut.

"I know one of the directors of the Facility is back at Mars Base Gagarin. Dick Thurman," said the foreman.

"I'm the cousin of his wife Kate. We've got a lot of catching up to do," Vladimer said excitedly.

"I should say so," said the second astronaut. "You come to Mars single and go back to Earth married to a fine looking lady. You lucky dog."

"Why don't we have someone drive you two to the base?" asked the third astronaut.

"Great idea," said the foreman.

"I hope you have more than just insulated jackets," Vladimer mentioned.

"We've got half-suits in the truck," said the foreman. "When we get to the work site we'll put them on. We'll take off our jackets first and then put them on. We just need to strap them to our pants to seal them and then turn on the oxygen. Our body heat will provide all the heat we need. Thank-you Madhouse."

Vladimer and Lonayha entered the building as a GSLP powered projectile was descending to the landing/launch pad behind the building. As most of the people in the base were watching the projectile descend, two saw the couple exiting the airlock.

"Where did you two come from?" asked one of the women. "We came from Reevane," Lonayha said. "It's below the surface of Kerian along with several other cities."

"You mean you're a Martian?" asked the second woman. "Kerianite. We call this planet Kerian just like we call your planet Vorion. Our planets are called other names on other worlds." "We're not going to argue with you since you come from here," said the first woman. "I need to bring you two to see the base commander, Major Bryant."

The four people entered the control room where everyone was shocked to see two strangers standing before them. They all turned from watching the projectile land and stared at Vladimer and Lonayha.

"Who are you two?" asked the major.

"I'm Vladimer Premakoff from Russia and this is my wife Lonayha Muns from Calofrene. If you had told me a day ago I would find out I had ancestors from Mars and that I was the one they were waiting for and I'd be married to a knock-dead gorgeous woman, I might have said you've been outside without a spacesuit on too long. But here I am. We'd like to go to Mars Base Gagarin." "We need to tell Earth that Mars is inhabited. This is the most significant discovery ever made on the Red Planet. How many people live below the surface?" asked the major. "Around 80,000 people," said Lonayha.

"I'd really like to see my cousin Kate Thurman. She's at Mars Base Gagarin. Could someone check to see if she and her husband are still there?" Vladimer asked urgently.

"I'm on it," said the man at the control panel who was back to monitoring the descent of the projectile. After it was clamped in place, the man called Mars Base Gagarin.

"Why did you two get married in the first place?"the major asked. "Come to find out, my great-great-great-great-grandparents came from Mars. Because of that, I've become sort of the ambassador for Earth on Mars. I'm supposed to be responsible for the treaties that are made between Earth and Mars. They'll trust me here since I'm part Martian. Being married to this gorgeous creature is more than just icing on the cake. I'll get the chance to wake up in the morning and the first thing I'll see is her lovely face. And she makes fantastic cookies too."

"They're still at the base," said the man at the control panel. "We need a ride to the base," said Vladimer.

"Follow me," said the first woman the couple met when they entered the building.

The trip to Mars Base Gagarin was a nonstop gabfest. The trio talked constantly. The woman at the controls wanted to learn as much as she could about Mars because she figured she wouldn't learn more about the planet than from someone who was born and reared there. She drove slower than normal so she could learn as much as possible.

When they finally arrived at Mars Base Gagarin, Kate, Maria, and Dick were standing outside the main building with half suits like the ones the astronauts were going to wear. Kate had the two suits draped over her shoulders as she entered the airlock entrance of the vehicle. She dropped the suits to the floor, removed her helmet and dropped it to the floor, and began hugging and kissing her cousin. She even shed some tears of joy.

As Lonayha was putting on the half suit, Kate asked her cousin, "Who is this beautiful woman?"

"She's my wife Lonayha. I'm the luckiest Vorionite on Kerian." "What?" she asked.

"That's the names of Earth and Mars to her people. I'm now the ambassador for Earth on Mars thanks to my great-great-great- great-grandparents Sasha and Irena. They came from Mars. The two old ladies she lived with knew them. I've got a lot to talk about on the trip back to Earth."

"We can catch up on everything when we're on our way back," said Kate as she wiped away some tears. She hugged and kissed him again before he put on the suit.

Kate left the vehicle and joined Dick and Maria as they walked to the spaceplane. Since the half suits weren't as protective as full suits, Vladimer and Lonayha ran to the spaceplane. It was a bit crowded in the airlock chamber for five people. But once the atmosphere was restored, the chamber opened and the five nearly fell to the floor. Once they were strapped in, the plane took off and a joyous ride back to Earth began.

Chapter 22

Thanks to the transdimensional chamber that followed Lonayha, Maria didn't need to rush back to Earth. There had been just enough food and beverages to last three days for three people for the trip back to Earth. But if anyone wanted something to eat, they could shift into the chamber and either have replicated food or "real" synthetic food. The kitchen didn't have access to Martian water since the chamber didn't have access to all of Mars. So the water that was stored in the refrigerator had to be added to the replicator material storage chamber. There was enough material to make over 20 kilos of food and beverages. When you added the synthetic food in the kitchen, there was more than enough food for five people for two or three weeks.

The quintet had plenty of meals at the dining room table with some of them being prepared by Lonayha in the oven. Her cookies were a big hit along with her cakes, pies, and candy. Kate praised her cousin for marrying a wonderful woman who could cook much better than she could.

When the plane landed back at hangar 3, an apartment was waiting for Vladimer and Lonayha at the Facility that had a king- sized bed in the bedroom. But with all the requests from around the world for interviews with Lonayha about life on Mars and requests from governments and institutions and companies for access to Mars for many reasons, it looked like the happy couple would be away from the Facility more than they would be there. And with teleportation links to some of the cities under the surface of Mars about to be established, Vladimer established a tourism company which would allow people from Earth to travel to Mars and vice versa. Since his wife was going to be busy traveling all over the world for interviews and talks about Mars, Vladimer would run the company. Eventually he would have to hire a team of tourism coordinators and was given a section of the Facility inside hangar Once he received six teleportation chambers and a cargo-sized teleportation chamber which BOSS would pay the government of Janvuor for, a separate building would be constructed near the hangar which would have access to the tube system which would allow people from around the world to take the tube to Siberia.

There was one major change that met Kate when she went to work the day after arriving back at the Facility. She entered the tech lab to see how much progress had been made with her companion brain for children. Andre was talking with a young man she had never seen at the Facility before.

"Welcome back," Andre said as he extended his hand in friendship. "I'd like you to meet someone you met the first day you were testing your companion brain. This is Michael Gregorian from Smirnoffgrad."

"You mean his father."

"No, I am the five year-old you met," he said. "I came back the day after you left for Mars and became the man you see in front of you."

"I was giving the children micromachines and construction material and he knocked the tins to the floor and ate the capsules like candy," said Andre.

"I blame you for that," Michael said. "If you hadn't made them banana and cherry flavored I wouldn't have eaten them like candy." "He ate six micromachine and eight construction material capsules and became a cybernetic megabrain."

"It took less than five minutes to go from having a child's brain to having a brain Einstein would have been envious of. I designed my biosynthetic body that day and had a fabricator make it the next day. Since the size of my cybernetic brain was limited to the size of my head, I told the surgeons in the medical department how to transfer it from my child-sized head to this head. My organs have been offered for donation to hospitals around the world. I developed an organ sustaining transfer chamber that allows the organs to function as if they were still in the body for as long as what is needed before they are transplanted. No longer is there a time limit of viability for the organs or a need for ice to keep the organs fresh. I even donated what remained of my biological brain, sensory organs, nerves, and muscles for transplantation."

"So in essense you donated your body to medicine to save countless lives around the world," Kate pointed out.

"Pretty much. I expect my entire body to be put to good use either for implantation purposes or for experimentation. Micromachines are still circulating through my old body."

"So I guess you no longer need a companion brain."

"My cybernetic brain has wireless connection access capability to most computer systems. I have no need for a device to be attached to the side of my head."

"Why are you here then?"

"I got a new job here in a new division of the electronic entertainment section of the Department of Culture. I may look like a 25 year-old man. But I'm still a five year-old boy. I will create and develop toys and other devices that should appeal to children and even parents.

"Yesterday, I completed my work on a baby translator. It is part telepathic communicator and part audio translator. When I was a baby a few years ago I spoke a strange language that sounded like gibberish as most babies do. But it was the way I communicated. My device reads the images that babies have and translate them into an understandable language. It also interprets the cries of babies to tell parents what each type of cry means."

"Have you tested it yet?"

"It is being tested as I speak in the main hospital in Smirnoffgrad. The last time I called out there, the obstetrics department head told me my device was working well. Many parents want to take the device home with them. I told her that the Facility will make as many devices as what is needed. I priced them at 10,000 rubles which the department head said sounded reasonable. It only cost 4,500 rubles to build one and it only takes ten minutes to fabricate one. But if I tweak the fabricators, I should be able to cut fabrication time to less than two."

"Do you know how many parents will want your baby translator?"

"It would make more sense to rent them out because by the time children learn to speak in a discernable language, my device won't be needed. That's why I will recommend hospitals renting them out for 300 rubles a month for as long as they are needed. If they are maintained well, one translator should last for years and help dozens of sets of parents to understand their babies in their formative months between birth and one or two years of age."

"I'm sure you've heard it so often that you're tired of hearing it—" "Yeah, yeah. I'm a genius. Tell me something I don't know. Oh, that's right. You can't. See you later. I'm testing out a military toy set today in my division."

The man/child left the room and headed for another section of the department.

"He is indeed a supergenius. But he has a super ego to match," Andre complained.

"Next time we hand out capsules, let's not present the tins like candy dispensors," Kate recommended.

Dick was in his studio picking up from where he left off developing the flying limousine the President wanted. He had sneaked the fabricator he used on the Aremulac into his studio and integrated it into the fabricator he had there. Instead of taking upwards to an hour to construct the vehicle, the microconstruction droids emerged from the fabricators and constructed the vehicle in two minutes. They immediately returned to the fabricators once the job was completed.

Dick opened the scissor door to the front section of the cockpit and entered the vehicle. It was exactly as he had designed it. All he needed to do now was take it outside and test it. The reactor was fully fueled and ready for initial beam injection. He inserted a beam initiator that was the size of an average magic marker into a receptical in the dash. In less than a second, the injection reactor was pumping out enough charged particles to sustain the reactor. He levitated the vehicle to 5 centimeters off of the floor and glided to the elevator that would take his vehicle to the surface.

The day was clear and frigid. There was a thick blanket of snow on the road leading to hangar 1. But the double-field motive system pushed the snow off of the pavement and the vehicle silently glided at 100 kph to the runway. Dick barely depressed the accelerator. When he was on the runway, he accelerated to 200 kph and lifted into the air.

He was at an altitude of 20 kilometers over the sea when he turned on the repulsion-drive engine. In seconds he was passing the moon and heading toward Jupiter. Ten minutes later he was passing Jupiter and heading for Saturn. He entered the Kuyper Belt less than half an hour after leaving Earth.

That was when he finally remembered to turn on the cameras that would record the journey. The sun was becoming an increasingly smaller bright dot in the rear and the next small bright dot was becoming increasingly larger until an hour later, the Aproxima Centauri system was entered. There were no habitable planets in the system. So he rounded the star and headed back to Earth.

Dick was landing his vehicle on the runway leading to hangar 1 little more than three hours after leaving it. He was glad his cameras used solidstate memories because images on video disks would have looked smeared. Even at a recording rate equal to 100,000 images a second, there was a bit of bluring.

The only person at the hangar was Joseph Simmeroff. Dick thought it was odd until he realized why he might be there. Maybe he wanted to steal the vehicle and fly it to Beijing or maybe a military testing facility in China. Dick quickly removed the initiator and turned off the reactor.

Joseph was standing a meter away from the vehicle when Dick exited it and walked toward the spy.

"I'm amazed that you were able to get your vehicle into the air a day after you returned from Mars."

"I just had a few things to do before I left. So it took almost no time to get it ready for testing," he lied.

"That's good. How was your trip to Mars? I heard some earthshaking news came from there. Is it really inhabited by people like you and me?"

"Yes it is. My wife's cousin is an ambassador representing Earth before the Martian government. I bet China will want to make some treaties with Mars through him."

"I…wouldn't know. It's good to have you back."

Joseph walked away from Dick toward an office in the hangar as Dick was heading for the horizontal elevator.

"Don't they need you back in the department?" Dick asked over his shoulder at him.

"I need to use the restroom. I'll get back to the department in awhile."

Dick knew what he was up to. But he didn't dare let on he knew.

The man entered the vacant office and entered the toilet as he said he would. But instead of lowering his pants, he removed something that looked like a cigar holder from his right rear pocket and removed half of the cover. A small satellite dish opened like an umbrella. He secured it by a clamp to the top of the toilet stall and placed the cover in his pocket. He pulled a device that looked like a pen out of his shirt pocket and clicked the end. He twisted a ring on the device until a low whistle was heard. He depressed the clip on the side of the device and spoke in Mandarin a message to someone he thought was his government contact.

"Today is a lovely day for flying. Number one returned from somewhere. Should I get a bird for you today?"

After releasing the clip, a voice in Mandarin said, "Later unless the market is about to close. Go back to work and we'll talk later."

The radio transmission ended and Joseph placed the radio back in his shirt pocket, placed the cover over the end of the dish after it was removed from the top of the stall and retracted, and left the stall to return to work. If he felt threatened of being discovered, maybe he could start up the vehicle Dick had tested and fly to safety. If that didn't work, maybe he could take one of the other planes in the hangar. It wouldn't be as big a prize for Beijing as the limousine. But it might be worth studying.

Chapter 23

Joseph Simmeroff went back to the Department of Military and Space Research to continue his work on suicide droids. He was having difficulty shrinking them to the size of peas and have them be destructive enough to blow up a tank. He also found it difficult to make them able to receive instructions and have enough energy to fly upwards to a kilometer. He had shrunk suicide droids to the size of marbles. But they could be seen long before they hit their target and taken out with an EMP burst. They would be exploded long before they could do significant damage. The things had to be small enough to not be seen by radar so they could reach their target and explode and do extensive damage.

One of Joseph's coworkers came up to him and asked, "Could you use my help?"

"I don't want to impose upon you."

"You're not imposing. Tell me what you're problem is."

"I'm trying to miniaturize my suicide droids. I've got them down to the size of marbles. But I need to get them down to the size of peas."

"If the work I'm doing pays off, you may not need to do that. Do you know about teleportation and how it is supposed to work?" "It is how an object or person can move from one place to another as if the object or person is being transmitted like a radio or TV signal. Are you working on teleportation?"

"Yes I am. I'm not sure if I'm supposed to tell you this, but we have been successful teleporting objects from one transporter to another. We've also teleported a synthetic from one transporter to another and nothing bad happened. All we need is a volunteer that is brave enough to risk his life to see if people can be safely teleported from one transporter to another. I might have to be that brave volunteer who does it. But we have found that teleporting from a transporter to a destination where no transporter exists is much more difficult if not impossible. If a person could teleport an explosive into a tank, that would be a real game changer in the art of war. If the ruler of a nation knew a bomb could end up in his bed and it couldn't be stopped, he might negotiate for peace with those that have the transporter."

"How far along are you in being able to do that?"

"We are working with interdimensional shifting from one dimension to another. Once we are able to shift from one dimension to another and combine that technology with destinational teleportation, it would be possible to shift from this dimension into another and when you arrive inside a room where a targeted person thinks he's safe, you could shift back into this dimension, kill the person, and shift into another dimension and escape."

"That would indeed be a game changer. When do you think you'll be able to do that?"

"I don't know. It could be today. We're that close." "Tell me when you are successful."

The man stared at him for a moment with a growing smile on his face. When he couldn't contain himself any longer he began to roar with laughter.

"Why are you laughing so hard?" "Did you see me enter this room?"

"I don't recall seeing you come in. Why do you ask?"

"I shifted from this dimension to an adjacent one, walked into this room, and shifted back into this dimension. We tried to combine shifting dimensions with destinational teleportation, but extreme precision is required."

"Are you using GPS location determination?"

"It's not precise enough. We're trying to thread a needle from 36,000 kilometers away. We are able to teleport objects into empty rooms. But most of the time the room has to be large enough to hold an army. We want to be able to teleport an object into a lead safe. But the object needs to shift dimensions because lead is difficult to teleport objects into something made from it. Once we can do that, no enemy would be safe from someone with such a transporter."

"Being able to shift from one dimension to another and back is impressive enough for me. Do you need to wear something that will allow you to shift dimensions?"

The man opened his shirt to show Joseph what looked like a metal fiber undershirt.

"That thing allows you to shift dimensions?" "This and a dimensional field changer. Watch."

The man had a thin cable attached to the garment and to a hand control that had knobs and buttons. He twisted the dial slightly and pushed a button. He vanished. A few seconds later, he reappeared several meters away.

"I shifted dimensions." "Could you let me try that?"

The man removed his shirt and the undergarment that had a small battery pack on the back. Joseph removed his shirt and placed the undergarment on.

"Twist the knob to setting one and then push the red button when you want to shift dimensions. When you want to shift back, push the green button. Don't touch the knob. That will have you shift to another dimnension."

Joseph did what he was told to do, walked through a wall and back into the room, and finally shifted back.

"That was incredibled. I almost felt the same way a ghost must feel when he walks through walls. Do you have more shirts like this one?"

"A few. But they're worn by members of my team. Now if I were a pervert who wanted to look at naked women, I could shift dimensions and enter the apartment of a gorgeous young woman and watch her in the shower. She would never know it."

"But if she saw you smiling a lot around her and getting excited she might suspect something."

"Maybe. But that garment is not for getting cheap thrills while wearing it."

Joseph removed the garment and gave it back to the man. He almost got the cable between the garment and the control caught on his belt. He decided he had to have such a garment and control. He had to form a plan on how to take the devices.

"I'd like to see you work on your transporter. It could make what I'm doing a waste of time."

"I'll check with the guys. If they say it's all right, I'll let you know." The man left the room through the door. Joseph left the room where he had been working on his droids and entered his office. He had a feeling that he was being watched, so he entered an EPU Internet system that the Madhouse in Arizona had perfected. It allowed people around the world to experience programs, people, work situations, and institutions. Joseph frequented various programs and visited with friends like Stanislav Robinov who was one of his connections with Beijing. He presented himself as a Russian in Eastern Siberia. But he was actually working for the Chinese military out of Nanjing. But in the program in which he met with Joseph, he looked like a broad-bodied Cossack with a thick moustache, a short sword, and a pair of ivory handled Colt 45 revolvers. They met in a tavern where Russian folk music was being played on the accordian and the barmaids were friendly and wore loose blouses.

Joseph entered the tavern and immediately was hugged around the neck and kissed before the woman rubbed his face on her ample breasts amidst shouts and laughter from patrons. Stanislav was sitting at one of the tables in the corner with a buxom black-haired beauty on his lap. He was nuzzling her breasts and causing her to giggle with glee. When he saw Joseph, he called to him and sent the woman to the bar to grab a bottle of vodka and two pewter mugs. "Sit down, my friend. Are you conquering the world out there?"

asked the jovial Cossack.

"I'm doing my best to beat it into submission."

They grabbed each other's hand as Joseph sat down and planted their elbows on the table and arm wrestled. They grunted and sweat until Stanislav slammed Joseph's arm to the table. They both laughed and kissed the barmaid who returned with the bottle and mugs. Stanislav poured the vodka to nearly the brim in both mugs. They chugged the liquor, slammed the mugs on the table, and Stanislav poured some more vodka.

"Do you have any news from that crazy place you work at?"

"I saw one of the directors riding a winged steed he will present to our leader."

"Wonderful. Are you allowed to ride it?"

"No. But I will attempt to seize the reins. Our leader can always be given another flying steed. I also donned a metal shirt that allowed me to become invisible and pass through walls."

"You jest. Have you been imbibing something stronger than what is in your mug?"

"I haven't touched a drop of strong drink since our last meeting. The shirt is owned by someone who can travel like lightning. He has other friends who own similar garments who also travel like lightning."

"You must possess such a shirt and show me the peculiar garment. What else have you learned that would interest me?"

"Since our leader visited the crazy place, he has ordered the construction of mighty war machines that can shake the world like a whoremonger shaking the ample breasts of a wench in a bed of love. They can turn walls of stone into partitions of paper.

"The war birds that will be given to the leader will terrorize their prey. Opposing birds are like sparrows when compared to the leader's eagles. And I've seen metal soldiers that are unstoppable."

"What you tell me sounds like the ravings of a madman. Allow me to have someone look into your mind to separate fact from imagination."

Stanislav spotted a fortune teller dealing with a client in another corner of the tavern.

"Gypsy," he shouted.

She glanced his way, excused herself, picked up her crystal ball, and walked over to the table where Stanislav and Joseph were sitting. Stanislav pulled a chair from a nearby table and as a gentleman pushed it toward his table as the woman sat.

"Gypsy, is the story my friend telling me a delusion or truthful?" The slim young woman with long black hair and coal black eyes looked into the eyes of Joseph and told him, "Place your fingers on my globe and I will read your thoughts."

Joseph did as he was told. She stared into the quartz crystal intently.

"I see you are a truthful man. Your story is not from the demented mind of a maniac. You have seen marvels beyond imagination. You work among people who create wonders that the world may not be able to comprehend."

Stanislav took a couple silver coins out of his money bag hanging from his belt and slammed them onto the table. The woman placed the coins in a money bag hanging from her belt, picked up her globe, and walked back to her client to continue her reading of the man.

"I apologize for not believing your account. You have never lied to me before, so why should you start now? Do you plan to roam around that crazy place you work at to see more wonders?"

"Of course. There are rumors that a beautiful woman with a brilliant mind has outrun the light from the sun. I will attempt to see if such a thing has been accomplished. If it has, I will return to tell you."

"Very good, my friend."

Joseph was about to leave when his friend asked, "Why must you leave so soon? You just arrived. Stay seated."

Stanislav whistled to the tavern keeper and shouted, "Tavern keeper, bring us thick slabs of beef and another bottle of vodka. We are famished over here."

After the meal which included two more bottles of vodka, Joseph left the tavern and the program to tour the Facility via microdrones that were the size of flies. He wanted to bring up the plans of various devices on his computer. But he feared his investigation would be detected and he would be exposed as a spy. He had already downloaded from the cybernetic portion of his brain information he had gathered into the program he left through the gypsy fortune teller. The information was eventually sent to Beijing.

As the microdrones were gathering information that was to be downloaded into his memory, Joseph decided to work on another weapon project since the suicide droid idea wasn't going anywhere if teleportation through other dimensions made them unnecessary. He decided to work on a concealed weapon that was in plain sight. It would be a multi-purpose weaponized glove.

It looked like a thin silver glove that was thin enough to allow one to pill a trigger. But it was connected to a cable that ran under the shirt, over the shoulder, and down the back to a nuclear power pack that was strapped around the back and chest. There was a second glove for the other hand that had the same abilities.

By pointing your index finger like a pistol, you were supposed to be able to fire a charged particle beam toward a target that was lethal enough to kill a person. If you laid your hand on someone, your hand became a taser or could be dialed up to discharge a lethal 100,000 watt jolt of energy. He was having some problems with his glove. He could fire the beam of charged particles. But the end of the finger of his glove looked burnt. And he had burnt the palms of nearly 30 gloves. He needed to be able to fire his beam and electrocute people without burning his glove.

He took a chance and contacted a coworker in the department to see if he could solve his problems. He contacted him over the computer video link.

"Hey Ted, could you help me with some problems I have with my discharge glove?"

"I'll try. What seems to be the problems?"

"I keep burning the glove when I discharge large amounts of energy. I know you work with various materials for military use. Your force field jacket can protect one from explosions that could destroy a vehicle. Yet it has no burn marks. What's your secret?"

"I ionize the fabric and circulate a field over it before I place the primary field over that one. The first field insulates the fabric from the primary field. In your case, I would use a metalic fiber that has an insulative inner fabric against your hand so you aren't shocked. Ionize the fabric, place the insulative field over it, and form an electromagnetic tube that is extended from your forefinger toward you target. If you're trying to use the traditional tri-beam system, the driving beam will be the initial beam that will be extended from your finger. You may need a solid tip at the end of your finger and three narrow tracks for the beams to follow around your finger. Or you could use microtubes that use electromagnets and linear induction to accelerate the charged particles around your finger. The solid tip at the end of your finger should be magnetized to repel the beams and prevent burning.

"As for your palm, do the same thing. Ionize, insulate, and energize. It will require more energy and the gloves will be nearly as thick as work gloves. But you might still be able to pull a trigger. Give it a try and call me back if it works or even if it doesn't work. Or you could try it out in a program and see if the computer thinks it will work. If it does, have your fabricator make a pair of the gloves along with everything else you'll need. Talk to you later. I need to conduct some tests with one of my projects."

The man logged off and Joseph went to work on his glove. He did the design work, designated the materials he needed, and entered a program before fabricating a pair of the glove to see if the computer thought the concept might work.

In the program he was back in time 1,500 years before the discovery of gunpowder which could be used for a weapon. But he had the gloves on and they were connected by cables to the nuclear power pack on his back. He wore a long robe over the power pack. Joseph was walking through a forest in Europe during a very dangerous time after the Roman Empire was destroyed and various tribes were ruling regions brutally. Bandits terrorized those that dared travel down the roads. And if a person was by himself, he was fair game for robbery and possible murder.

As Joseph was coming upon a fallen tree that blocked the road, three men emerged from behind huge oaks with their swords drawn. "Hand over your money bag and maybe we'll let you live," said one of the robbers.

Joseph pointed his forefingers at two of the robbers and punched holes in their chests. The third robber ran for his life as his partners dropped to the ground dead. Joseph punched the air toward the third robber and discharged a burst of energy that ripped the man's head off. He had no idea throwing a punch would allow him to do it litterally.

The fallen tree offered no resistance to his punches and the beams emitted by his fingers. When he pretended his hands were axes, he found he could slice the obstacle into firewood. He felt emboldened to continue his journey through the forest and eager to take on more robbers.

He didn't need to wait long. Minutes later, half a dozen men jumped out of the trees and tried to overwhelm the traveler. His energy fingers and fists dispatched the attackers with ease. One man jumped out of a tree onto him and tried to stab him with a rusty dagger. The blade nicked Joseph's neck. But since he had micromachines in his bloodstream, in the program the wound was healed in seconds. The attacker fared much worst because when Joseph grabbed his head, he began screaming. The energy from the gloves set the man's hair on fire and blood gushed from his ears and eyes. Smoke came out of his mouth as he strangled on the blood in his throat. Eventually the man died in intense pain.

In an opening appeared five men on horseback with drawn bows pointed at him.

"Drop your money bag or our arrows will hit their marks," one of the men shouted.

Joseph raised his hands as if he was surrendering. But in a flash he waved his hands and cut the bows in half and knocked the men off of their mounts. They drew their swords and rushed the traveler who cut them in half with the sweep of his hands.

In the distance he saw a castle that was being attacked by a small army. Archers from the walls were shooting at the attackers. A dozen men were using a battering ram to try and smash in the thick wooden doors shielded by a couple dozen men who held their shields over them to protect them from the rain of arrows.

Joseph ran toward the battle and waved his hands toward the attackers. Even from more than a kilometer away, the beams that were emitted by his fingers were deadly. The attackers turned toward him and fired arrows his way. He flailed his arms and shattered the arrows long before they could reach him. He also cut archers in half until there were fewer than three left and all the men who tried to smash in the doors were cut to pieces. The remaining attackers mounted their horses and rode away.

Shouts of joy were heard from the walls that were higher pitched than that of men. When Joseph arrived at the doors that were splintering from the assault with the ram, they were opened and women came out to greet him. He was brought into the courtyard where a dozen women hugged and kissed their savior. He had removed the gloves and unplugged them from the power cables. He tucked them into his belt so they couldn't hurt anyone.

An older woman came to the front door of the palace with two of her daughters. She smiled and said, "Welcome, stranger. You have saved this castle and the lives of its inhabitants. Come in and help us celebrate this victory over Jeffery Crow and his army of infidels. Are you a God-fearing gentleman?"

"What if I said yes?"

"Then you are welcome to join us in the great hall." "Of course I'm a God-fearing gentleman."

Shouts of praise and exaltation were raised. Joseph entered the castle with several women trying to get close to him. He entered the great hall where female servants were bringing in food on large platters and beverages in metal containers and setting them on the banquet tables. The older woman and her daughters strode to the main table and left a chair between the daughters for Joseph to sit upon. The first man inside the walls of the castle complex that Joseph saw was a priest who stood behind the chair the older woman stood in front of. He raised his hands and everyone became quiet and bowed their heads reverantly. Joseph followed their example.

"Dear Lord of Heaven and deliverer from evil, we praise you now for the great deliverance from our enemies. We thank thee for allowing this man who with only his hands slayed our attackers who undoubtedly would have sacked this structure and ravaged the women. His appearance was a miracle in which we will be eternally grateful for. Bless this celebration. Bless the food and liquid refreshment and the hands that prepared it. May it give us strength and make our hearts merry. But may we always acknowledge that you are the eternal deliverer of our souls from Hell. Though our bodies could have been torn apart or burnt by our enemies, we have the assurance that we will live forever in your presense. I thank thee for all perfect gifts you give us everyday and may we always deserve every blessing you bestow daily. In the name of your dear son Jesus we thank you. Amen."

Everyone looked up and the woman said before anyone sat down, "This is indeed a most wonderful day. We have been delivered from our enemies by this fine gentleman who appeared like an avenging angel to rescue us from certain death. State your name, sir."

"Joseph. I am from a distant land where my people do wonders beyond your imagination. I am pleased to be of service to you fine women. If I may be so bold, where are the men besides the priest?" "Dead. They were slain by the army that nearly took this castle.

We are the widows and near orphans that remain. We will forever be in your debt. After the feast, you may join us in the communal bath to luxuriate in the warm mineral water that all people enjoy.

Afterwards, you may spend the night in a huge comfortable bed large enough to accommodate a dozen sleepers. We have received the blessing for the food. Let us now enjoy the meal."

As she sat, everyone else sat and started to enjoy a meal that lasted for a few hours. Musicians played ancient music and entertainers danced and juggled and sang until late into the evening. Afterwards, Joseph and a couple dozen bathers removed their clothes and entered the soothing warm mineral bath that relaxed the bathers. He made love to all the women; even the older woman. Afterwards, they dried themselves in fluffy towels and headed off to bed in the nude. The older woman and her daughters along with four other buxom beauties joined Joseph in the royal bed for play time until they all fell asleep.

Joseph awoke in his office with a huge smile on his lips and wonderful memories of what happened in the program he had experienced. He had his fabricator make the gloves and energy pack that powered them.

After the gloves and power pack were fabricated, he tested the gloves to see if they could do the things they did in the program. To his relief, they were capable of everything they had done in the program.

That was when he got a call from Dick to come to his office. Joseph wasn't sure why he was called up. But he didn't want to show he was uneasy. So he walked in confidently and sat in front of his desk.

"I'm sure you're wondering why I called you in. I was here one full day and never got a chance to get to know you. I met you at the reception after the recital. That was less than two weeks ago. Tell me about yourself. What are you working on in the Department of Military and Space Research?"

Dick read his mind as he spoke so he could see if there was any deception.

"Before you came to the Facility I was working on something I call a suicide droid. I began working on the device while in the university in Moscow. It started out the size of baseball. The work you did at the Madhouse in Arizona to build a levitated vehicle that used a double-field motive system was brilliant. I was able to make my suicide droid fly, follow a target if it were on the move, and blow up. I was able to power it with a small injection reactor that was the size of a ping pong ball. I coupled the reactor with the explosive which made the droid not only potent but more dangerous to unintended victims. I would probably use the first version of the droid to destroy a base or city.

"But I wanted to miniaturize it to make it less detectable and not as radioactive when it exploded. I got it down to the size of a marble with a flying range of ten kilometers. But it could be disable by an EMP burst. So I tried to make it even smaller. But I still had the EMP burst vulnerability.

"That was when I learned about shifting to other dimensions to deliver an explosive. Are you familiar with that technology?"

"Yes I am. Ten years ago it was science fiction. There was some theoretical work being done. But even at the Madhouse in Arizona it was still theoretical. But in the last couple years, work has been done on interdimensional shifting. I was surprised how easy it was to shift from one dimension to another. It also helped to have people from Newgate, New York come out to Arizona to help us out. I didn't know them personally. But I knew they were doing some amazing work. I didn't realize work was being done here with interdimensional travel. And they're also trying to merge teleportation with interdimensional shifting. That will be a real game changer for the military."

"That's why I decided to stop working with suicide droids and work on my latest innovation; an energy discharge glove that might turn out to be better than I originally thought it might be. I was testing it out when you called me. I'd like to get back to testing it."

"Sure. If I need to talk to you later, I'll give you a call."

Both men stood and shook hands. Joseph left the office and went back to work while Dick entered an EPU program where he met with the watcher who had told him about Joseph. He appeared as a bearded cowboy with Dick. They both were riding horses and driving a small herd of cattle on the open range 170 years ago in Texas.

"Did you get a read on the young Chinese fellow you were talking with?" the watcher asked.

"As best I could. Did you know it would be so difficult to read someone with a partially cybernetic brain?"

"Why do you think he had it done to himself? What did you get out of his metal brain?"

"Very little. I have a shower curtain as my defense against unwanted mind snooping. He has a bank vault. Is there any way I can crack that safe?"

"I've managed to read some of it by using a transdimensional probe. But when I tried to get information from his innermost components, he erased that portion of his cybernetic brain. He is an unusual spy. He can gather information and download it into a computer. But if he knows someone is trying to get to the information he has locked in the vault, he makes it go poof. What do you plan on doing with him?"

"I'll let him think no one knows he is a spy. His latest idea is a novel one that would help soldiers without fighting suits or force fields have an edge over conventional soldiers. Did you see him testing it?"

"Yes I did; both in his studio and in the program he enjoyed. And I do mean enjoy. I was one of the archers on the wall of a castle I was defending. I knew he couldn't pass up showing off in front of a lot of people. He saved the castle, had a feast, took a bath with a bunch of gorgeous women, including me—"

"You mean he likes women with several months of facial growth?" Dick joked.

"Yeah. He also wants his women to have big packages and legs like shag carpets. He's good in bed too."

"I think you also enjoyed yourself, didn't you?"

"About as much as getting it on with one of these steers. You need to find out where he deposits his information that he retrieves after he erases it from his cybernetic brain. Make sure you don't scare him off until at least you get to that information. I have a feeling he has at least one contact with the Beijing government because my friends watching down there know information is getting through that I thought had been blocked. If Beijing knows too much, the next war that Russia may fight with China could go China's way unless your president is allowed to use the good stuff."

"What do you mean by good stuff? Hyperlight reactors?" "Yes."

"Transporters?" "Most certainly." "Weather control?"

"You already know the answer. Those guys are getting into dangerous territory. If they're not careful, they could wreck the climate. Imagine what they could do with hyperlight reactors."

"They could rip the ozone layer out of the sky. Human life could end," said Dick.

"You know I can't tell them. I'm not assigned to them. I'm pushing the envelope just talking to you. So tell them that they should be careful with the technology available at the Russian Madhouse."

"You don't call it the Facility like everyone else does?"

"You wanted it to be known as the Russian Madhouse from the start. Some of the people working there make it an appropriate name. But if you want to call it the Facility, go ahead. You know deep down in your heart it's the Russian Madhouse."

"What if the ones that assign you to watch me and Joseph find out that you've been talking with me and interfering with my dimension and the way things are? What could they do to you?"

"Back in 1941 here in Russia a Jewish Christian watcher from Newgate shut down a Jewish death camp in a town that doesn't exist today because the Nazis bombed it out of existence. That was after over 20,000 Jews were shifted to another dimension. Another 15,000 Russian gypsies, and homosexuals were rescued and shifted to another dimension."

"If a town that was used as a death camp had over 35,000 people in it, why didn't the world know that those people vanished?"

"It was a humiliating defeat for the Nazis and the Soviets weren't about to admit such a place existed where Soviet citizens were tortured and overworked and starved to death. The Soviets made sure the town of Bravnia was removed from all records and even the history books. Even people who knew it existed at one time were paid off to forget about it or be thrown into the gulag. The generation that existed when Bravnia existed died out. So as far as Russians know, it is a huge field of sunflowers and a cattle ranch near the Caspian Sea. Even the graves were dug up and the bodies were ground into powder."

"Why didn't the West know about the camp at Bravnia?"

"The Nazis weren't going to let the world know what they were doing there and the Soviet government had an efficient means of erasing and changing history. If the world hadn't been reporting on the invasion of Israel, you can be sure President Kursolov would have ordered the humiliating defeat to be officially forgotten."

"Again, what would they do to you for talking with me?" "They used to be much stricter a century ago. But the main office in another dimension and the office in Newgate has relaxed its standards and allows a lot more interaction with other dimensions that are being watched. The world has become much more dangerous and it is important to keep the world from being destroyed by the stupidity of people. The relaxation of standards began in 1945 after the atom bomb was dropped on Hiroshima.

The Office of Interdimensional Monitoring and Interaction still frowns upon its agents becoming too known by the general public and has fired many watchers. The watcher who has become known as the Savior of Bravnia was rejuvinated in the coffin in the Newgate Municipal Hospital around 80 years ago. He isn't allowed to be a watcher. But the Messianic Jewish congregtion in Newgate feel honored to have him as a member. When they celebrate Hannukah each year they present the series Bravnia on one of the TV stations in Newgate and people can experience the Battle of Bravnia EPU program at Temple Messiah there in Newgate."

"So why are you disguised as an old cowboy on a cattle drive in Texas?"

"Sometimes I like to experience transdimensional programs and this is one of them. When a program is designated as TEPI, that means it's transdimensional and interactive. See the cowboys on the other side of the herd? They exist in your dimension and their dimension which means they might not exist in the adjacent dimension I watch from. The woman driving the chuck wagon exists in still another dimension as well as this one."

"Does that mean I shifted to another dimension when I entered this program on my computer?"

"Yes. This program exists simultaneously in 35 different dimensions at this time and has the capability to coexist in over 100. A lot of people in other dimensions as well as yours like to play cowboy. In this program we're headed for Abilene, Kansas. When we leave the program, the two cowboys behind us will remain and will take over for us. There's another one that just joined the program. "You had better get back to work. It's generally very relaxing out on the trail. Sometimes the people experiencing the program have to fight off rustlers and Indians every now and then. But that's going to happen during the evening. I'll try to track down where Joseph is storing his information and tell you where to find it. Don't spook him before that happens. Talk to you later."

Dick left the program and removed the EPU headset and placed it in the drawer. He decided to spend some time in his studio working on more levitated flying vehicles while his watcher attempted to track down the locations of memory dumps Joseph was using.

CHAPTER 24

Dick wanted to design and fabricate levitated flying vehicles that could be used for racing. With levitated cars becoming more popular with the public, it would be only a matter of time before there was a demand for races. He needed to line up racing venues around the world and recruit drivers willing to fly around tracks and road courses a few centimeters above the pavement at speeds approaching 500 kph and above.

He was into designing an open cockpit levitated car when he got a projection message from President Kursolov. A tone was heard in the studio and the voice of the President Kursolov alerted Dick to his projected presence.

"Welcome back to the Facility. How are you coming along on my flying limousine?"

"I got it done. I hope you like it. Is your projection in my office?" "Yes it is."

"Good. I'll see you in there shortly."

Dick walked from the studio to his office and found the projection of the President sitting in a chair. Dick sat down behind his desk.

"I was flying your limousine earlier today and it's a great vehicle. Since you're not physically here, you could join me in an EPU program and I'll fly you around. Ready to ride?"

"Sure."

Dick brought up the program designated as KURSOLOV'S LIMOUSINE before putting on the EPU headset. In seconds, Dick was in the driver's seat and the President was sitting in the back. Dick turned on the vehicle and in seconds was gliding out onto the runway at 100 kph. Seconds later, the vehicle was traveling over 300 kph and a few hundred meters in the air heading east.

"How are you doing back there?"

"Great. I could live back here. There's plenty of food and vodka back here and I can even go to the bathroom by opening the seat I'm sitting on. There's no toilet paper though."

"No problem. If you have to shit, once you're done, a wet cleaning system will wipe your butt and an air blower will dry it. I got the idea from watching a TV show called 'Lexx' that used to be on SyFy. They used a giant tongue on the show. At least you don't need toilet paper or even use your hands except to take off and put on your pants."

"How fast can this thing go?"

"I don't know. We're doing over Mach 5 at the moment and the field displacement engine is operating at 12% capacity. Would you like to fly to Mars?"

"I need to go to a state dinner tonight."

"This vehicle can reach Mars in less time than it takes to fly from the Facility to Moscow. This program has been updated with the latest conditions on Mars. The Americans and Chinese are erecting field towers to generate electromagnetic fields to retain an oxygen-rich atmosphere. In time they'll help Mars Base Gagarin erect field towers."

"Go for it then."

Dick turned on the repulsion-drive system and within seconds was hurtling toward the Red Planet at the speed of light and increasing in speed.

"I thought I would feel the boost in speed and would be clawing my way out of the back of my seat."

"It's the gravitational modification system. That's why I didn't tell you to buckle up."

"I normally don't buckle up back in Moscow. What if this thing ran into a space rock at the speed of light. Wouldn't I be killed instantly?"

"No. There is a force field around this vehicle. If we were to slam into an asteroid going as fast as we're going, we'd turn the thing into gravel and not affect the limousine. Would you like to see if I'm right?"

"No, no. I believe you. Anyways, this is only a program. So if you're wrong, we wouldn't be dead."

"We'd just leave the program. When you come out to the Facility physically—"

"Couldn't you set it on autodrive and have it fly itself to Moscow?" "Sure. You could have it tomorrow if you want."

"Do it. Oh, by the way, when will the weapons I saw at the Facility be added to the Russian arsenal?"

"This week. I'm sure of that. The plans have been sent to various factories along with some fabricators to make production faster. I'm surprised the factories aren't up and running yet with the new equipment yet."

"I'll look into it. Are there some things I need to know that are going on at the Facility?"

"Like what?"

"With so many people working there, I can't believe everything is running like clockwork. Any problems I shuold know about?"

"Nothing that we can't handle. No sabotage."

"The planes that I ordered. Will any of them be as fast as my limousine?"

"Yes. It wouldn't be fair to have the Russian air force deprived of warplanes that aren't as fast as this thing."

"Good, good. Will they be able to destroy any enemy plane that goes up against them?"

"Possibly."

"I don't want to hear possibly. I want assurance that my planes will be able to destroy all other planes that are flown against them," the man demanded.

"If you want your planes to outperform the planes of China or America they'll need to be totally AI-controlled. Do you want that?" "If that is what it takes to make my planes the best in the world, make them all AI-controlled. The same goes for my tanks. I want the Russian military to be feared. And make sure the space weapons your former employer has in orbit can be taken out. Can you do that?" "Uh…yes."

"You were hesitant. I know you're an American. But you work in my country; Mother Russia. You should be loyal to me and the people of this nation first and the rest of the world second."

"I hate to admit this, but…Oh never mind."

"Go ahead. Speak your mind. I want to hear what you think." "I hope you don't take this wrong, but you seem to be turning into another Joseph Stalin. I hope I'm wrong."

"You are wrong. If I were another Stalin, I'd turn the Facility into a sweatshop and your people would be forced to make only the things I want. But you have freedom at the Facility to work on projects I couldn't care less for. And when this program ends, I won't have you removed and sent to a prison for your candor. So don't worry. I'm not going to let ego overpower logic. I'm not going to plunge the world into a war that could destroy it. Some people have told me that China will wage a 13-month war that will destroy a third of the world's population. It's in the Bible they say. Do you believe it?"

"Yes I do. I've heard it since I was a little boy in Sunday school."

"More of a reason to keep that from happening."

"The Bible said in symbolic language that Russia would invade Israel and be destroyed militarily. But you went against what the Bible said would happen anyways. Why?"

"I have to admit I was warned not to do it by the same people who say China will have a 200 million man army. They nearly have that many right now. I was wrong to not listen to them a few months ago. But I'm going to listen to them now. So believe me when I tell you I'm not planning on going to war against China or America. I just want protection against them and my Muslim enemies that are thinking the destruction of most of my military will allow them to defeat Russia."

The limousine approached Mars and slowed to Mach 3 when it entered the atmosphere. By the time it was over Mars Base Gagarin the limousine was flying at 500 kph. Field towers were almost to the area. Dick landed the limousine between the American and Chinese bases.

"We don't have space suits," complained the President. "I guess we'll just have to sit here and take in the view."

Dick checked the atmosphere and found it was 19% oxygen. He opened the driver's door and walked over to the back of the car. "Do you want to just sit there or would you like to get out for a breath of fresh air?"

The President pushed the door button that opened the passenger hatch and exited the vehicle.

"It's too bad I couldn't land at Mars Base Gagarin."

"By the time you physically have this vehicle the towers might be erected past the base."

"It's not as cool as I thought it might be. It's a little warmer than back in Siberia."

"Imagine how it might be on Mars in a couple genertions. No one will need a space suit and there should be large bodies of water to swim in."

"Is this program set up for me to visit with real life Martians that live below the surface?" he asked excitedly.

"I'm sorry, but no. You'll have to meet with my wife's cousin Vladimer to see if you are allowed to meet with Martians. Ready to go back?"

"Sure. I guess I'll have to wait."

"You may not have to fly in your limousine to come back to Mars. I heard that BOSS is going to purchase transporters from the government in Janvuor to allow people to teleport here. Vladimer will start a tourism business at the Facility. You should be able to meet his wife Lonayha while you're there. She's a knockout."

"More a reason to come back to the Facility."

Instead of remaining in the program, President Kursolov and Dick left the program and Dick placed his EPU headset in the drawer.

"So you will send my limousine to Moscow after we're done." "Yes. In fact, I'm going to install an autodrive system after we're done here. Just send me the GPS coordinates for where you want it delivered and it will fly there."

The projection of President Kursolov vanished and Dick returned to his studio to fabricate an autodrive system to install in the limousine. As he was doing that, Joseph was on his way to hangar 1 to try and gain access to the limousine to fly to Beijing. He was disappointed that he didn't have the shirt which would allow him to shift to other dimensions. But he had sent off a tremendous amount of information to Beijing already. The gloves and the limousine would have to do.

As Dick was heading for hangar 1, the watcher shifted from an adjacent dimension and entered the horizontal elevator car where Dick was seated.

"Why are you physically here?" Dick asked.

"Joseph is waiting for you at hangar 1. He wants to take the limousine and might kill you. He has his energy discharge gloves so don't say or do something that will tick him off. Give him the vehicle. You can always fabricate another."

"Thanks for the heads up. I just hope he gives me time to integrate the autodrive system into the controls."

"Good luck."

"Have you found out where he stores his memories?" "Not yet."

"Keep on it. Thanks again for the warning. I don't know what I'll do. But I'll think of something."

The watcher shifted back to the adjacent dimension while Dick headed out to hangar 1.

Joseph was patiently waiting for Dick to come out to the limousine and stood by the driver's door.

"Joseph," he said in mock surprise. "Why are you out here?" "I'm sorry, but I need this vehicle," he said as he patted the top of the vehicle with a gloved hand. "What do you have in your hand?" Dick looked at the autodrive unit and said, "This is an autodrive system. It will let the owner of this vehicle sit in the back seat and drive him to wherever he wants to go. May I install it?"

Joseph considered the question for a moment before saying, "Sure. Go ahead. My president in Beijing will appreciate it."

"Your president in Beijing? I thought you were a proud Russian," Dick lied.

"Do what you need to do and don't set off an alarm. I know you're a man of your word. You won't set off an alarm, will you?"

"No I won't. Besides. This vehile is so fast that you'll be over Chinese air space long before one of the planes here can catch you." Dick opened the door and immediately went to work installing the autodrive system. It was the size of a credit card but had the ability to drive the vehicle using AI. He unscrewed the cover of the computer and placed the device in a slot among six empty slots that were available for upgrades to the systems. After he secured the cover, he left the cockpit and allowed Joseph to enter the vehicle. "I won't take advantage of the system you installed to be taken for a ride as a passenger. But I'm sure President Xian will enjoy it once I get this vehicle to Beijing."

The door closed and seconds later the vehicle was gliding out onto the runway. Less than a minute later, the vehicle was in the air and headed for Beijing. But that was until the autodrive system took over and corrected course to head for Moscow. Joseph tried to get the vehicle to head back toward China, but it was useless. The vehicle had a mind of its own and Joseph couldn't change it.

CHAPTER 25

Joseph was desperate. He couldn't return to the Facility since he was discovered as a Chinese agent. But he had to escape the vehicle before it arrived at its destination which Joseph had a feeling was Moscow. He found he could slow the vehicle and change the altitude. But it was still headed for Moscow. Joseph lowered the altitude to 5 centimeters above the ground and the speed to 20 kph with great effort. He had to push the brake pedal to the floor, but it wouldn't stop. He managed to open the door and jumped out. He almost got his right foot caught in the car because as soon as he took his foot off the brake pedal, the vehicle began to accelerate.

The man rolled down an embankment as the vehicle sped away. If he had snatched a dimensional shifting shirt, he would have been able to travel to Beijing undetected. But at least he had his gloves so if he needed to kill someone to steal the vehicle they were in, he could do that.

Joseph walked a short distance and found a fallen tree. He removed his satellite antenna and radio transmitter from his pocket and secured the antenna to a limb. At least he didn't need to speak in coded language.

"This is Hu De Hong. I'm away from the Facility. I tried to escape with a flying limousine and fly it to Beijing. But it was programmed to fly to a certain destination and I had to jump out of it while it was moving. But I am wearing a pair of energy discharge gloves that our soldiers can wear and use. The reactor on my back is something our military needs to power the weapon systems our soldiers will use. It is very potent. It can even power vehicles.

"You have my GPS position. Tell me what I should do."

"We will send a VLV to a clearing that is 3.8 kilometers to your north. Wait for the VLV. We will track your signal, so extend your antenna when you reach the clearing. We will rescue you."

Hu knew it would take awhile before the craft came, so he had to be wary. He hoped no one was in the area to turn him in to the authorities.

He had forgotten to wear a coat or hat, so he was cold. He hoped he didn't die from exposure. He used his gloves to light some dead wood by grabbing some wet limbs and holding onto them while generating a tremendous amount of electric current. In a minute he had a smokey fire that produced enough heat to warm him at -15 degrees centigrade. There was little wind, so the smoke didn't get in his eyes. He hoped no one saw the smoke or smelled the burning wood. He sliced logs from a dead tree and added them to the fire. He held onto the wood to try and dry it.

Ten minutes later, two hunters came out of the woods and were surprised to see someone that had no reason to be out there. "Good morning, stranger," said one of the men. "Kind of cold being out here with no coat on."

"My car ran out of juice about a kilometer away. I called for some assistance and will be picked up in about an hour at a clearing a few kilometers north of here," he said convincingly.

"Why didn't you stay with your car?" asked the other man.

"I needed to start a fire. So when I saw the wood, I naturally ignited some of it to provide some warmth."

"With what? You don't have any lighter or lighter fluid," said the first man.

Hu showed the men his gloves and said, "Watch this."

He picked up some bark and clutched it in both hands. It started to smoulder before bursting into flames. He tossed it on the fire in front of him as the men stood amazed.

"Are you from the Russian Madhouse?" asked the second man. "We call it the Facility. I'm doing some field testing of my gloves." "Why didn't you stay around the Madhouse to do your testing?"

asked the second man.

"That would have been too much a controlled condition. I wanted to see if my gloves could work in real-life conditions like the woods when it is either make a fire or die from exposure."

"Kind of smokey, isn't it?" asked the first man.

"When you need to survive, you have to take things the way they are. I see you two haven't shot anything yet. What are you hunting?" "Almost anything with four legs and fur," said the second man.

"What type of guns do you have?"

"EMD rifles. I used to shoot conventional rifles and pistols. But EMD weapons have a muzzle velocity of over 2 kilometers per second," said the first man.

"I have mine dialed up to 3 kps. It has no kick and since it uses 11 mm steel shot, it has tremendous stopping power. I just have to remember to wear my earmuffs because it's like holding a stick of dynamite it's so loud," said the second man.

"How long did they say it would take before they picked you up?" asked the first man.

"Probably a couple hours."

"Well, stay warm," said the second man.

"If I wanted to do that I wouldn't be out here."

The men walked back into the woods and headed west. Several minutes later, Hu picked up a burning log off of the fire and headed north toward the clearing. He came upon a house a kilometer south of the clearing and was about to walk on until the front door opened and an old man and woman called out to him.

"You look mighty cold out there without a coat on," said the man.

"Come inside and warm up," said the woman. "A good strong mug of Russian coffee might be what you need to take the edge off of the cold temperature."

Hu entered the house and followed the couple into the kitchen. The woman placed a mug in the coffee maker and dispensed half a cup of black coffee. She removed the mug and opened a bottle of vodka and poured some into the mug. Hu thanked her for the mug and drank half of it. He noticed that it was a bottle of caramel Russian Madhouse vodka she had poured from.

"I guess you could call it Russian Madhouse coffee," Hu said. "At least I won't freeze to death out there falling down drunk."

"You need more than coffee, young man," said the woman. "I've got some bread and cheese and sausages in the refrigerator. I could make you a sandwich."

"Thank-you."

The woman removed the cheese and sausage from the refrigerator and the bread from the vacuum container near the refrigerator by opening the air valve. Air rushed into the clear container and seconds later, the woman removed the container and moved it to the left on the counter. She put the sausage on a plate and popped it into the microwave for a couple minutes as she took a slice of cheese and placed it on a slice of rye bread on a plate. After the sausage was hot, she pulled it out of the oven and sliced it in half and placed the meat on the cheese.

Hu grabbed the sandwich and was about to take a bite out of it when the old man grabbed his arm.

"We aren't infidels in this house," the man announced. "Let me ask the blessing first."

The three people closed their eyes and bowed their heads. "Heavenly Father, thank-you for the food this young man is about to eat and bless it for his body. And since it looks so good, bless the food I am about to receive—"

"Me too," said his wife.

"And what my wife is about to receive. May it sustain our bodies and please protect this young man as he makes his journey through the snow and cold. I ask this in Christ's name. Amen."

"You're not going to go out without a coat and hat. I see you already have gloves. They don't look too warm," she scolded Hu.

"They're plenty warm. But if you have an extra coat and hat, that should keep me warmer than just holding a flaming log."

After some more small talk and lies from Hu that the couple seemed to believe, Hu was given an old insulate coat and an insulated cap which he thanked the woman for. He left the house and headed north. Why two total strangers would help him was a mystery.

Eventually he reached the clearing and waited nearly half an hour for the VLV to arrive. When he sighted the familiar Chinese flag on the side of the craft he breathed a sigh of relief. The VLV landed and the door behind the cockpit opened and steps came down to make it easier to enter the craft.

Two Chinese men welcomed him inside in Mandarin which made him feel more comfortable. He sat in one of the seats and buckled his seat belt as the other two men did and seconds later the craft lifted straight up and flew west when it reached an altitude of 10 kilometers. It sped up to Mach 2.

"You can remove your gloves," said one of the men. "It's plenty warm in here."

"No, I think I'll keep them on. I'm sort of attached to them." Hu looked out the window and saw a VLV that also had a Chinese flag on the side for a split second. Fear suddenly seized him. "You're not from China are you?" he asked.

The men jumped from their seats and grabbed at Hu. He cut them with beams from his fingers. Their wounds healed in seconds. He grabbed them and discharged over 100,000 watts of energy into them. But the energy gave them severe burns and caught their hair on fire. But they were still standing. They beat out the fire with their hands.

Hu finally sliced off their heads. Their bodies and heads dropped to the floor. Metal strands came out of their necks and grabbed their disembodied heads. The strands snapped the heads back on the men's bodies and within seconds, the men were ready to fight again.

Hu used his beams to chop up the heads and bodies and kicked the pieces around the cabin hoping the human jigsaw puzzles couldn't be put together again.

He ran to the pilot and demanded, "Fly me to China now." The pilot put the VLV into a dive.

"Pull up or I'll have to kill you," he warned. "I've been dead a couple times. It's no big deal."

Hu grabbed the man's head and twisted it 110 degrees. Seconds later, the head was turned around and the pilot was facing forward and laughing like a maniac.

"That makes three times now and in seconds It'll be four times." The VLV slammed into the ground and crumpled into a mangled heap of metal and synthetic materials. This time, all four men were finally dead and incapable of coming back to life. One problem had been solved. But it was more like solving the equation one plus one compared to an enormous problem that was created which was more like discovering how to shift into other dimensions. With Hu dead, someone who covertly helped the Chinese military, China was sure to retaliate. And with a Russian President desiring to take on China with advanced weapons, a military showdown was inevitable. But which side would win or would both side lose and take the world down too?

CHAPTER 26

News of the death of Hu became an obituary buried in the newspaper web sites in Beijing wedged between the death notice of a woman who was on the Great March with Mao as a child and above the death notice of a teen who died from exhaustion after spending 180 hours experiencing programs without eating or drinking anything or taking a break.

President Xian wasn't asked about Hu's death in a press conference he held a couple days later because he only wanted to talk about the Gobi Desert Reservoir that was going to be excavated with plasma equipment built by companies associated with the Madhouse in Arizona. He even quoted the Bible when it mentioned that the desert would bloom. With severe drought plagueing China due to a colder climate and less rain as a result, the reservoir would have to be used to store water. In order to fill it, a tunnel that reached from the desert to the Yellow Sea that was ten meters in diameter bored out by a giant plasma mole built by the Madhouse in Arizona was about to break through to the sea. An enormous desalinization plant was ready to take the inflow of seawater to not only turn it into fresh water but to also remove minerals from the water to be used for various purposes. The Pentagon and Russian military feared Xian would use the submerged entrance to the Yellow Sea as a means to send out a new generation of AI-controlled submarines to patrol the Pacific.

But unofficially, the death of Hu hit the Chinese military hard. He had supplied China with enough information to advance their weapons technology by nearly a generation. The Chinese defense factories were turning out weapons they couldn't have developed without the help of Hu.

In Russia, President Kursolov prepared for the Chinese threat by having his defense factories turn out even more advanced weapons systems thanks to the Facility. He came to the Facility more often flying in in his limousine Dick had built for him. He was like a child in his own personal toy store. He also had shipments of Russian Madhouse vodka sent around the world to international leaders and sampled bottles of it at the distillery.

The President couldn't declare war on China on a whim. He needed a good reason for it and so far, the Chinese hadn't done anything provocative enough to justify war.

It became harder all the time to keep knowledge about the most advanced technology being developed at the Facility from President Kursolov. After awhile, he knew the Facility was holding back and insisted that the best technology had to be shown to him or else he might hold back billions of rubles in funding. It became a game of hide-and-seek at the Facility and also an act of diversion to make the President think he was getting his way by demonstrating a new piece of equipment or a weapon for his approval.

There were some tense times in the Facility in areas far from the attention of the President. Kate, Maria, and many of the women at the Facility tolerated the programs "Mr. Channel 10" produced and presented on that adult channel. They felt uncomfortable being shown doing sex acts in his pornography. But when he began distributing it around the world without their permission and began cashing in big time, something had to be done to stop his international pornography production company.

A three-woman committee went to see the pornographer in his studio while he was recording an orgy that would make Caligula blush. A mix of humans and synthetics were performing all manners of acts of perversion and Boris even participated in some of the disgusting acts along with "Miss Channel 10."

After he was through for the day with the live action portion of his production, he met with the three women; Kate, Maria, and Dollia the wife of Dr. Vlandner. They met on the set which was being cleaned up at the time and sat on the floor since the beds and chairs had various bodily fluids and excrament on them. At least Boris was wearing a speedo.

"You lovely ladies just missed out on some fun times here on the set," he said with a sly grin. "What brings you here today besides wanting to get it on with me?"

"You usually push the envelope in the limits of decency," said Kate. "We know you're free to do whatever you want whether we like it or not. But you went too far lately. You used our images without our permission in your productions that were distributed outside the Faciity."

"And you three want a cut of the profits. I can understand." "The men that used me when I was another woman were more gentlemanly than you are," Maria complained. "What do you mean another woman?" he asked.

"When I was younger and more of a sexual toy, I thought I was happy. Men lusted after my body and I enjoyed the attention. But then I met the ultimate gentleman, Jesus Christ, and he changed my life for the better. I'll never watch your filth because it reminds me of when I was a different woman."

"I can always use the 25% rule and distribute your assets to four ladies and you can't stop me," he bragged.

"I don't know why there's that stupid rule at the Facility. It should be 0%. There are plenty of silly girls that love the attention like I used to crave it. But I'm a Christian and want to be treated like a Christian even if it's in an EPU program."

"But you are just as popular now as you were when you were 'another woman.' I thought you would like that."

"You are a sick person. Don't you have any sense of decency?"

"I wouldn't be doing what I do so well if I had one."

"The other night I happened to see a little bit of one of your programs that had naked ballet dancers in it. The music of Stravinski caught my ear," said Dollia.

"Ah, you saw my classy program of 'Rites of Spring.' I'm glad to hear a robodancer enjoyed my stuff."

Dollia glared at him and said coldly, "I didn't like to see me portrayed as a priestess who sacrificed lovers that didn't please her. You are indeed a sick person."

"I was wondering. Can you really please a man better than a human woman can? Boy, I sure would like to do you," he said as he smiled broadly.

Dollia gave him a death stare as he laughed. She began to do something no one expected. She removed her clothes and laid on one of the beds pleasuring herself to excite the pornographer. He nearly ripped his speedo when he took it off and threw it to the floor. He jumped onto the synthetic and sexually assaulted her with gusto. When his penis entered her vagina he had a look of ecstacy on his face. Seconds later, his look of joy began to change into a look of pain.

He began to scream as urine, blood, and sperm started squirting out of Dollia's vagina as if it were a plugged hose that was squirting water. When the pain became too much to bare, Boris pulled his penis out and cursed at her and how he felt.

"What in Hell did you do to me? My balls feel like they're on fire," he screamed.

"Trade secret my people will never reveal," she said with a smirk. "Imagine if we had had rough sex."

"You're a monster! I'm suprised your husband has survived this long."

"He likes it rough."

"He's insane. Get out of here," he demanded as he put his speedo back on as Dollia started putting her clothes back on.

"Ready to meet our demands?" Kate asked. "Yeah, yeah. What are your demands?"

"None of the women of the Facility will be portrayed in any way in your programs. There are more than enough real and computerized women outside of the Facility to choose from," said Kate.

"And don't show any of us as we may have looked when we were younger," Maria added.

"Fine, fine. What else?"

"Your sexbots—" Dollia added.

"Come on! You're killing me. The Japanese can't get enough of them. And then there are the geeks that can't get it on with real women. Do you want me to leave them high and dry without objects of their desire?"

"I guess since they aren't based on real women they'll be allowed," Kate conceded.

"Thank-you."

"And the naked dancers—" said Dollia. "You're really a bitch," he complained.

"I'm not objecting to them as long as they're tastefully presented," said Dollia.

"I can do that. I just won't portray any of your friends unless they give me permission."

"I know a few that might not mind. I just hope they don't regret becoming sex toys because I know you'll do that to them."

"Hey, they'll be taking their chances of becoming objects of desire."

"If you ruin their lives I'll be back for a visit," Dollia warned.

Boris grabbed his crotch and said, "One visit is more than enough. I'll try to behave myself."

"You better or I'll have my friend Dollia come back,"Kate warned. "I'll behave. Believe me. I'll behave."

The women left the set and walked toward the elevator. "What did you do to him?" Kate asked Dollia.

"Decades ago when synthetics were being improved, a cybernetic engineer named Frusia Kalor in the dimension I came from who had been a rape victim decided to make synthetic females less vulnerable to sexual assault. She made synthetics able to protect themselves from sexual predators with micromachines that destroyed their sperm and others that went straight to the pleasure center of the brain. The next time he produces pornography and fantasizes about women in it, the micromachines in his brain will give him painful thoughts. He'll also feel pain below the belt. But if anyone deserved being treated so badly, he does."

"Why didn't I know you had the ability to counter-attack rapists?" Kate asked.

"I didn't think it was a big thing."

"Maybe you should see your husband in Frankenstein's Laboratory and be back-engineered to develop protection from rape for human women," Maria suggested.

"You know, that sounds like a good idea. I'll make that suggestion." "I've seen you dance on the stage. You're incredible," Maria gushed. "Are your fellow dancers jealous of you? You would make Najinski envious of your leaping ability."

"None of them are jealous as far as I know. They are all professionals. I even help those that ask me for assistance. I dance secondary roles like when I played the nurse for Juliet in Prokofiev's 'Romeo and Juliet.' I needed to take a break from the usual dance routine."

"I bet some of your friends would like to be enhanced," said Kate. "They've all been enhanced to one degree or another. They appreciate my connections with the medical division." "Have you ever danced naked?" Maria asked. "Many times…with my husband," she giggled.

The women went to different floors and went to their apartments. Kate entered her apartment and found Dick eating lasagna and garlic bread.

"How was your day?" Dick asked.

"I got a lot done that needed to be done. Hopfully I made Boris more manageable."

"I'm not going to check out channel 10 to see if you succeeded." "What you're eating smells good. Do you have any more?"

"Yeah. It's in the freezer. It's hard to believe it was dirt, stone, and water 24 hours ago. But a guy from Newgate, New York brought two replicators; one for food and one for objects to the Facility. He's going to integrate the object replicator with the fabricators just like we've been able to integrate our fabricators since we left Mars."

"Hear anything about trouble with China?"

"Not lately. President Kursolov hasn't been here for a week which is a blessing and a curse. It's a blessing that he hasn't been nosing around to find stuff he's not supposed to have. But it's a curse in that I haven't read his mind in a week. I have no idea what he is thinking. I might ask my watcher if someone who is watching him might know what is on his mind."

"Any good things happen to you today?"

"Yeah. I was in a race with 11 other drivers testing out my flyers flying to Moscow, up to Saint Petersburg, and out to Lake Baikal and back. I came in second. But I enjoyed myself for a couple hours." "Let's hope and pray your racing circuits can go on without being eliminated by war with China."

That evening, a naval task force out of Vladivostok entered the Yellow Sea. It consisted of an aircraft carrier, two brand new battleships, destroyers, cruisers, and submarines. Kursolov had sent it off to try and provoke the Chinese into waging war. President Xian knew what the Russian President was up to and didn't want to play his game. There was no way his navy was going to start a war intentionally.

A Russian sub approached the tunnel that was allowing seawater to enter to fill up the Gobi Desert Reservoir. That was when two attack subs emerged from the tunnel. Since they were programmed to defend Chinese territorial waters, they fired directed energy powered torpedoes at the sub which slammed into the Russian sub in seconds. There was now a reason to start WW III and President Kursolov was eager to proclaim its beginning.

CHAPTER 27

Pesident Kursolov got the message that a Russian submarine had been destroyed near China in the evening as he was having a state dinner in the same meeting room he had met with Dick Thurman and others who founded the Russian Madhouse a few years before. One of his assistants whispered into his ear the information and left the room quickly to gather more information when it came in.

President Kursolov stood and his guests became quiet as he said, "We are unofficially at war with China. One of our submarines has been destroyed with no provocation on our part. We must retaliate for the destruction of Russian lives and retaliation will be swift and sure. To avoid escalation of the aggression, we must present a powerful show of force and demonstrate to the Chinese government our overwhelming military dominance in the world.

"For years we have seen China become a growing military threat to world peace. It has built islands to extend its territorial claims well into the Yellow, East, and South China Seas. Much of the material used to construct those islands came from material excavated from the Gobi Desert Reservoir. The largest of the islands is located in the Yellow Sea. At the present time, it is seven times larger than Metropolitan Moscow. It has a naval port and also an air base with the longest airstrip used by the Chinese air force. There are reports that a tunnel running from the mainland to the island will be completed later this year.

"Our two newest vessels, the battleships Brezhnev and Putin, are off the coast of China in international waters. Each have the newest and most powerful types of weapons ever used on a warship. Each have twelve 45 centimeter main guns that can fire a round that has a maximum range of over 500 kilometers. That means one of those battleships could hit

Beijing from international waters. This should strike fear in the heart of President Xian.

"Our newest bombers based in Eastern Siberia can strike any major city in China in less than two hours. We can place space- based weapons in orbit over China from space facilities in Western Siberia in less than an hour. If the Chinese decide to confront our forces on the ground, our latest T-40 tanks and potent fighting suits will obliterate their forces. We also have weapons I am not at liberty to mention that are superior to anything they can field against us.

"To show I am not a warmonger bent on world domination, I will give President Xian 24 hours to apologize for the destruction of our submarine and pay 10 billion rubles in restitution for the loss of nearly 400 lives; 400 precious lives that had a lifetime of potential. Mother Russia has lost a future that might have benefitted from what those nearly 400 loyal citizens that loved their nation more than life itself could have given us. I will not let their deaths be in vain. Let us bow our heads and have two minutes of silence in honor of the loss of those brave sailors."

For two minutes, President Kursolov and his guests bowed their heads reverantly. Afterwards, he sat down and the meal continued. The conversations were more quiet and the mood was much more somber. They eventually left the room and went their separate ways or went to various apartments dignitaries spent the night in.

President Kursolov entered a smaller conference room to talk with advisors and military experts to seek their guidance. Two generals, two admirals, two GRU agents, and two personal advisors met with the President at a big oak table with a holographic projector in the middle.

"Gentlemen, what's the situation out there?" the President asked. The projector projected the image of an admiral above the table. "This is Admiral Vosslov. So far we have seen no warships out here and our radar and sonar hasn't detected anything that could be considered a threat. We saw the explosion of the submarine. But after that, it's as if nothing happened. We'll be on watch for anything. So far, it's peaceful out here. I'll alert you if anything happens. Admiral Vosslov of the battleship Putin signing off."

After the image vanished, President Kursolov said, "He is hiding something he doesn't want to tell us. He is doing a good job hiding that fact."

"I've known the admiral since we were cadets at the academy," said one of the admirals at the table. "He tells the truth no matter how painful it is. If he says nothing is happening out there, nothing is happening."

"Are you willing to wage war against the largest standing army and second largest navy and second largest air force in the world?" asked one of the generals.

"Six months ago we could have held our own against China.

Not today," said the other general.

You could almost see steam coming from the ears of the President. "You're lucky you didn't say that to my predecessor a century ago. If you were lucky, you would have been thrown into the gulag for the rest of your life. How dare you tell me that?"

"Sometimes the truth is a tough thing to hear. But it had to be said to you," said that general.

"I know our military has acquired advanced weapons systems," said one of his personal advivors. "But you've only seen them demonstrated under controlled conditions and not used during battle. You better hope none of our ships are lost off the coast of China. It couldn't be prevented when a tsunami sank much of our navy off the coast of Israel last December. We can prevent losing any of our ships by not provoking an attack. You know how much each of our battleships cost; a quarter of a trillion rubles. Two million- ruble missiles can sink each ship. If both of them were sunk, the loss of life could be over 5,000 sailors even if some of the crew members were rescued. Losing nearly 400 sailors was a tragic loss. But losing over 12 times that number would be an absolute disaster."

"If they face our navy with their navy, we would send them to the bottom of the Yellow Sea," the President bragged.

"But our navy wouldn't be facing just their navy," said the second advisor. "The days when one navy slugged it out with another navy passed nearly a century ago. If the Chinese have ray weapons in orbit, our navy could be at the bottom of the Yellow Sea in a matter of minutes. Why did you have the task force set out from Vladivostok and enter the Yellow Sea?

Did you want to provoke a response from the Chinese and not expect what happened to happen?"

"Cowards! You're all cowards," he screamed at them. "Get out of here," he demanded. They left the room grumbling about the President.

After the meeting, the President left the room and went to the toilet to scream and curse at the mirrors. He pounded the sinks and nearly broke them off the wall. He finally decided to relieve himself in one of the stalls.

As he was sitting on the toilet, the knob on the door turned and the door opened. Standing in front of him was someone who looked exactly like him.

"Who the Hell are you?" he asked the man. "In a moment I'll be you."

Before the President could call out for assistance, the man slapped an interdimensional shifting tag on his shoulder and he was shifted to another dimension. The man left the restroom and saw one of his assistants who feared what was going to happen.

"Peter, after nearly breaking my fists on the sinks in the toilet, I finally came to my senses and realize you and the others are right. For too long I have been allowed to get my way when people should have stood up to me. I've told people for years I never would become like the man I look like. But during the last few months I have become more and more like him."

"Are you all right? I've never heard you talk like this before."

"Sure you have. Remember how I was years ago when I was a political novice?"

The man began to smile thinking about the past.

"I almost forgot about how you were back then when we used to talk about politics until the sun came up."

"I almost forgot too," Kursolov confessed. "I wanted to make Russia great again and even admired the boldness America's President Trump had to take on the establishment. I wanted to be just as bold."

"I must say, you have suceeeded. But nearly 400 of our people have been killed by the Chinese. What will your response be to that?" "I am responsible for their deaths because I indeed did want to provoke a response from the Chinese. I had our men and women go into harm's way and hundreds paid the ultimate price for my arrogance."

"You are talking more like the young idealist I met in the coffee houses of Saint Petersburg so long ago. I like how that young man seems to be re-emerging."

"My friend, I do too. I will immediately order the task force out of the Yellow Sea and order it to go on maneuvers in the North Pacific."

The men embraced and the President entered the conference room and contacted the admirals in the Yellow Sea to order them to head for the North Pacific. They were all relieved.

The next day at noon, Moscow time, most of the nation stopped to hear a speech by President Kursolov as he addressed the nation about the incident in the Yellow Sea.

"People of Russia, I must publicly appologize for the way I have been acting since our humiliating defeat in Israel. I let my rage poison my mind and I foolishly put thousands of people in harm's way with nearly 400 being punished for my foolishness with the loss of their lives. That is why I ordered the fleet out of the Yellow Sea and into the North Pacific. It is not a demonstration of weakness because personally, I believe our navy is the equal of the Chinese navy. But if our navy provokes a deadly response beyond what happened last night which cost the lives of nearly 400 heroic men and women, the loss of lives could be over 20 times that many. I don't want their deaths to haunt me for the rest of my life.

"From this day forward, I will attempt to do what is best for Mother Russia. We will still build up our military to make it so strong that no nation would dare challenge us. But we will balance spending on our military with domestic spending to help the majority of the people of this proud nation.

"We have a place called the Facility which is located in Northwest Siberia. It is where brilliant men and women work on projects that will help the world. Our future may depend on what they do. Pray for their success. Our survival during this period of global cooling could be in their capable hands. My government will give the Facility its full support.

"Greater days are ahead for us. With God's help and our mutual cooperation in making Mother Russia a mother proud of her children, we will eventually become a nation that all other nations will admire. Help me fulfill this nation's potentual of becoming greater than it has ever been in its history. Let us start today. God bless Russia and the great people of this proud nation. Good afternoon."

The people of Russia rejoiced and the people at the Russian Madhouse praised God for the change that had been made in the heart of President Kursolov. Dick Thurman and a few others knew how the change of heart had been made. There was a physical change of personnel. Dick's watcher told him what happened. He told Kate and she told Maria. Somehow, the replacement of President Kursolov with a biosynthetic replicate was known by only a handful of people like Dr. Sorchen Vlandner who worked with watchers to create the more than perfect replicate who could make the people of Russia believe their president was someone they could support. If the people around him knew he wasn't the authentic President Kursolov, they didn't let on they knew there was an imposter controlling the nation. He was a better man than the one who nearly plunged Russia and China into WW III.

That night was the premier of the ballet "Andria" which featured Dollia Vlandner. Her children were at the performance too sitting beside their father on both sides of the proud father. Trav was with his human wife and showing the first signs of pregnancy.

The performance was brilliant and could have only been performed by a synthetic or an enhanced human. Everyone in the theater knew they had witnessed greatness. And in the years to come, the Facility, the Madhouse in Arizona, and the other places started by BOSS would help the world enter a brighter future where nearly anything was possible as long as people believed it and were willing to make it possible.

THE END